F. J Kiefer

The Legends on the Rhine from Basle to Rotterdam

F. J Kiefer

The Legends on the Rhine from Basle to Rotterdam

ISBN/EAN: 9783337377052

Printed in Europe, USA, Canada, Australia, Japan

Cover: Foto ©Andreas Hilbeck / pixelio.de

More available books at **www.hansebooks.com**

THE
LEGENDS
OF THE
RHINE
FROM
BASLE TO ROTTERDAM

BY

F. J. KIEFER.

TRANSLATED BY

L. W. Garnham, B. A.

SECOND EDITION.

MAYENCE.

Published by DAVID KAPP.

—

1869.

INDEX.

V

RHINE-LIFE.

On the Rhine blooms fine life!
From the Destruction's dust,
The Ancestors' spirits strife,
Which long were the Graves' rust;
And songs there resound
With harmonious stream,
In the spirit again found,
And again must I dream.

See I the birds flying
High the blue air through,
See I the ships striving
In distant grey-fog anew,
Is me, as if in flight
The birds words sing,
As in quick despite
To ships others cling.

Spirit-words on the moor
And quick moving flood;
There round the Convent-door,
Where Pilgrims once stood —
And the Ivy branch waves,
So high and sadly wild
Binds tendrils round the graves
There tone fairy songs so mild.

KIEFFR, Legends of the Rhine.   1

Yet the wall regarding
Of dilapidated mountain,
So rises a slight trembling
In my bosom's fountain;
For in the solitary fragment
Tones like struggle and storm power,
Soon I hear gentle lament
From deep dungeon in round tower.

Soon speak Ore, Stone, and Wine
Of the strange past Times,
Sometimes talk the folk on Rhine
Of the fabulous old Rhymes.
We inherited many traditions
And ever believe anew,
Who ventures useless additions:
Or asks if they are really true?

Truthfully I announce to others too,
What I once, in old time heard and found,
He may wander, believing it not true
To our beautiful country bound.
And on the heights and foundations
Listens he on an evening still —
The heart can ever make translations,
If it only seeks and has the will.

Adelheid v. Stolterfoth.

Basel.

One hour in advance.

asel was once surrounded by enemies and hard-pressed. The besiegers were in agreement with the malcontents in the town, and arranged with them to conquer the fortress, by attack on a dark night. The attack was to happen on the clock striking 12, but accidentally the watchman of the Tower heard of the intended storming some minutes before its execution; there was no time left to warn the Commander of the garrison, or the guard. Cunning and reflection alone could help, and the Watchman quickly knew a safe expedient; he prevented — in advancing the clock one hour — the announcement of the midnight hour, and made the hammer strike 1 instead of 12. This caused doubt and misunderstanding both in the town, and among the enemy outside the town, both believing to have neglected the concerted hour, and while they reflected what was most advisable to be done, the Watchman had time to communicate with the Magistrate and Commandant The traitorous plan completely miscarried; and the Enemy at last tired of the siege, retired without having obtained any advantage.

The Legend does not relate if the brave Watchman saved the town, or was rewarded, but in remembrance of the remarkable manner by which this safety occurred, the Magistrate ordered that the Town Clock should remain advanced as the Watchman set it, and since, it struck 1 o'clock in Basel, when elsewhere it struck 12 o'clock. This singular regulation, which continued till 1798, gained the inhabitants of Basel the satirical praise, that although they were a Century behind, yet they were an hour in advance. Now, of course, they keep the same time as other towns.

Another remarkable thing was the so-called Lallenkönig, a very large strangely carved head placed on the Clock of the Basel-bridge steeple, which at every movement of the pendulum turned its eyes and thrust out its tongue, this head had been placed there after a dispute, to mock and ridicule the citizens of Little-Basel. In 1839 the tower was pulled down, causing the disappearance of the Lallenkönig.

Zähringen.

Zähringen's Origin.

Ⅰn the wooded valleys of Zähringen, there, where the First ascends to the summit called the Rosskopf once lived a young Charcoal-burner, a stately brave fellow; he could have been satisfied with his occupation, in which also his parents found a sufficient subsistence, however he could not feel himself happy. Being sent once to the town by his parents, he had an opportunity of seeing a Tournament which excited in the youth an inclination for Chivalry — his parents being dead, and filial duty not binding him more to his paternal hut, he wished to leave the wood for ever, and take service by the most renowned knight, as he was revolving these thoughts an old hermit came to him and said: I know what you meditate, however believe me the means to attain your wish lies only in this wood, and your hitherto occupation, but you must choose a better place than where you have till now burnt Charcoal. Come with me I will show you a better place. In astonishment the youth followed the old man: Here, said the old man, continue to burn your Charcoal, and with these words he disappeared before the Charcoal-burner could ask for an explanation. The old man's words he thought will explain themselves

in time, in every case, it cannot hurt if meantime I obey him, and with great exertion he
hewed down the strong trunks which surrounded
the hill, erected a kiln, and covered it, before
kindling, with the rocky earth of the eminence;
how great was his astonishment as he, after the
kiln had burnt-out and taking away the cover,
found several pieces of Gold, which had formed
themselves by the heat out of the stones; he
prudently concealed the treasure in a near cleft
then built a second kiln, and afterwards several
others, and all produced similar booty; so that
he soon found himself in the possession of an
immense fortune. Occupied with several plans
to invest his gold, one evening he went to bed
late, the care of his treasure tormented him and
he could not sleep. There he thought he heard
a light tap at his door, he rose, and in still doubting a strong knock convinced him he was not
mistaken. Courageously he opened the door,
and by the weak light of the moon he saw before him a man who demanded admittance. The
Charcoal-burner was the more astonished at this
nocturnal visit, as it was very seldom that a
wanderer came in this solitary wilderness, and
therefore hesitated to receive the unknown, but
as this asserted that he was a pursued unfortunate and only concealment could save him, the
humane youth did not longer resist to afford him
a hospitable sojourn. The deeply hidden situa-

tion of the hut was the best protection for the
fugitive; no pursuer appeared, and the stranger
soon recognised in the young Charcoal-burner a
faithful upright heart in whom one could trust
implicitly. I dare without danger, unconditionally
discover myself to you said he therefore one
morning to the youth, you are incapable of
Treachery, and as it appears to me a man of confidence, and such a friend is necessary for me,
I could never find my way in these thick woods,
therefore I require a guide who will conduct me
to my people, know! young man, who it is to
whom you have opened your hospitable doors;
I am your unfortunate Emperor. Attacked by over-
whelming enemies I have lost all in an unequal
ruinous battle, my army and treasure are gone,
and I must fly far from here, to lament in deep
concealment my destiny. From you I demand
the last service, to lead me by secret paths to
those who expect me, a service which I, once so
powerful, am not able to recompense. The Charcoal-burner heard these words with astonishment,
and in shedding tears of sympathy, he sank on
his knee before the Emperor. But then rising he
seized the right hand of the illustrious guest and
spoke: now I recognise the dispensation of Providence who let me find here, in a wondrous
manner, a great treasure which enables me to
offer to my dearly beloved sovereign, probably
a successful service. See, contined he in leading

the Emperor to the place near the hut where
the gold was hidden. I demand nothing for it,
but your permission to count myself to the number
of your dependants, and to devote my arm to
your just cause. Affected and full of new hopes
the Emperor embraced the excellent young man.
Still the same evening they departed with the
great treasure, and by secret ways, and many
nightly adventures they reached trusty friends.
The gold enabled the Emperor to levy a new
army, and before long, the sovereign saw himself at the head of a well equipped force, so that
he felt himself sufficiently strong to attack the
enemy. The bravery of his troops bore-off a
complete victory, and before all, and under the
eyes of his sovereign the Charcoal-burner acquired
honour and celebrity. On the field of battle he
was knighted by the Emperor, who gave him the
name of Zähringen with the instruction to build
a castle for himself and successors, on the dominating eminence of that secluded valley.

Alsace and Breisgau.

The holy Odilie.

Attich, duke of Alsace had an extraordinary beautiful and amiable lady, and for the completion of his happiness he only wanted the enjoyment of a father. But so much as he wished a scion, as often as he prayed to Heaven for marital blessing, his longings never seemed as if they would be accomplished. Once he prayed fervently, and vowed that he would devote the child entirely to the service of God, and his prayer was at last heard, the duchess felt the throes of child-bearing, and bore a lovely daughter which was baptised Odilie. Yet the parent's pleasure was not unalloyed at this birth, for the girl (as if Heaven had retained a pledge for the fulfillment of the vow), was blind. However Odilie grew a blooming maiden, but still more than by bodily beauty, she early distinguished herself by pre-eminence in goodness and by pious sentiments, and this sentiment increased daily, so that she was the delight of all good persons. But as she wanted the gift of sight, she could only have imperfect ideas of the exterior world and nature, and the more charming descriptions one made her of God's glorious creation, so much the more Odilie deplored her blindness. Ever when so very sad she sought consolation in prayer, and

in her childlike piety she prayed incessantly to
the Almighty to unclose her eyes, and to allow
her the high enjoyment of the sight of his beautiful world. What nobody expected happened;
the Heaven wrought a miracle on Odilie, she saw.
With indescribable joy the parents saluted this
unexpected happiness, and offered thanksgivings
for the costly present, praising the goodness and
power of God. But men are too inclined to withdraw from the fulfillment of an engagement, and
not to keep a promise for which it was given,
when it is completed. Since Odilie enjoyed the
light of day, and the glance of her eyes increased
the charm of the graceful maiden, she did not
want wooers, and the honourable offers which
were made to the Duke, caused him often to
regret that he had dedicated the child to the
service of God. For a time Attich had thoughts
of giving notice of such a changement of opinion,
and as count Adelhart an excellent knight who
had done him great service begged as reward
the hand of Odilie, the duke thought it not necessary to regard the vow, and gave his consent
to the count. With terror the pious maiden heard
that she was to marry. She had already hoped,
(according to her former destination, and inclination), to be received in a convent, and she believed to be obliged the more resolutely to resist,
the intention of her father as so much the more
sinful it appeared to her against God, she there-

fore ventured to represent to the Duke his wrong,
and to declare decidedly her refusal, and seeing
that arrangements were making to compel her,
she fled from the castle into the wood where she
hoped to remain concealed. It was however
soon found out whither she had gone, and Attich
drew ont his servants and huntsmen to catch her.
Soon she heard her pursuers. As a hunted deer
she fled.before them in the impassable thicket,
but at last the fugitive's steps were hemmed-in
by a steep broad rocky wall; already the servants and her father were near, the maiden called
on God for help sinking on her knees, and see,
the rock opened, took the pursued, and closed
after her again. All who saw this stood immovable from terror and astonishment, but the
most perplexed was the Duke, and the wickedness of his action was heavy on his conscience.
While regarding the rock which hid Odilie, her
voice sounded from the stone. „My father if you
wish to see me again so fulfill your Vow faithfully, if you insist on my marrying I am for ever
taken away from you." Attich who now distinctly
knew that his daughter was irrevocably destined
to Heaven, swore not to act more against this
destination, and then the rock opened and Odilie
stept forward. But in remembrance of the miraculous event, and to atone for his wickedness,
the Duke had a cloister built where the pious
Odilie was withdrawn from her pursuers; Odilie

became the first Nun of this Nunnery, and later Abbess. After her death she was declared holy by the Pope.

Thann in Alsace.

The dreamy beautifully situated small town Thann is, in a double regard, remarkable to the lover of old romantic legends, not only on account of the steeple but principally of the neighbouring Lyingfield. The steeple was built in a time when by great drought and heat, a severely felt want of water dominated, and springs and fonntains scarcely yielded sufficient to allay the thirst. But just at this time the wine had thriven so luxuriantly that persons not prepared for this abundance, could not procure sufficient vessels and barrels to store the rich blessing. Therefore it happened that the citizens of Thann prepared the mortar, for the building of the steeple, with wine instead of water, which changed the lime to a sort of must, spreading a most lovely fragrance. By such application of the sweet grape-juice it is said not only to have acquired an extraordinary solidity, but even to the present day the walls occasionally yield an agreeable exudation when the delicate plant is in blossom.

One indeed asserts that the tolling is then more euphonious and harmonious. Not so charming but rather terrific and dreadful is the legend of the Lying-field. An uninhabited, barren waste, uncomfortable sterile wilderness, stretches itself before the wanderer's eye, and the defamed field is unwillingly visited, which Nature seems to have chosen as the seat of Death. No tone of a living creature is to be heard, no green ear shoots from the wide pasture, the only change of color on the dark mossy ground is offered by the bleached skulls, which like an obnoxious seed are here scattered about. Once, so says the Legend, a wanderer surprised by night, lost himself on this wide plain. The clocks of the near town announced midnight, and directly the solitary was aware of a subterranean strange rustling, a rattling as of weapons, and a tumult as of fighters. Suddenly there appeared before him the figure of an armed knight, in menacing position and harangued the terror-stricken so „What are you searching here miserable, and why do you venture to enter the field that already since many centuries loaded with the curse, is a field of Terror and Death?" Are you a stranger in this country, so know that you stand on the place, where once Louis the Pious arranged his army to struggle in open battle with his enemy. The venerable king wished to stand an honourable battle, but his own sons reflected on treachery,

and Lothar the Infamous bribed the warriors
with gold and soft words. And as the pious
Louis confiding in the faithfulness of his troops
would begin the battle, he experienced the shameful desertion of his own troops who tore the
crown from his head, and delivered him to his
antagonists. The deceived old man, with uplifted
hands cried with bitterness to Heaven. „There
is no more fidelity on earth, for all my warriors
betray me. Cursed be they, and this field the
witness of such an act, for ever.“ This curse oh
stranger! has been most terribly fulfilled, „Here
under this black plain lie in mile-wide graves,
collected bones of the perjured warriors, and as we
by our faithlessness robbed our king of happiness
and quiet, so our bones will never enjoy repose,
and never will the curse be taken from this field,
which since that event, is called the Lying-field.

After these words the spectral warrior sank
in the ground which opened and closed with
hollow menaces, but the stranger seized with terror
and horror hastened away, and the next day
announced what he had experienced on the plain.

Staufenberg in Ortenau.

The foot on the Wall.

In the fine times when there were fairies, nymphs, and other lovely creatures of the world of Fable who cultivated a gay and happy intercourse with men, lived at his castle Staufenberg, a rich young count whose amiability and virile beauty had almost become proverbial in the neighbourhood. He was passionately addicted to the pleasures of the chase, ranged daily mountain and wood, and not seldom he made an excursion to the distant banks of the Rhine, which then, were little inhabited. It once happened that tired from the useless pursuit of a stag which had led him to the banks of the stream, he encamped in the shade of a tree and fell asleep. On awaking he saw a young maid of incomparable beauty, sitting in the grass who friendly saluted him. Just as much astonished at the unexpected appearance as attracted by her charms, he asked after her origin and dwelling, the sweet maid related him that she was a nymph of the Rhine and her house was built in the rocky-ground of the river. This answer astonished the count still more, and raised in him the impression which the fabulous being had made on him so much, that he, bewitched by the supernatural charm of the nymph, did not separate from her, till

she had promised to be on the same place the
next day. The count directly renounced the chase,
and different pleasures which he had had before, he
had only mind for the charming enchantress who
bound him with magical love-bands. He saw
her daily on the quiet confidential place where
she first appeared to him, and nothing disturbed
the enjoyment of sweet happy love. The oath
of eternal true love, which the Fairy demanded
of him, the count had willingly given with the
assurance that it would be impossible for him,
ever to belong to another, for which the beloved
promised him continual joys, and a long life.
Could you, she said sometimes with warning voice,
could you once forget your oath and break your
vowed Faith to me, nothing would remain for
me than to weep eternally, for I can only love
once, and never another than you. But your
faithlessness would be ruinous to you, for you
would hear my plaintive cry in this castle or
wherever you might be, and even if I were invisible you would see a foot of mine, and this
would be a sign, that after 3 days as punishment
of your perjury you would become the prey of
Death. Long the calm band of love was more
than in one manner a blessing for the count, for
by the magic of his adored, every endeavour
and action succeeded. He was always victor in
Tournament, as in serious battle ever his lance
struck his adversary, never failed his sword, and

the high renown of his arms spread wide into the
country. No wonder therefore, that many a
beauty rivalled for the favour of the beautiful
count, yet he remained faithful to his nymph.
It happened once that the Emperor, sojourning
in the Rhine-country arranged a grand banquet,
and as then the most noble knights took part, so
also the Staufenberger. The Youth's stately figure
and noble manners soon attracted all eyes, but
the most the glance of the only daughter of the
sovereign. She was inflamed with love for the
knight, and did not conceal from her father that
she must either be the count's wife, or never
marry. The Emperor cordially responded to the
wish of his child and sought an opportunity to
make the count acquainted with this wish. This
declaration was accompanied with such splendid
offers, and alluring promises, that the thereby
blinded knight declared to the Emperor his oath
of love to a nymph of the Rhine, and this was
the obstacle which prevented his conducting home,
as married wife, the daughter of his powerful
master. The emperor opposed, that a love connection with such a being, and that an effected oath,
could have no validity, and in every case the
Bishop would be able to release the count from
the fairy, from all guilt and from all evil consequences. Allured by ambition, the count consented
to the emperor's offer, and in the loving caresses
of the Emperor's love-inflamed daughter, the

youth soon forgot all of that threatened him by
the nymph, and drunk with joy, he sat at the
wedding-feast beside the highly-blessed in beauty,
blooming young wife. But see! as all were jovial,
and the health of the newly-married was enthu-
siastically toasted, there was displayed on the
wall, opposite the festal-table an extremely beautiful and elegant feminine foot, which visible to
the knee, had penetrated through the wall, although it remained undamaged. At the same
time toned in all ante-rooms a heartrending long
continuing wail. By this infelicitous sign the
count paled: „Woe to me!" he cried that is the
punishment for my faithlessness, that is the
announcement of my near death. Seized with
madness, and as if chased by Furies he ran forth,
after 3 days he was found in the near Forest
killed by lightning. But the unhappy bride sunk
in grief and mourning, renounced the world, and
ended her days in a cloister.

Castle Niedeck.

The Gigantic toy.

In that time when in the German countries still unnatural beings were in abundance, a giant race had their seat on the castle Niedeck. Although this castle is since long in ruins, yet the sayings of the people testify of their, and their former inhabitants, extraordinary size and strength. It was these, so says the legend, immense giants who kept aloof from the impulsive men, and good-natured, hurt nobody. It happened once, that the castle-owner's little daughter in promenading, wandered further than usual. The young giantess traversed the adjacent woods and arrived at a wide plain on which fields and meadows extended themselves. She perceived a peasant with horse and plough which she had never seen! Admiringly she regarded the man for a time, how he ploughed the field, and full of childlike pleasure at the sight, she clapped her hands so that the mountains echoed, and frightened by the noisy sound the good husbandman stopped, and his horse fell. „What a fine toy" cried the giant child and before the husbandman knew whence the words came, the girl had hurried to him, snatched up horse and plough as easily as if they were

Tyrolean carved-work, and covered them up in her apron. Joyfully she hastened with them to her father at the castle, „look here" said she, beside herself with joy, and placed the peasant with the put-to horse on the table before the giant „look here" what charming elegant figures I have found, a living toy. Oh! that shall make me more pleasure than all my dolls, which are only of leather and immovable. But the father said seriously, my little daughter „Do you know what you have done, and what you have brought with you?" You have taken the peasant from the field, torn him from his work, he the most useful of all the children of men, exerts himself in heat, wind, and rain, that the fields are productive. Therefore quickly carry the man back with horse and plough, and once for all remark: „He who practices injurious play and will on the diligent peasant, draws Heaven's curse on him." And at the father's command, the giant's daughter carried the husbandman with plough and horse to the field whence she had taken them.

Strasburg.

The Clock and the Cathedral.

As the world-renowned building of the Strasburg Dome was completed, the Magistrate had the wish to ornament the high steeple with an artistic clock. Long no master was to be found, to whom one could confide the execution of such a work, but at last one announced himself from a foreign country, named Isaac Habich, an already venerable old man, who offered to arrange an incomparable clock-work on the steeple. The offer was joyfully accepted, and the master began the laborious work. After several years unremitting endeavours the work was finished, and all who saw it, regarded it with justifiable admiration. The clock not only indicated the hour, but the day and month of the year, there was also added a large World-ball with the rising and setting of the sun, which as well as the appearances and eclipses of the Moon and Sun each time exactly as they occurred in nature, Mercury standing with his staff pointed out all changements, and each constellation stepped forward in its turn as soon as its domination commenced. Besides many artistic arrangements of different sorts, was also remarkable, that beside the clock which announced the hours, stood the personification of Death, who shortly before the strike of every quarter advanced to seize the clock-hammer, while at the same time from the other side the figure of the Redeemer appeared and sent back Death; only the full hour Death struck with the hammer. This ingenious clock as well as an excellent chime belonging to it, which toned the most edifying church-psalms seemed to be a real masterwork and the city glorified itself in its possession. But even the excellence of the work excited in the minds of the magistracy the wish that Strasburg might be and remain the only city that could boast of it, and this wish led to the horrible design, that instead of reward-ing the master for his art and diligence, to put-out his eyes. In order to have a pretence for this cursed act, and because they feared to exe-cute such cruelty on a man so highly honored by the people, they took refuge to the easy de-ceptive superstition of that time.

They accused the master of not being able to complete the work without demoniacal help, was in connection with the Devil, and effected by imprisonment and torture the master's con-fession of his guilt. However before the infamous men could carry-out their Judgment, the master declared, that he must do the last work to the clock and finish the wheel-work what would be impossible for any one else to complete, and begged to be still once allowed to ascend the steeple. This explanation appeared so weighty with the chiefs of the city that they could not but comply with it. They had the condemned conducted to the steeple, and after he had filed and altered some time, he declared that all was completed. Immediately afterwards the dreadful act was committed of depriving the old man of sight. But soon it was known that the chimes and works were still. The cruel authors of the inhuman act perceived now too late, that the master of the artistic movement had intentionally destroyed it, to revenge himself on the barbarous vanity and ambition of the Magistracy. And so indeed it was. The badly treated artist said he had annihilated his own work, and that nobody would ever be able to repair it and set it in motion.

Even to the present day one shows the immovable wheel-work to the stranger visiting Strasburg-dome; whoever regards the endless artistic work and the fine mechanism can only regret that as the blind master predicted, till now no artistic hand had power to order the machine and to bring it into activity. In the clock made by Schwilgue 1838—1842 some parts of the clock were used; at midnight of 31st Dec. of every year, the clock regulates itself for the next year.

Castle Trifels.

Richard Lion-heart.

On the Upper Rhine boundary of France between Weissenburg, Bergzabern, Landau, Edenkoben, Neustadt on the Hardt and Dürkheim as far as Grünstadt is one of the finest countries of Germany, possibly of Europe. Provided with woods, vine-clad eminences, and fruitful fields, and richly ornamented with villages and hamlets, and crowned with old castle ruins, this country, although little known, can vie with all, and equal to every other in changement of beautiful and interesting objects. The Vosges the summits of which already begin to incline to the plain have not more the same wild character which surprises the traveller on the Swiss frontier and in Upper Alsace; so much the more lovely and softer is the country, and so much the more fruitful the ground, and only here and there one is reminded of the neighbourhood of the mountain by the proud projecting rocks. One of these eminences allows the free View to the North and South. The Domes of Strasburg and Speyer besides the churches of Worms, on the right bank of the Rhine the ruins of Heidelberg castle, to the left the Donnersberg with its projecting cupolas are the principal objects of a Panorama which charms the spectator. Not far from the Landau and Anweiler lies as if thrown in, a row of wooded mountains and rocks with ruins. Three of these mountains render themselves particularly remarkable, they seem to have belonged to one, and to have been the property of one master who had his dwelling on one of them. The name Trifels signifies this unity, for it is the collective name of the 3 rocky ridges, although also only the most important with its castle-ruins is called so, and the 2 others are named Anebos and Scharfenburg. The ascent of Trifels is tiring, but this labour is repaid a hundred-fold by the lovely prospect of near and distant environs, and particularly of the splendid Rhine-valley with its finely situated districts. Landau before all attracts the notice of the spectator, it lies in the midst of numerous villages and one says therefore there proverbially, that the inhabitants of 200 districts visit its Market without requiring more than 1 day to do so. The founder of the castle Trifels is (as many buildings of the Middle Ages) unknown, one knows only that it is mentioned, in old chronicles, as of the times of the Salic kings, and that it passed over to the Dynasties of Hohenstaufen and Habsburg, but in the year 1410 was the property of the Duke of Zweibrücken. Frederic Barbarossa has often, according to the legend, and willingly resided in the castle and enlarged it, and also built the once celebrated marble-hall, of its plan however scarcely a trace remains.

In the Middle-Ages Trifels served with its fortifications a three-fold purpose. It was Imperial fortress, state prison, and a place of conservation for jewels and treasure; and its possession often of great importance, because the height and strength of the place defied every attack. Just on that account it was adapted to hold important prisoners. The blood-thirsty Henry 6th Barbarossa's successor has here incarcerated many of his enemies and several state-criminals, and had them executed with unheard-of cruelties.

About Easter 1193 Richard Lion-heart was delivered as prisoner to Henry 6th by Leopold of Austria, and by the order of the latter brought to Trifels. For the heroic King a terrible destiny might have been intended, for he was, as so many bloody-victims, thrown into one of the strongest and well built dungeons of which there were several. However the courage of Richard remained unconquered, he even amused himself with singing and harp - playing, but there was scarcely a hope that he could escape his bitter enemy, and he was obliged to resign himself to the idea of a cruel death.

The king had in England a faithful adherent of his former years a singer by name Blondel. As he learned that his beloved master had disappeared, or rather incarcerated, he vowed with an Oath indefatigably and incessantly to search for the place of sojourn of Richard, and

to venture all for his deliverance. Only a few
devoted and valiant knights followed the faithful Blondel who wandered to Germany, traversing
the whole country inquiring at all castles and
making inquiries in all towns, and could never
discover any traces of his master. Already he
had searched out almost all places on the banks
of the Danube and Rhine as one day he arrived
in the wild valley of Anweiler, and perceived
the tower of Trifels. A strange presentiment
seemed to strike him that it was the king's
prison, and he resolved to arrange his inquiries
with the greatest care and prudence.

His companions were obliged to conceal themselves in the wood, while he would inspect the
castle. Being on his road there he met a maiden
who entered into conversation with him, and who
living near Trifels related him many things of
the castle, and its sights. As she wished to separate from him Blondel begged her to stay still
some minutes, wishing to reward her communi-
cation. Thereupon he took his Zither and sang
an old moving song which was also Richard's
favourite song. „Ah that sounds“, indeed said the
joyfully surprised, „exactly as the song which a
poor captive kinght, in the north tower of Trifels
sings, when I pasture my sheep in the neighbourhood.“ With these words spoken so unsuspiciously,
but so important for Blondel, the maiden sprang
away. Full of happy hope to have at last reached

the object of his wandering the singer crept,
by twilight, as near as possible to the marked
tower, sang, with accompaniment, the same song,
which the king had set to music, and composed.
Scarcely had the first strophes ceased, the attentive listener heard the continuation of the song,
which resounded from the window of the tower,
and soon afterwards asked a well-known although
suppressed voice from the same place: „Art thou
my faithful Blondel? „Yes it is I my royal master“,
replied the singer, „who thanks Heaven that he
has at last found you. Depend upon my, and
some friends', zeal to free you.“

The following day the stranger tried and obtained entrance to the castle, but he was obliged soon to learn, how dangerous his enterprise
was. The tower well watched and provided with
a numerous garrison could neither be taken by
force nor by surprise. It only seemed possible
to attain the desired object by cunning. Blondel's
lively manners and gay songs obtained for him
the favour of the governor as well as the other
guardians, and what was more useful to him also
the love of the gaoler's daughter with whom he
soon was on a confidential footing. After convincing
himself that she loved him deeply, and resolved
to fly with him, he believed to be able to discover himself. She promised her assistance to
liberate the king, and so it was possible to accomplish the dangerous undertaking. Mathilda

so was the name of the maid knew exactly all
the passages of the Tower-where her father kept
the keys, and how she could unperceived obtain
possession of them. On a dark stormy night,
Blondel and Mathilda, after having arranged all,
proceeded to act, they opened the king's Dungeon,
handed him a helmet and a sword, and conducted him to the castle-yard, surprised the two
sentinels, and compelled them to open the door.
Before the garrison drawn together by the noise,
could offer resistance, Blondels companion penetrated into the open castle, and after a sharp
struggle, he succeeded in delivering the king,
and to get clear-off with the heroic maiden on
a steed which had been before hand kept ready.
After long wandering they all fortunately arrived
in England.

Blondel then conducted his beautiful Mathilde
to the Altar, and received from the king the
richest reward for his rare lasting fidelity. Also
those who had accompanied the valiant Blondel
were rewarded with royal liberality.

Carlsrhue.

Charles' rest.

The Margrave Charles of Baden returned victorious from the battle - field, where great
actions had made his name celebrated. He
thought, after long wars, to devote time and
strength to the happiness of his subjects in the
enjoyment of peace. With his capital Durlach he
wished to make the beginning, the same should
be enlarged and be embellished with suitable
pleasure-grounds; but obstinacy, and short-sighted
court-intrigues opposed so many difficulties to the
benevolent intentions of the Margrave that the
plan was not carried-out.

One day hunting in the Hardt wood for his
recreation, it happened that in pursuit of game,
he lost his suite and after wearily wandering
about reposed himself under an oak-tree. Sleep
overcame him, and strange reveries occupied his
senses.

High over his head in the top of the tree he
perceived a crown ornamented with the most
precious stones on which glanced the words: „This
is the reward of the noble" and round it, stood
directly as if by the power of magic, a splendid
large city with Towers, Pinnacles, and a noble
castle worthy to be the seat of a sovereign.
While the charmed Margrave admired this vision,

it at once dissolved, he awoke and standing around him the the hunting - party who had discovered their missed master.

„I had", said Charles to them, „here a delightful dream. What I saw, around me in spirit, a large fine city I will found, the crown which soared above shall be an idea to me to make the new city my residence, and the place of the tree under which I reposed shall be the spot of my sepulchre."

To this dream Carlsrhue owes its foundation, for the Margrave accomplished what he had promised.

Philippsburg.

The Recruit.

At a siege of Philippsburg by the French a storm-attack on the works was ordered, twelve grenadiers were ordered to mount the rampart secretly at a retired, apparently unoccupied place. Here stood, besides a single recruit, not another man of the garrison, taken from the Imperial-army, because no one supposed that anything would be undertaken against this part of the Fortress. The recruit was however as sentinel, an attentive observer of what happened near him, and stood fully prepared, behind the parapet, holding his halberd ready for defence. Suddenly he remarked before him, the face of a moustached inimical grenadier, who was about to place his foot on the wall.

„Ho, ho“, growled the recruit to himself, „that is an impudent fellow I must show him the way“; and with a strong push, he thrust the enemy from the ladder. But see, a moment after again grinned a bearded grenadier, and a bullet whistled past the recruit's ear. „Oh! that for you“, cried the recruit, „already there again, have I not struck you well?“ and with all his strength he pushed his halberd against the breast of the climbing-up opponent, so that he fell backwards.

But how great was the astonishment of the young recruit as the grim face of an attacking face appeared for the third time. The valiant defender of the rampart made if possible a still more effective thrust, and thought: „With that the so often rejected will have enough“, nevertheless the threatening enemies continually appeared; and only after 12 had been precipitated into the trench, did the attack cease.

After the lapse of some hours the guard was relieved, and the sergeant asked, if anything had occurred: „Nothing particularly“, answered the recruit, „only that an impudent, inimical grenadier had the boldness to climb the wall, I gave the fellow a couple or two of thrusts, so that he fell backwards into the trench, however he always

returned, and only after I had set him right 12
times with my halberd, he has been contented,
and not troubled me again.

The sergeant had the Trench examined, and
there lay to his no little astonishment 12 dead
grenadiers, which the brave recruit had successively thrust from the storming-ladder.

The act was announced to the commandant,
who handsomely rewarded the brave recruit.

S p e y e r.

The Clocks.

Among all sovereigns who sat on the German
Imperial-throne none experienced a sadder
Destiny, suffered greater humiliation, and
found a more lamentable end, than the unfortunate
Henry 4th.

A great part of his sad fate was due to himself, but not a little due to his tutors. From
childhood his wrongly-directed mind, his passions
and his irregular character, allowed severity and
kindness, firmness and mildness, ever dominate
at the wrong time; and all what he did only
tended to the disadvantage of himself and his
Empire.

The world-renowned humiliating spectacle at
Canossa was the principal cause which lessened

Henry's authority, and attracted the contempt of
the Vassals of his empire. His irreconcilable
opponent Pope Hildebrand's submission could not
reconcile the effected ignominy, nor satisfy the
Princes who so unwillingly saw the Imperial
crown so disgraced. Numerous enemies conspired
against Henry and even his only son was his
opponent. After the eldest Conrad had died at
Florence; the second Henry attempted the deposition of his father, and did not shun cunning and
intrigue with all filial duty for the attainment of
his object. He won by different manners allies;
had himself chosen successor by his weak father;
and then seized an opportunity to rebel openly,
and arranged that the Pope declared outlawry
against the Emperor, in consequence the Emperor's hitherto adherents gradually left their proper
master, and went over to the son.

Left by all who had obeyed his commands,
Henry 4th saw himself obliged to go into exile
to Ingelheim on the Rhine; and in order to obtain his personal freedom, at last to sign his
renunciation of the throne. Deeply humbled by
such strokes of Fate, the dethroned old-man
(accompanied by an old servant, Kurt, still with
him, and singularly devoted to him) made a pilgrimage to Liege. Here died the once mighty
Emperor, at a distance from his family, in Poverty
and Misery. For several years his corpse was
unburied, because the ban of the Pope was still

on him, Kurt alone protected it, and under dep-
rivations of all kinds he prayed incessantly a,
the coffin of his Royal-master. At last, however
admonished by the princes of Germany, and possibly more so by his own conscience, Henry 5th
requested of the Pope the abolition of the Bant
obtained it, and ordered that his father's rests
should be brought to Speyer, and should be solemnly interred in the Dome.

As they were brought from Liege one found
still there, the faithful Kurt, the watcher and
guardian of the corpse, and out of respect for
his great love, and attachment he was allowed
to follow the procession to Speyer, and there
witness the interment which was carried out
with all the splendid ceremony customary with
crowned heads.

The long experienced privations, and the great
age of the pious servant, the unremitting watching and praying had consumed the old man's
strength, and the care which was devoted to him
at Speyer could not lengthen his days. He died
after some months, and as the legend relates, in
the moment of his dying all the clocks of Speyer
tolled, without anyone putting them in motion,
as if an Imperial-burial had taken place.

But even in this city Henry 5th was dying, days
and years. Horrible were the sufferings which
visited the sovereign in his last illness, who had
trampled upon the most holy duties, and had

made his way to the crown by shameful, unnatural treachery. No treasures and no flatterer's
words could now quiet the voice of conscience,
and the memory of the despised, in misery dying
father stood as an apparition before his soul.
When at last Death freed him from the nameless
torments, hark! there tolled at once (to the astonishment of the citizens), strangely from the
steeples of the city. It was not tolling which
announced the decease of a sovereign, by invisible hands rang sharp and clear the bell of the
poor sinner; and each asked the other, what
criminal one conducted to execution to-day.

As the people heard the emperor had just
died, horror and terror filled every breast, and
silent prayers ascended to Heaven for the soul
repose of the departed.

Heidelberg.
The Wolfs's spring.

As the Jettenbühl, near Heidelberg, was still
a thick wood there lived in its shade a prophetess named Jette. She had a tall, noble
figure, and in dignity and grace she resembled an
immortal. A noble youth of the Franken-people
heard of the prophetess, and resolved to visit

her and learn his destiny. His heart knew no
fear, but when he stood before her and she appeared to him as a maiden from Walhalla, he
answered rather hesitatingly to her question.
What he wanted? Mighty prophetess you possess
the power of Divination, let me know my destiny?
Jette threw a penetrating glance at the handsome
heroic youth, and a sudden changement seemed
to take place in her heart.

Come again to-morrow, as soon as the sun is
about to set, meantime I will ask the Runen. The
youth appeared the next day at the appointed
hour. What have the Runen said? asked he.
She shook her curly head and sighed. The signi-
fication has not been quite clear to me said she,
but I fear our natal stars touch each other. Then
I should be too happy exclaimed the youth, and
sank at her feet, seized her hand wich he covered with burning kisses. Will you join your
destiny to mine? asked the maiden. The youth
swore it by all the Gods.

Our happiness must remain concealed from
human eyes said the prophetess, and showed
him the spring, now known by the name of
Wolf's spring, as the place of their nightly rendez-
vous. But in the first night as the youth came
to the spring, a fearful spectacle met his view,
the maiden lay on the earth, and on her corpse,
mangling her tender limbs stood a terrible wolf.
The moon illuminated the ghastly scene. The

youth immediately drew his sword, and rushed
at the monster which defended itself, but in a
moment, struck by the deadly steel, it fell dead.

The Legend of Wolf's spring.

Already glances on the Neckar's flood the Moon's twinklinghorn,
Who wanders quickly and good-humoured iu the wood to the
green Born?

Beautiful Jetta it is, of Jettenbühl the holy prophetess —
Faithful Love's powerful feeling encourages the actress —

Every evening to the Waldborn came a strange huntsman;
A youth bold and loving, who Jetta's love had much won —

Oft by the moon's dusky light has she to the Nymph listened,
When kiss on kiss, the stranger stole from loved lips pinioned;

To-day too she veutured him to homage, by late pilgrim way,
From ardent Heart's impatience, how long the path she
could not say.

So long and anxious, the Moon paled, thoughts were torment's touch,
The forest-birds sang blithely, ob Nymph „Hasten not so much!“

Yet now after almost completed course, she sees by bush hidden;
Her gallant already „My love look up“ He does not as if bidden.

The Maiden flies languishingly - quick to him — with impetuosity
Embraces her, not her companion — a greedy monstrosity.

A Wolf, which there its thirst satisfied, greedily its instinct
renewed,
By blood, which from her breast gushed is bush and moss,
bedewed.

O source of grief! Hears no ear her heart-rending scream?
O hunter, hunter come forth to preserve thy lover's life-stream.

He approaches, he hears, he hurries-to, as lightning struck
his blow,
The monster sinks, the maid is free, yet deadly cold, and low.

She glanced still once at him, happines and death her
power gave,
„Farewell dearly-loved hunter my bride-garland falls into
the grave."

Her eye glazed — In Jettenbühl where living she dwelled —
There rests the maiden deep and cool by Neckar flood welled.

Still complains the Palatinate the legend of Jetta's sorrow,
And Wolfs-spring, was the source called from that morrow.
                                        Edward Brauer.

Seckenheim.

Frederic the Victorious.

About the middle of the 15th Century the Elector Louis of the Palatinate, called the bearded,
died, and after a few years his successor and
eldest son Louis 4th was deceased, it looked very
bad for the welfare of the country, for he to whom
the Palatinate should be as inheritance Louis 4th
only son, was a child scarcely 1 year old; and
a powerful Regent was the more necessary, as

the more dangerous attacks from outwards menaced, and the greater acts of power exercised
by impudent robber knights. The states transferred, although against the will of the Emperor,
the government to the Uncle of the Minor, the
younger son of Louis the bearded, the valiant
Friedrich, and not easy could a choice ever have
been more excellent.

With energy Friedrich met his opponents,
and in powerfully steering the deeply-seated
disorder; he succeeded in introducing prosperity
into his country.

The respect and the renown which he acquired,
excited against him jealousy and enemies. Among
these was before all the Archbishop of Mayence,
Diether of Isenburg, who laid claim to the prin-
cipality of Lorch. But Friedrich conquered the
Bishop near Pfeddersheim, and in consequence
of this victory, there was made not only peace
but also an alliance, offensive and defensive, so
that the Victorious, as he was called, could with
increased strength now act against his other
opponents. These were, namely Earl Ulrich of
Würtemberg, and Charles of Baden, Earl Louis
the black of Saarbrücken, and the Bishops of
Speyer and Metz, who encouraged by Pope and
Emperor collectively formed a League against
him. They conducted a desolating war, their
hordes infested the Palatinate, burning places,
country-houses, mills laid in ashes by the hostile-

troops, and the fruitful corn-fields were completely ruined. The banks of the Neckar, and the neighbourhoad of Heidelberg more especially, experienced such devastation; and with despair the Husbandman saw his hopes entirely annihilated. But Elector Friedrich who lamented the misery of his subjects, did not allow them to wait long for him; with a select, yet in number feeble troop, he pursued the enemy, resolved to meet them in open battle. Near Seckenheim, not far from Mannheim, he came upon the Allies. An excellent position which he took, favoured his attack. At the head of his brave troops, he pressed irresistibly into the masses of his opponents, scattered their strength, and used his advantage so well, that he not only obtained a brilliant victory, but also got in his power a great number of his enemies, among them many nobles, the Earl of Würtemberg and the Bishop of Metz.

With his victorious army and the prisoners, Friedrich made a splendid entrance into Heidelberg, but he treated his prisoners magnanimously, and on the same day even, he invited the most noble of them to a grand banquet, which he arranged at the castle. The magnificently spread table savoured of fine dishes and delicious wines, only one was failing the most indispensable — „Bread.“ The Earl of Würtemberg who wished it, called a servant, and bade him fetch the missing article, but the Elector Friedrich took the captive guest by the hand, led him to the window and said. „To the warriors, who unmindful of the laws of humanity, devastate the fields, and wantonly stamp down the seeds, and with the villages, burn the mills, belong no bread.“

Ashamed and with gloomy glances as Friedrich so spoke, the Earl regarded his Allies, but the Victorious soon enlivened them by friendly conversation, and proved himself during the whole dinner as an attentive and affable host.

After the prisoners had been kept in custody a considerable time, Friedrich released them and their knights against considerable ransom, and reciprocal bond, never more to invade the Electoral-Palatinate.

Oggersheim.

Hans Warsch, the valiant Shepherd.

Once in the 30 year's war, a commander of Spanish troops chose the Rhine palatinate as the object of his enterprise, and in his excursion he arrived in the neighbourhood of Oggersheim. The terrified inhabitants fled in all haste, with their best effects, of all men one only remained behind, Hans Warsch the shepherd, who would not leave his just confined sick wife.

When the Spaniards appeared before Oggersheim; according to war-usage the gates of the
town, were closed by the courageous shepherd,
and from the watch-tower on which he had placed
himself, he answered the enemy's trumpeter
who demanded its surrender, that admission
should be allowed to the Spaniards, for which
their commander would insure the citizens protection for their property; in case of refusal of
such reasonable conditions, the garrison were
resolved to defend themselves valiantly. The
commandant of the Spaniards consented to the
conditions, and gave his word of honour for the
conscientious fulfillment. Thereupon Hans opened
the gate, and as the warriors entered Oggersheim they were astonished to see nobody in the
streets, and still more astonished were they, to
find (besides a woman and a baby lying in a hut)
not a single person in any of the houses. Inter-
rogated by the general the shepherd declared
the other inhabitants had fled, but that he, in
order not to leave his wife, just in confinement
without help, had remained.

Such true courage, and devoted affection to
wife and child, moved the Spanish commander,
he praised the brave shepherd, punctually fulfilled the conditions of the Capitulation, and even
stood Godfather at the christening, which Hans
Warsch kept in the most joyful manner.

W o r m s.

Siegfried.

After Siegfried had returned from the Nibe-lungenlande, and brought with him great trea-sures, he thought he would again sally forth to search for fresh adventures. This time he wished to go towards the south, for he had heard of Worms, in Upper-Rhine, and of Gunther the powerful king of Burgundy, and of his sister, whose beauty was said to excel all that one had ever seen of admirable beauty.

With 12 selected horsemen and numerous retinue, he set-out, and made his entry in the most splendid manner into the finely situated Rhine-town. Clothed in red garments, embroid-ered with gold, and richly ornamented with splendid silver-helms on their heads; shields of the same metal and carrying glittering arms, they rode on fiery noble chargers, so that dif-ferent persons regarded with astonishment the strange guests. At the court of Königsburg, noble pages and servants received the procession, and announced to the king, that Siegfried, son of the king of the Netherlands was arrived to salute him. As soon as the king, who had already heard of the mighty Dragonslayer, learned his arrival he advanced towards him, and conducted him and suite to the knight's saloon, where all

the notables of the kingdom were assembled,
as well as the different members of the royal
family. Siegfried was astonished at the gigantic
figures he saw here, especially at the members
of the royal-house, among whom particularly the
brothers of Gunther, Gernot, and Gieselher, as
well as their mother Ute. To the combat exercised young men in the retinue of the king, belonged the knight Hagen of Troneck, his brother
Dankwart, Ortwin of Metz, Volker of Alzey
Rumold, Sindold, Hunold, and many other chosen
swords, as Siegfried, by questioning, declared that
he was come, because he had heard, here at the
court was to be seen the most valourous king
of the world surrounded by the most daring
young men, and because he intensely longed for
a battle for Life and Death, and for Kingdom
and Crown, then regarded the bold with angry
looks, and there would certainly have been an
unequal struggle, if the King's brother Gernot
had not interfered, and by soft words and regal-
ing with sweet wine directed their thoughts to
other subjects. But more than this, worked on
Siegfried the remembrance of the beautiful
Chriemhilde whom he desired to see. He placed
himself at table and caroused gallantly with the
king and his courtiers.

Siegfried passed a whole year, in the most
agreeable manner with festivals and tournaments.
He conquered in all warlike exercises the most

powerful opponents, and the renown of his dexterity in battle spread far into the country. In the chase too, he displayed his bodily strength in overthrowing the Boar, and wrestling with the Bear. To complete his happiness failed only the sight of Chriemhilde, which was not yet allowed him, although she, behind the silk curtains of her chamber, had often listened to and pleasingly regarded Siegfried, when he pranced his horse in the court of the palace, or broke a lance with others.

One day, appeared at Gunther's court ambassadors from Leudeger, the Saxon sovereign, and Leudegast the Danish king. They came to announce war, and to inform that within 12 weeks their sovereigns with mighty armies would march to the Rhine, and would attack the Burgundians. This embassy caused the king much anxiety, because he knew the great power of his enemies, but Siegfried calmed him by the promise that he at the head of his 12 young men, would move out with the Burgundian army, and that he certainly should succeed in repelling the Saxons and Danes. After the ambassadors were dismissed, Gunther armed himself with all his might. People were chosen as standard-bearers, and the army was soon together. After the king, at the advice of Siegfried, had consented to remain at home; the troops marched out against Saxony. There stood the collected power of the enemy already

encamped, and many bitter engagements took
place. One day, the valiant Siegfried perceived
the Danish king Leudegast in golden armour and
immediately dashed at him. A furious combat
began, but the gigantic power of Siegfried struck
the northern combattant deep wounds, and unhorsed him. Several Danish combattants came
to the assistance of their vanquished sovereign,
these however were put to flight by the hero
Siegfried, who then took the Danish king prisoner
and sent him to Worms.

After this heroic feat of arms Siegfried tried
to engage the Saxon king. As he soon afterwards
saw him behind his army, he hurried through
the drawn-up warriors, direct to Leudeger. This
a still more redoubtable combattant than Leudegast, received Siegfried with flourishing sword,
and both delivered mighty blows. After a mu-
tually useless attack, the Saxon king recognised
that he fought with Siegfried, the son of King
Siegebert, and considered it not advisable to continue the combat. He therefore called to his men
to surrender, and delivered himself with 500 of
his troops, to the Burgundian. All these prisoners and many thousand wounded, made by
Balmung's sword fell into Siegfrieds power, were
sent to Worms, where the message of Victory
excited great Joy.

The war was now finished, and the valiant
troops returned to the Rhine with song and music.

In Worms Siegfried and his men were joyfully received; and the fair of the town handed them garlands of flowers and laurels. Only Chriemhilde still did not appear, however, as soon after the return of the victorious army a great festival was celebrated; Gunther did not longer resist Siegfried's entreaty to persuade the sister, and the much praised came to the festival surrounded with the splendour of her beauty. All the knights and magnates of the kingdom who had not seen the Beauty were astonished at the maiden's grace and charm, but the most, Siegfried, who was beside himself, and inflamed with love for the king's sister. From this moment he was her constant companion, and thought no more of returning home.

The report spread that in the extreme north, on Iceland was living a queen whose beauty exceeded all others in the world, and was at the same time endowed with such bodily strength that she unhorsed the most powerful combattant. She would give her hand, it was said to that knight who could conquer her in wrestling, however many had lost their lives in the attempt.

As Gunther learned this, he felt much desire to go to Iceland, and try his chance with the Queen. However his vassals dissuaded him from the dangerous undertaking, but Siegfried promised not only to accompany him, but good success if the King would give him Chriemhilde for wife, Gunther was satisfied with this proposal, and it was resolved that besides Hagen, Dankward and Siegfried, not any other knight should accompany the kin. Immediately all was arranged in secret, and the 4 brave combattants with chosen servants embarked and sailed to the distant island.

On the 12th day, they came to the longed for coast, and disembarked near Isenstein, the capital of Iceland, and the residence of Brunhilden. The Queen herself stood surrounded hy her ladies on the balcony of a castle, on the sea, and saw the arrival of the strangers. Already at a distance she shone in infinite sweetness, and king Gunther could not wait for the time to see her, face to face. When he had announced himself at the court, splendid carriages, came to fetch the arrivals, and each could admire, after his pleasure, the glittering court, and the beautiful, but at the same time gigantically strong sovereign.

As soon as Brunhild learned for what purpose Gunther was arrived, she had everything prepared for the approaching struggle, and named the day on wich it should take place. If Siegfried had not excited the king's courage, he would have been discouraged, and not have ventured the battle, for he thought of those conquered by the powerful queen, and he feared to share the destiny of the conquered.

On the appointed day, Siegfried clandestinely
visited the ship, put on the celebrated Tarnkappe,
which he had formerly taken in the Nibelungen-
lande, and which possessed the property of making
its wearer invisible, and then repaired to the
field of battle, where the whole court was already
assembled. The queen appeared in splendid
armour, sword and spear were carried behind
her, so heavy, that 4 men could scarcely carry
them. King Gunther came glitteringly arrayed,
and the first game began. As Brunhilde would
throw the immense spear and sword, Siegfried
stepped to his side, and seized the royal shield.
„Stand firm“, spoke he, „I am here invisibly for
your assistance, only make the movements of
the battle; I will do all for you.“ These words
encouraged the king very much, he took his
position and awaited the throwing of the spear.
The throw was so powerful that from it 2 men
fell to the ground, but they quickly rose again,
and Siegfried who did not wish to wound the
queen turned Gunther's spear, and threw it, with
such strength at Brunhilden that she also fell to
the ground. But as the throws were not decid-
ing, so began slinging with heavy stones, Brunhilde threw one 500 feet. Siegfried thereupon
seized a stone of equal weight, and in throwing
still further, he decided Gunther's victory.

Gunther immediately advanced to the conquered, who blushed with anger, and said: „Now,

beautiful Brunhilde, you will give me your hand
and accompany me to the Rhine." „That will",
not happen she said, „before I have asked the
advice of my generals, and knights whom I have
had invited here." Such an answer appeared
suspicious to the king, and as he informed Siegfried, who meantime had secretly taken off the
cap, this said: „The Queen has some bad intention; I shall immediately depart and fetch assistance, in a few days I shall be returned again."
With these words he hastened away, embarked
and sailed secretly to the country of the Nibelungen, where he had formerly experienced
Adventures.

After a short passage, he landed there, and
went to a castle, which he saw in the distance.
After knocking and demanding admittance, the
door opened, a gross giant came out, and ran
against him. A terrible combat ensued, but Siegfried in wrestling, threw him to the ground, and
bound him fast. By the terrible howling of the
giant, the dwarf Alberich hastened to the place,
and seeing his friend bound on the ground, he
attacked Siegfried running at him with a long
spear. The hero would not kill the, to him well-
known, guardian to the Nibelungen treasure;
therefore he ran against the aggressor, seized
him by the ring, he wore on his body, as well
as by the long beard, and bound him too. Alberich
seeing himself vanquished, regarded the Victor

and in again recognising Siegfried, he said: „It appears, that I am destined to be your subject, therefore I will now obey you, free me from my bands and command your servant." „For which you swear", answered immediately Siegfried, „to place a thousand fighting men at my orders, with the necessary ships to carry them to their destination, and deliver to me the Nibelungen refuge?" Alberich swore to do so, and Siegfried set the 2 captives at liberty.

The following day, the Dwarf came with a thousand of the best giants of the country, all splendidly accoutred, and placed them under Siegfried's command. They carried the Nibelung treasure which had been concealed in the rocky clefts, and after embarking, the fleet sailed to Iceland. ·

Queen Brunhilde stood on the parapet of her palace as the ships arrived; she recognised Siegfried from afar, who with all the giants stood on the deck, and inquired of Gunther the meaning of the fleet. He answered it was his suite which he had left on his way to her. Brunhilde now saw, that all resistance was useless against such a power, and consented to accompany him to the Rhine. In all haste preparations were made, then with a numerous, and splendid court-suite; and after a touching farewell from all the Queen entered the ship, and sailed towards her new home, accompanied by Gunther and his companions; as well as the warriors of the Nibelung country.

As soon as the fleet had reached the mouths of the Rhine, Siegfried, with some servants landed, to hurry on horseback to Worms, for the purpose of announcing the return of the King. Here the Hero's narrative caused much joy; and the beautiful Chrimhilde who received Siegfried particularly friendly presented him, as a token of her favour, a number of gold buckles set with precious-stones. The preparations for the reception of the King and his bride occupied all persons. Dame Ute was the most active, and all was carried-out according to her directions.

On the day the ship was expected, a number of splendid tents were erected on the banks of the Rhine, and in them was held a grand festival, then the whole court, Chriemhilde, Siegfried on splendidly caparisoned steeds rode out to meet the New-comers. As soon as the ship with the royal flag was seen, a shout of Jubilee arose from the people collected on the banks; and with continued cries of joy from the crowd, the sovereign pair with suite landed. Gunther conducted his bride to the bank, who was embraced and welcome by Dame Ute, and Chriemhilde. Then the others disembarked and reposed in the tents, and the procession was arranged for a solemn entrance into the town. In the royal palace all was prepared for the Marriage and delicate

Wedding-feast. As, the newly married, with the guests had seated themselves at the magnificently illuminated Saloon. Siegfried stepped before Gunther and said: „Now, my king, I remind you of your promise, to give me Chriemhilde as wife." And the king turned to his sister and said: „I have promised you as wife to a noble cavalier, will you be his wife?" „Yes", answered she, „inasmuch as it is Siegfried the bravest of all combattants to whom you have destined me."

As Siegfried heard this he could not resist from embracing Chriemhilde, and thanked the king who rose, and announced to all the guests that Siegfried and Chriemhilde were about to be married. All were joyful, with the exception of Brunhilde who deeply loved Siegfried, however she appeared contented, and the two lovers were then united.

Siegfried enjoyed with Chriemhilde the happiness of Love, but from the first it was not so well with Gunther. As he entered with Brunhilde the bridal-chamber, and strove for the reward of his love, she resisted and requested him to desist, for she intended to remain a virgin. As he, nevertheless was the more violent, she seized him with much strength, and so bound him that he could not move, and then hung him on a wall, where she left him till the next morning, when he was freed. The king was extremely angry at this disgrace, and complained to Siegfried, who promised to assist him the next night; clothed with the invisible cap, he slipped unobserved into the royal sleeping apartment, threw Brunhilde violently to the floor, tore away the magical girdle, and wonderful ring which lent her great strength, and retired unobserved. The Queen believing herself conquered by her husband, resigned herself to Gunther's will and rewarded his love.

After some time Siegfried felt great desire to remove, with his wife, to his father's court. After being overwhelmed with presents; and given a splendid suite by the king they embarked, and after 9 days they arrived at the Castle in Xanten. The parents felt great joy in seeing the long missed son, with his beautiful wife, and celebrated magnificent Festivals during several days. King Siegfried being old and requiring rest, transferred his kingdom to his son, and this he governed with justice and clemency.

After 10 year's uninterrupted peace, during which his mother died, and Chriemhilde bore a son; came messengers who brought an invitation from the Queen Brunhilde to Siegfried and his wife, to repair to Worms. This invitation was sent in the most cunning intention. She had, often thought with envy, that Siegfried to whom the Nibelung country was subject, and owned the invaluable place of refuge, possessed such great power and riches. She therefore reflected

on all sorts of ruinous plans. Siegfried, Chriemhilde and the old king, accompanied by more
than 100 knights, set-out on their journey and
arrived happily in Worms, where they were
received with royal magnificence. Feast succeeded feast, interchanged with combats and
other recreations.

One day as the Queens regarded the warlike
exercises from a balcony, and Chriemhilde praised
the dexterity of her husband above all others,
not excepting Gunther; the two high ladies fell
into a dispute concerning this, which at last
was so violent, that Chriemhilde mockingly reproached her sister-in-law, by saying that in the
bridal-night, it was not Gunther who had overcome her, but Siegfried who had snatched away
her girdle and magical ring. Raging, Brunhilde
ran to her husband, and complained of what she
had been obliged to hear, and although Gunther
was angry that Siegfried had confided that secret
to Chriemhilde, yet he was so mindful of the
services rendered to him, that he should cherish
hatred against him. But the more furious was
the rage in the breast of Brunhilde, and she
applied to the knight Hagen, whom she knew
did not love Siegfried, because his strength
caused himself and other combattants to be disregarded. The knights Gernot, Ortwin an several
others were gained by him, who, as himself,
were of the opinion that Siegfried must be punished

with death. Hagen knew that Siegfried armed
with dragon's fat was insured against thrust and
blow, but also that a place on his shoulder had
remained free from this arming, and was vul-
nerable.

At the instigation of Hagen, a great hunt was
arranged in the Odenwald by king Gunther, at
which Siegfried was present. The strong combattant accomplished wonders, killed several
boars, and wolves, and as an immense bear was
being pursued he overtook it in its course, threw
it to the ground, and loaded it bound, on his horse.
Tired from hunting they encamped for a repast,
but wine was wanting, and as the king and Siegfried felt thirsty, Hagen proposed to hasten to
a near spring. This happened, they took off their
swords and were soon at the place. Siegfried
waited till the king had drunk, then he satisfied
his thirst, but in drinking in a stooping pasture,
Hagen treacherously pierced him deeply in the
shoulder with a hunting spear, so that a great
stream of blood gushed out. Directly Siegfried
seized the assassin by the shoulder, and threw
him violently to the ground, however sank soon
himself and he had only still time to recommend
Chriemhilde to the king Gunther, when his heroic
spirit fled, and all bystanders lamented the terribly traitorous act.

The single combat.

At Worms, the old town was announced a Diet of the Empire by the emperor Max 1ˢᵗ to advise concerning the means to restrain the arbritrariness, and to keep peace and order. At the same time there was arranged a grand Tournament, and invitations sent to near and distant princes, knights, and nobles. Each capable of tournament, and even foreigners were to be friendly welcomed.

Among the numerous guests, who found themselves at this feast in Worms, appeared also a French knight, „Claude de Barre“, sent by his king to guard the renown of the French arms, and there was scarcely a combattant to be found, whose dexterity and strength equalled that of the Frenchman. The character of the Invincible had preceded him; and the gigantic structure of his body, confirmed this fame. Scarcely arrived, the Frenchman had his arms hung over the door of his lodging, and invited, by a Herald, every one to a life and death combat. None of the knights present, would enter the lists against the mighty one. In vain the emperor himself summoned the most vigorous combattant to meet properly the derision of the Frenchman. Nobody announced himself for the dangerous combat, and Max saw with pain the increasing haughtiness ol the vain-glorious fellow. The Emperor could

not longer support the mockery of the faint-heart-
edness of the Germans; he himself therefore
accepted the challenge, and with admiration, the
people saw the arms of Oestrich and Burgundy
hanging beside those of the Frenchman.

Thousands of spectators, on the fixed day for
the combat, pressed round the lists, and expect-
atingly beat every heart, as the emperor and
his opponent appeared on the plain, completely
equipped, and mounting splendid chargers. With
immense strength, the disputants charged each
other, and their lances broke without unhorsing
either, then they dismounted, and seizing their
swords continued the combat on foot. Blow succeeded blow, the powerful strokes of the Frenchman penetrated the Imperial armour, and blood
flowed from gaping wounds. But now Max's
strength seemed to double itself, and with renewed
power he attacked his opponent, and applied such
vigorous blows that the giant fell.

Prodigious cries of Joy filled the air, but
Maximilian quickly reconciled, magnanimously
offered his hand to the conquered, and invited
him to the banquet, as well as to the recreations
of the following day, but the humbled Frenchman
thought it better, still on the same day to leave
Worms.

Flörsheim.

The maiden of Flörsheim.

Not far from Tripptown situated old ruin Wilenstein the remains of which still yet overlook the wood-mountains of Westrich, once lived knight Bodo of Flörsheim. He had had a pious, affectionate wife too early taken from him by death, and an only child Adeline, who bloomed in grace and youthful beauty, was the only joy left to him.

When Adeline had attained a marriageable age, the charms of the maiden; and the riches of the knight attracted many suitors, but the maiden's heard disregarded all solicitation, for none of those who courted her had made any impression, and she loved her father too much to wish to leave him. In domestic occupations, and the enjoyment of the beautiful free Nature, she passed her days, and no passion dimmed the clear mirror of her soul.

One day there appeared at the castle a strange young man of noble fine exterior, however in the costume of a shepherd, and begged permission of the knight Bodo to share the protection and tending of his numerous flocks. The situation of a shepherd, added the youth, was the position of his choice, and he could boast of being so known with it, that it would certainly be of advantage, if the offered service was not refused.

During the conversation the stranger displayed so much knowledge not only of cattle-breeding, but of agriculture, and excellent ideas, that Bodo did not hesitate to transfer to him the superintendence of his shepherds and flocks. Only one thing the youth declined to give, his name and home, because he asserted powerful reasons compelled him meanwhile to keep it secret. Till he was allowed to declare himself, he begged to be called Otto. The beneficent consequences of his shepherd's position soon showed itself, the flocks flourished and increased in an until now, unknown manner, and the timely care of the enigmatical stranger extended to other, to him not transferred, objects, so that he rendered the knight important service, for which this remunerated him with benevolent gratitude. But notwithstanding the blessing which rested on Otto's arrangements, the youth was not of a joyous disposition. A deep melancholy lodged in his soul, he was occupied with his own thoughts, sought solitude as much as possible, and not seldom, believing himself unobserved, he shed tears.

Adeline had heard much from her father of the strange youth; and wath was related of the shepherd excited her complete participation. Till now she had not yet seen him. It happened accidentally that once passing through the forest, she met him. The impression which her appearance made on the youth was great and surprising.

For a time Otto stood speechless, lost in astonishment and feeling, and as if the remembrance of a distant dear person suddenly stood before his soul, he regarded the maiden with doubt and admiration. Only slowly he recollected himself as it seemed, then he begged to be excused on account of his strange conduct, and ventured, Adeline making herself known as the castle maiden, to offer his company. With the utmost attention he listened to each of her words, and as, not far from the castle, he respectfully took his leave, he expressed the hope, that he might, soon be allowed to see her again. Still occupied with the impression which he had just experienced, he retired to his country lodging. He confessed to himself, that if it were ever possible to reconcile himself with the world, with which he unfortunately so early already had quarrelled, if he might still hope happiness would smile on him, Adeline could conduct him to it, whose almost wonderful resemblance with his beloved ah! already departed sister, excited him so powerfully.

Also the maiden felt herself magically attracted to the educated stranger, whose pale suffering features bore the expression of deep grief. His noble conduct, the feeling in his discourse spoke for him, and if she did not confess that she felt more than friendly to him, so had however the still dreamy manner that now took the place of her former joyous spirits, convinced a spectator that in the young heart love was become awake. It was also more than accident, that already the following day Otto and Adeline met again, they saw each other almost always at the same place, sat themselves on a mossy bank, and talked till the setting sun reminded them of the course of time. From that time, they passed each evening together, soon they confessed their feelings to each other, and nothing resembled the bliss with which they swore eternal love, and fidelity to each other.

In one of these hours of happy meeting; Otto confided to his beloved the fate of his former life. Prematurely losing a tender father, who had been a most respected, wealthy knight in Thuringen; Otto had, with a loved younger sister, suffered the cruellest treatment from an avaricious, unfeeling step-father. Then Death had by the loss of their mother, entirely delivered them into the power of the rude man. To escape the ignominy of being abused as a shepherd, Otto fled at last to a distant uncle, at whose castle he found apportunity to obtain a knightly education, and to exercise himself in arms. After several years he returned home, and found his step-father in possession of all the property, and the dear sister dead. The monster had continually ill-treated the girl, and as she in consequence became ill, he left her without care, indeed,

according to well evidenced suspicion, had hastened
her death by poison. Beside himself with grief,
Otto questioned the villain, challenged him, to
answer for the death of the sister, and demanded
the immediate delivery of the unjustly retained
property. A revolting answer was the decision,
and the young man stung thereby to the utmost
anger, drew his sword, and stabbed him whom
the world called his father. But this rash bloody
action had for Otto the most fatal consequences.
He was obliged (if he would not be bound by
the servants of the murdered and killed), to fly;
and secure himself from the pursuers, into the
thickest woods. His own uncle till now favorable,
cursed him, and soon shared the property with
a near relative of the murdered. Then Otto
wandered long till he found admission as shepherd
by Adeline's father.

With the deepest sympathy the beloved heard
the tale. Then she sketched plans for the future.
Otto was to discover himself to Bodo, a faithful
friend to be sent to Thuringen, to obtain information of te uncle, and the state of things and the
property belonging to the young man, and leave
no means untried, to obtain an agreement with
the uncle, and what could be obtained of the
paternal property. The lovers hoped that no
abstacle would oppose their early union.

On the day following this confidential com-
munication, Bodo sent for his daughter, and said

to her: „Hitherto you have refused all offers of
honourable knights, and I have pardoned this
from regard for your youth and inexperience,
but retain to myself to assert my paternal
respect by the next acceptable suitor, and hope
that no longer childish obstinacy, or affectation
will be an obstacle to your advantageous connection. Such a connection now offers itself.
The knight Siegebert has solicited your hand,
he is the richest in our district, and has obtained
great renown in Palestine, whence he is lately
returned. To-morrow he will come to solicit for
you, and I confidently expect that you will gladden him with a friendly promise.

Adeline stood as if annihilated, she could not
love the strange knight, however rich and renowned he might be, and she abjured the father to
force on her no husband, to whom her heart did
not incline, and not to hazard the happiness of
her life, but to leave the choice of a husband
to herself. But the knight Bodo remained inflexible, and excited by the resistance of Adeline
he forgot himself so much, that he ill-used her,
and even locked her up.

The next day the knight Siegebert magnificently accoutred and with a splendid retinue made
his entry into the castle. He had chosen Adeline,
whose beauty had been praised to him, and
hoped to find in the maiden, joy at the prospect
of such an advantageous, brilliant connection, but

the striking paleness of her face, and the weeping eyes were not witnesses of a joyful meeting, and Siegebert was disagreeably affected by these discoveries, his vanity was most sensibly offended by his friendly words finding no response in the course of the day, and not being favored with a favorable regard.

This behaviour embittered the knight Bodo. He confined Adeline in a dark room, and swore that he would send her to a convent, and disinherit her if she did not give, even on that day her promise to Siegebert. At the same time arrangements were made for a splendid marriage-feast, and invitations sent to the neighbouring castles.

Meanwhile Otto passed tormenting days. He had, since his last meeting not seen his lover, heard of the visit of a strange knight, and of preparations for a grand banquet. Besides it was not unknown to him how anxious Bodo was for Adeline's marriage, and therefore with increasing anxiety he expected the hour when he could again speak with the beloved. But Adeline came not more. He was seized with unspeakable pain, and the thought the beloved had thoughtlessly forgotten her oath, made him take the resolution to leave the country for ever. Like a madman he wandered through the woods, and distant plains, cursing himself and his fate, that had destined him to misery, and so he strayed about

days and weeks: till at last the irresistable power
of ardent desire brought him into the neighbourhood of Flörsheim. He wished to hear at least
news of Adeline, in fact, he wished to speak
with her father, discover himself to him; and if
the beloved had not forgotten all faith, beg for
Bodo's consent, but as he went to the castle with
such intentions, he heard from shepherds whom
he met, that on the next day the marriage
ceremony with Siegebert was to take place. He
was seized with despair on hearing this news,
without giving any answer to the shepherds, he
turned to a bridge, which led to a deep stream,
now swollen by violent rains, and threw himself
into the raging-flood.

Adeline was, to the day on which her marriage with Siegebert was to take place, so much
the more strictly watched, because meanwhile,
she had declared to her father her love for Otto.
This severity, as well as the exhortations and
menaces with which Bodo unremittingly tormented
her, and still more so the news, that since some
time her lover had disappeared, brought her at
last to such a state of mind, that she unwittingly
yielded to her father's will. But as she should
go to church, dressed in her wedding - garments,
as the marriage bells chimed for the nuptial
ceremony, the poorest believed to be obliged to
escape her misery, and watching a favorable
moment she hastened, unobserved out of the

castle-door, and to the place where the beloved
one's hut stood, „Otto, Otto", cried she, „have
you really left me?" and look, there stood at
the brook some shepherds, who, as it seemed
to her, endeavoured to draw a human body out
of the water. A terrible presentiment saized her,
drove her to the shepherds and oh! horror, a
corpse was before her, it was the corpse of Otto
which had just been landed. Now the power of
despair seized Adeline, and quick was the unhappy maiden's resolution; before any one could
prevent it, she sprang from the lofty bank, and
the waves swallowed her.

Some days afterwards, the bridal-dressed corpse
was washed on shore; and the knight Bodo full
of bitter repentance, at the folly of his obstinate
severity, had the two lamentable victims buried
together in one grave.

Heppenheim.
The Monk at Lorch.

Not far from the, [on the mountain street
situated small town Heppenheim, and near
the place Weschnitz, stands on an island, still
the ruins of the formerly rich and powerful „Bene-
dictine abbey Lorch." Founded under the

government of the French king Pipin; and richly
presented by successive sovereigns, this abbey
had existed during centuries. To the devastation
of the 30 years war succumbéd the fine large
building, the treasures and jewels it contained,
were lost by the plundering of the war parties.

To this abbey, arrived once late in the evening
Charlemagne, who according to his habitude
travelled through his kingdom, in going from one
royal court to another. He wished not only to
pass the night there with his retinue, but to
repose from the fatigue of a long straining ride,
for the great sovereign had reached a high age,
and the acts and cares of a very active life had
consumed the strength of a former vigorous body.

The Abbot and the other inhabitants of the
foundation, received respectfully and joyfully the
mighty guest, whose piety honored their calling,
and whom they had to thank for many gifts.
A banquet finished the festival day of so high
a visit.

It was already midnight, as the king kept
awake by harassing thoughts left his chamber,
to relieve his heart by prayer in the near church.
Alone and unremarked he strode through the
consecrated halls, and knelt before the altar.
The profound stillness which dominated here,
and the feeble light of the eternal light which
clothed the objects with a magical half dark
shine, raised the impression of the sacredness of

the place, and the Emperor uttered his prayer
with so much the more fervent devotion. He
would just return, as a noise behind excited his
attention. He looked round, and saw with
astonishment the figure of a venerable and as
it appeared blind monk, who, led by a boy tottered along the pillared corridor. Just before
the Emperor, the old man sat on a form and
then sank on his knees and offered-up a long
prayer, often interrupted by sighs: Charlemagne
felt himself uncommouly attracted by the venerable apparition, he believed to be obliged to
honor in him the ideal of a God-devoted; and
it seemed to him, as if a halo surrounded the
head of the old man. In the shadow of a pillar,
to which he had retired, he waited till the monk
had finished his prayer. and had retired with
his youthful guide; then he also left the church.
and went to his repose.

In the morning he related to the Abbot the
nightly apparition, and inquired after the name
of the old monk, but he could not receive any
other information concerning the problematic
person, than that some years before, the same
person by the name of Bernhardus, arrived from
another Convent, of what lineage he was, and
the name of the cloister where he had formerly
been, he had continually and obstinately refused
to mention.

Driven by curiosity and sympathy, the Emperor

had himself conducted to the monk's cell; as he
attentively regarded the monk's traits, he seemed
to know the features. Many remembrances passed
through his memory, and the inconsistency of
Fortune stood clearly before his soul. He reflected, that descended from princely-lineage,
Thassalio once governed the Bavarians; how this
duke excited by the, to him married daughter
of the dethroned Longobard king, had revolted
against the powerful emperor, and lawful feudal
lord: how then the undutiful, after he had been
vanquished and again generously rewarded, again
broke his oath of Vassal, and how at last, again
in the victor's power was banished to a distant
convent of the Franken-country, in order to expiate
in strict life-long penitence the past wrong. All
these recollections rose lively in his thoughts,
inquiringly his regard rested on the sorrow-
stricken features of the monk, and a tear of
sadness shone in the sovereign's eye. Then he
stepped nearer, seized the old man's hand and
said: „Pious father, you and I stood often antag-
onistic; however those times of hate and struggle
are long since passed. We are now of an age
when the passions cease: when the earthly
stand in the background, and the thoughts of
Heaven are in the soul. Duke Thassalio! you
have heavily enough expiated the errors of former
years. It is Charlemagne who stands before you,
who feels no more rancour against you, and who

herewith offers you pardon and reconciliation.
Let hate flee from your heart, if you still have
any against me." A convulsive movement passed
through him as Charles named simself, then he
fell at the feet of the emperor seized his knees,
and said: „I have heavily sinned against you my
king and sovereign. Privation and strict atonement be my expiation till my death. As I heard
of your arrival in the convent, my former life
passed before me, and more devoutly than ever
have I prayed to Heaven for forgiveness. That
you might also pardon me was my last earthly
wish." Exhausted by the extraordinary emotion
Thassalio fainted, and deeply moved Charles
retired, and gave the order that every attention
should be given to the neccessitous monk.

The next morning, before departing the
emperor wished to see Thasalio still once, and
beg his pious blessing, but the abbot announced
that in the night he old man had quietly departed this life.

Frankenstein.

George of Frankenstein.

In ancient times the neighbourhood of Frankenstein on the mountain-way was infested by a
huge monster, which had chosen for its sojourn

the vale of Modaubachs, covered with reeds and underwood. The monster had a serpent-like figure of powerful length, having a regularly formed thick head and jaws that could have swallowed an ox. The terror which was spread among the inhabitants of the country by the presence of such a monster, was so much the greater, because it not only regarded their flocks and herds, but even men as its booty; and almost daily a human being was its sacrifice.

Uselessly some bold champions had made the attempt to destroy the dragon, they were obliged to pay, with their lives, their temerity, and soon nobody more was to be found who had the least wish for a combat with the monster; complete pusillanimity overpowered all spirits, and whoever could, removed far from the country as if the plague ravaged there.

Not far from this place of terror, however on the other side of Eberstadt; lived at that time, George of Frankenstein at a castle, the ruins of which still look down upon the beautiful Rhine valley, from its far seen woody eminence. He was a brave knight, and celebrated champion, his gigantic bodily form, and the strength of his arm had always procured his arms the victory, so that also in gymnastics nobody ventured to enter the lists with him.

George heard the lamentation of the poor inhabitants of the Modaubach valley, who wan-

dered about homeless, their necessity affected
him, and he resolved to try a combat with the
monster however furious and terrific it might be.

On a war-horse suitable to the size of the
champion, armed with sword club, and armour,
he rode into the abandoned valley, and soon he
saw the monster in the willow-ground, rolled
together and comfortably sunning itself. Awakened
by the noise of the approaching knight, it rose
hissing, and in making a long spring, at the hoped
for booty; opened its immense jaws as if he would
swallow, at once, man and horse. But of firm
courage, although his horse reared, the knight
waited for his monstrous enemy, and as it was
near enough, the courageous made a dexterous
side spring, and avoided the greedy snapping of
the dragon, and seeing his advantage, he thrust
his sword into the neck of the salamander. Then
he seized his heavy club, and struck the monster
(that attacked him again grazing him with its
bloody teeth), so violently on the head, that it
fell stunned to the earth, and could be killed
without trouble.

In the meanwhile the squires of the knight,
and many people waited in the distance the
announcement of the hero's enterprise, and the
result of the struggle, and as now one blew the
hunter's horn as joyful sign of the victory, and
the hurrying persons saw the monster lying in
its blood, a joyous cry arose, and thousands of

voices praised the heroic act. But suddenly the knight's face was deadly pale, he sank to the earth, and could only say, with weak voice that he felt himself deadly wounded, by the poisonous teeth of the animal. Terrified, the knight's armour was loosened, and not to be mistaken was seen a slight wound on the hip, into which the terrible serpent's gift had penetrated.

The general joy for the obtained victory, was now changed into mourning for the hero, like that celebrated Saintly hero George, treading on the dragon's neck, died, after some minutes. His memory is still with the grateful inhabitants.

In the village of Nieder-Beerbach, one sees near the church-door, still to this day; a grave stone on which is represented by an artistic hand, the knight. triumphantly advancing to the dragon.

Darmstadt.

Walther of Birbach.

Walther of Birbach distinguished himself above all knights of his time, by fervent undissembled piety. To the holy Virgin Mary particularly, he directed early and late his ardent prayer, one could say that he seemed to devote to her his whole existence.

Once he rode to Darmstadt for Tournament, it was the first time that he would enter the lists, and he knew, that among the many knights were many who exceeded him in bodily strength, and in the dexterous handling of arms. He was therefore very anxious, that he would not stand the struggle with honour, and perhaps could be overthrown to the mockery of the spectators. But this thought was increased by thinking on the lady of his heart, whose colours he wore, and who was to be present at the tournament; and he believed not to be able to survive, if he should suffer a shameful defeat before the eyes of his mistress. As Walther full of tormenting thoughts crossed the fields, suddenly he saw in his way an erected altar, upon which was the figure of the Virgin Mary. Directly he dismounted from his horse, which he tied to a tree; and performed his devotions, in urgently begging the Holy Mother to assist him in the approaching struggle, and to lend him victory and honour. In the fervency of his prayer he lost his senses; a sort of convulsion ran through him, and long he lay there like a dreamer at the foot of the figure.

But the holy Virgin had heard the supplication of her zealous worshipper, she descended from the Altar, and unremarked loosened his helmet, armour, and sword, armed herself with them, and mounting his horse hurried away. After a considerable time she returned, armed, unperceived as before Walther with his own weapons, and again took her place on the altar.

Now the pious first recovered his sensibility. He raised himself hastily, bowed still once to the blessed, and gallopped to the not more distant town. Here at the door of the town he was received with joyful acclamations, and as he came to the place of combat, his acquaintances crowded around to congratulate him, and with astonishment he learned that he, in the already finished tournament, had conquered all champions. At first he did not believe his ears, but soon an interior conviction made it clear to him, by what high power he had become the victory and who had stood for him in the lists.

In consequence of this tourney; Walther became the happy husband of his beloved; and out of gratitude, he built over the figure of Mary on the plain, a fine roomy Chapel in honour of the holy Virgin in whose worship, he found happiness and blessing to the end of his life.

Frankfort.

Foundation of the City.

When Charlemagne fought against the Saxons the fortune of war, often was unfavorable to him, a brave liberty-loving people offered him powerful resistance, and not often, repelled by their superiority he fell into great distress. So also once as he was obliged to retire before them on the banks of the Main. A thick fog covered wood and river, no vessel showed itself, and it was impossible to find a place which could afford Charles and his army a passage. There sprang, alarmed by the noise of the army, out of the thicket, a deer which bore a young one, and as if she would show the emperor the way to safety, she waded with her young one through the river. Charles did not delay to use this discovery, he followed, with his army, the deer, and fortunately escaped the enemy to whom the fog hid the passage.

But on the other bank, Charles full of gratitude for the saving ford, stuck his spear into the sand, and said „Here a town shall rise to be called Frankenford" in memory of this event. And as in consequence he completely overthrew the Saxons, he founded Frankfurt, which later became so celebrated by the Imperial coronations, and in beauty and riches still now thriving commercial town on the Main.

The Knave of Bergen.

In Frankfort at the Romer was a great mask-ball, at the coronation festival, and in the illuminated saloon, the clanging music invited to dance, and splendidly appeared the rich toilets and charms of the ladies, and the festively costumed Princes and Knights. All seemed pleasure, joy, and roguish gaiety, only one of the numerous guests had a gloomy exterior; but exactly the black armour in which he walked about excited general attention, and his tall figure as well as the noble propriety of his movements, attracted especially the regards of the ladies. Who the Knight was? Nobody could guess, for his vizier was well closed, and nothing made him recognizable. Proud and yet modest he advanced to the empress; bowed on one knee before her seat, and begged for the favor of a waltz with the Queen of the festival. And she allowed his request. With light and graceful steps he danced through the long saloon, with the sovereign who thought never to have found a more dexterous and excellent dancer. But also by the grace of his manner, and fine conversation he knew to win the Queen, and she graciously accorded him a second dance for which he begged, a third, and a fourth, as well as others were not refused him. How all regarded the happy dancer, how many envied him the high favour; how increased curiosity, who the masked knight could be. Also the emperor became more and more excited with curiosity, and with great suspense one awaited the hour, when according to mask-law, each masked guest must make himself known. This moment came, but although all others had unmasked; the secret knight still refused to allow his features to be seen, till at last the Queen driven by curiosity, and vexed at the obstinate refusal, commanded him to open his vizier. He opened it, and none of the high ladies and knights knew him. But from the crowded spectators, 2 officials advanced, who recognized the black dancer, and horror and terror spread in the saloon, as they said who the supposed knight was. It was the executioner of Bergen. But glowing with rage, the king commanded to seize the criminal and lead him to death, who had ventured to dance, with the Queen; so disgraced the empress, and insulted the crown. The culpable threw himself at the feet of the emperor, and said „Indeed 1 have heavily sinned against all noble guests assembled here, but most heavily against you my sovereign and my Queen." The queen is insulted by my haughtiness equal to treason, but no punishment even blood, will not be able, to wash out the disgrace, which you have suffered by me. Therefore oh King! allow me to propose a remedy, to efface the shame, and to render it as if not done. Draw your sword and knight me,

then I will throw down my gauntlet, to every
one who dares to speak disrespectfully of my
king. The emperor was surprised at this bold
proposal, however it appeared the wisest to him;
„You are a knave he replied after a moment's
consideration, however your advice is good, and
displays prudence, as your offence shows adventurous courage. Well then, and gave him the
knight-stroke, so I raise you to nobility, who
begged for grace for your offence now kneels
before me, rise as knight; knavish you have acted,
and Knave of Bergen shall you be called henceforth, and gladly the black knight rose; three
cheers were given in honour of the emperor,
and loud cries of joy testified the approbation
with which the Queen danced still once with the
Knave of Bergen.

The 9 in the Vane.

Hans Winkelsee the poacher was in bad reputation with the people of Frankfort; he in-
trenched upon their rights, and shot their best game,
at last they succeeded in capturing him, and placing
him in the tower of the Eschenheimer door, and
the gallows was before him. The view he had,
from his high prison was possibly not so bad,
for if at that time, the town was not surrounded
by magnificent promenades, splendid gardens,
houses, and cheerful places as now adorn it; he

could however look over the wall, and see the
woody ridges of the Taunus, and his small window
allowed him to see the blue sky. But the more
extended his view, so much the more Hans felt
himself confined in the prison, and when he had
tormented himself with longings for liberty during
the day, the creaking vane of the tower made
his careless sleep disagreeable.

He had already passed 9 days and nights
there', as he cried out full of ill-humor, cursed
wall hole, still more cursed the vane creaking
over my head. If I were allowed, and had my
rifle I would leave behind me a memorial for
the destroyer of my rest. The Frankforters should
see how artistically I can shoot, with 9 bullets
I would draw exactly a 9 in the vane. The jailer
who well understood how to listen, heard these
words. Odds! murmured he, I should like to see
such shooting; and directly he carried his news
to the mayor and council what Winkelsee had
spoken. To most of these, the poacher's words
seemed only the boast of ill-humor. But the
mayor said it would ever be for us, and the
citizens an amusing sight if we allowed the poacher
to make the trial. If he shoot the 9 as he said,
we could spare his life and set him in liberty,
for such a shooter .would be well worthy of
pardon; however we will have him hanged if he
fail only by a hair. The proposal was unanimously
approved, and communicated to Winkelsee.

The next morning early, many sight loving people had collected at the Eschenheimer door and young and old waited with impatience, to see the shooting of the 9. Released from prison, Hans stept amongst the crowd, and joyfully he received his rifle, which by his arrest had been taken from him. The trial he had to stand, was so much the more difficult, as the vane just then was set in motion by a strong wind, and therefore offered no sure aim. But Winkelsee knew how to use the favorable moment, and the first shot struck exact, as well as the 2nd 3rd and all the others, forming 9 holes in the vane. At each shot, the people applauded by each success, the admiration increased, and as the shooter completed the work; there was no end to the joyful cries. Hans Winkelsee spoke the Mayor, you have obtained your liberty, and because you are so clever with the rifle, we will make you the Captain of our shooting corporation. But Winkelsee refused this offer. The vane of the tower, and Frankfort said he, may ever think on me, also I shall not forget the days and nights, 9 in number, which I have passed there, yet longer I do not wish to remain in your town, I prefer the woods. Should you ever see me again you may hang me up there above on the vane; and with these words he went out of the door, and Frankfurt never saw Winkelsee again.

Taunus.

The knight of Falkenstein.

At the time when Emperor Rudolph of Habsburg was endeavouring to restore order and peace in the empire, and with strong hand resisted the sword-law and disorder of the Robber-knights, lived in the castle of Falkenstein a knight of the name of Kurt, a very venturous and powerful highwayman. Not only did he rob the harmless wanderer, and the peaceful merchant who went quietly on his way with goods, but with his numerous men he surprised very often castles and towns, which he hoped to find unprovided for such attacks. For the success of most of his robberies and to his far feared might, was to be ascribed the circumstance, that he could at the same time multiply himself, for with him he had 7 strong sons, who carried-out his plans equally quick and effective, and occasionally carried out robberies on their own account.

The cry for help from the, by Falkenstein oppressed district, echoed soon to the Emperor's throne, and as the warnings sent to the evil doer remained unheeded, the monarch set out from Worms where he was at the time, with a sufficient troop against Falkenstein and invested the castle. The knight and his soldiers offered a valiant resistance, but a storm attack, effectively

carried out from all sides, placed the castle at
last in the power of the Imperial troops, Kurt
and his 7 sons were made prisoners.

The emperor had sworn that every knight-
robber taken with arms in hand, as well as the
accomplices should be executed, and so he commanded the execution of Falkenstein.

On the extensive castle platform, the Imperial troops formed a circle, in the middle of
which the Hangmen waited for their sacrifices;
and Rudolph himself was present, with a numerous
retinue to be witness of the execution of his
commands. It was a surprising and affecting
sight, as Kurt with his 7 sons were led into the
circle, the strong old man at the head of his
manly fine sons, and among the numerous spectators one heard voices, who ventured to beg
pardon for at least the sons. Also in the Emperor's breast there moved feelings of deep pity
for these unfortunate sacrifices; and willingly
he would have pardoned the youths who had
acted more in obedience to their father, than
from inclination and so become criminals; but
the Imperial oath was inviolable, and so the
monarch could not allow motives of clemency
even also not, as among his people many had
begged for the life of one at least of his lamented
sons. And however to yield somewhat to so
many and urgent solicitations, and however remain firm to his oath, Rudolph permitted the

pardoning of one of the youths, but under conditions the fulfillment of which, bordered on impossibility. „I will grant life and liberty to that one of the Falkensteiners, to which the father, after execution will step, and thereby designate for pardon." And now the old Kurt, with gloomy look until now, regarded Heaven, with the expression of inspired certainty, and courageously offered his neck to the executioner's sword. And see! as the head rolled in the sand, the headless with firm step advanced to the eldest who stood next to him, and from this to the 2, and the 4 others, when staggering to the youngest and last, he suddenly fell to the ground.

Astonishment and horror seized all who saw the spectral round visit. But the emperor ordered the 7 sons to be set at liberty, and had them taken into his army, so that by really noble actions they might efface the disgrace of their former lives, and that they might be worthy of pardon and condition of knights.

Mainz.

Heinrich Frauenlob.

Heinrich of Meissen according to some reports Canon, by others Doctor of Divinity, living in Mainz, at the beginning of the 14th century devoted himself besides the sciences, especially to Poetry, as then with him is said to have begun the incorporated principal school in Mainz. He dedicated his songs mostly to the holy Virgin Mary, in which he sang the ideal of the highest goodness and piety, but later his poems praise the female sex principally, and especially many separate women, so that with right, he received the name of Frauenlob, and under this name he is also known in the history of German poetry.

The love and veneration which the grateful sex paid him was so great, that his death spread a general mourning, and that the maidens and wives of the named town arranged him a burial as by the fair ones no man had ever before received.

The tolling of all bells announced the mournful day, and a long funeral procession moved along the streets, to the Dome, where his grave had been prepared. The greater part of the very numerous train were women in mourning garments, and eight of the most beautiful carried the coffin which was adorned with roses, lilies,

and myrtles. At the grave resounded songs of
lamentation from female mouths, and a quantity
of the most delicious flowers were strown upon
it. The favorite drink of the poet, which had
so often inspirted his poetry, the delicious, noble
Rhine wine, was here in death lavishly spent
on him, so that, as the legend relates, the entrances of the Church were flooded by the Liba-
tion. Only late, and amid many tears the women
left the grave.

A stranger who had come to Mainz on this
day, would have believed a great prince, a great
benefactor to the country, had been accompanied
to his last resting place. In the Dome, on the
place of an old damaged Monument of Frauenlob
in the year 1842, was erected a figure stone by
Schwanthaler (a beautiful female figure in white
marble, placing a wreath on the master singer's
coffin).

Rabbi Amram.

This most learned Rabbi was born in Mainz
in the 13th century, and lived in Cologne, where
he founded a high Jew's school, of which he was
the principal, and by his widely known learning
and piety, made renown also in foreign countries.
During a severe illness, he expressed the wish
to his scholars to be buried beside his parents
in Mainz. By the representations of the scholars,

that this could not be done without danger, he
ordered the following: „When I am dead, clean
me, lay me in my coffin, place it in a little
vessel on the Rhine, and let it go wherever it
chooses." When he died his wish was fulfilled,
and the small ship, without guide, floated up the
Rhine towards Mainz, as here the people seized
the vessel, to draw it on land it floated back,
so that it was not possible to hold the vessel.

The news of this miracle was heard of by
the bishop, who went to the Rhine, to convince
himself of the truth of the affair: indeed the
whole population of Mainz had streamed to the
bank to see the strange and inexplicable ship.
Naturally were also Jews on the Rhine, to whom,
to the greatest astonishment of the multitude,
the ship floated, but if Christians attempted to
take it, it floated back, so that apparently the
vessel would only go to the Jews. The bishop
allowed the Jews to bring the vessel to the bank,
in order to see what it contained, meanwhile they
had brought the vessel to land, and found in it
a coffin with a dead person in a Jewish death
shirt, and an inclosed letter, with the following
contents: „My dear brethren and friends, Jews
of the holy communion of Mainz, I am come to
you, for I have died in the holy communion at
Cologne, and beg you to bury me beside my
parents, who are buried at Mainz, and wish you
all much happiness and a long life. This begs

the Amram." The Jews brought the coffin to land, but the Christians struggled with the Jews, to get the coffin, but they could not carry it from the place. The bishop now ordered the coffin to be kept there, that it should not be carried away by the Jews, and had a crypt built over the coffin, from which one formerly believed they have given the name, and origin, to the present St. Emeran's church, which was very large. All applications and requests to keep the coffin were useless. However meantime the Jewish students in Mainz succeeded by cunning to bring away by night the body of the Rabbi Amram; and according to his last wish to bury him with his parents in the present churchyard.

On the wall of one of the formerly standing houses, of the streets running to the Rhine from the Bocks street, which disappeared 1850 by building; one remarked a half effaced Fresco, representing a ship driving up the Rhine, and standing on the banks a multitude of people.

Ingelheim.

Charles and Elbegast.

The Emperor Charles in his palace on the Rhine had just fallen asleep one evening, as in dreaming an angel appeared to him, surrounded with splendour, placed herself, before the Monarch's bed and said: „Rise great Emperor it is the will of Fate that you still in this night go away secretly and alone, for you shall steal.

Charles awoke, the dream appeared to him most singular and wonderful. While he reflected upon it, he slept again, and anew the same angel appeared, repeating the warning yet more pressing and emphatical. „Do not tarry", she said, „arise and steal, it is for the honour of yourself and kingdom, it is the order of a higher power announcing its power through me."

Alarmed at this repeated warning, he could not more consider it accidental dreaming, the Emperor rose from his bed. But in vain he tried to explain the meaning of the words, which the angel had spoken, the to him more than singular command, to him the richest sovereign of the East, to commit a humiliating dishonorable action.

But the appearance had announced to him the will of a higher power, to which Charles was accustomed to yield with pious resignation, and so he resolved to obey implicitly, to set out,

and to leave the consequences to Heaven. He
dressed and armed himself, left the chamber,
and after going to the stable, and saddling his
favourite charger, he rode out of the castle-gates.
But of all this not one of his servants, or the
castle-guard had remarked anything, for they
all lay, as if bound by magic in a sort of death-
like sleep. He took his way to the next forest
in saying to himself: „Because it is evidently
the will of the Lord to do what I ever detested,
I will submit to the command, but as I do not
know how to begin stealing, I could wish that
Elbegast the defamed thief whom I have hitherto
so much prosecuted were with me. I would reward him if he learned me to fulfil the nightly
work, or helped me, so that I might not grow
faint-hearted.“

While the king so reasoned with himself he
perceived, by the feeble light of the moon a
single knight advancing towards him. He also
seemed to have remarked Charles, and rode for-
wards so that soon they stood opposite each other.
The strange knight was in black armour from
head to foot, and rode on a black charger with
black horse-cloth. He appeared to regard the
emperor inquisitively, and the emperor had willingly known who rode so alone through the
forest at midnight; the black colour and the
silent Being did not seem of good omen, and the
Emperor was convulsed with the thought it could

easily be the Evil one himself, who would cause him damage and mischief in the hour that Hell has power over Men.

„Who are you“, the stranger first interrupted the silence, that you in full armour wander about by untrodden paths by night in the forest? Are you a servant of the king, come to find out how you may catch the Elbegast, whose retreat is in this wood; then you ride in vain. He is quicker than the wind, more cunning than the council at the Court of Ingelheim, and more known in the wilderness than the fox and the deer.“ „My ways“, answered Charles, „are not yours, and nobody but the Emperor dare demand an account of my actions, but if my words do not please you, I am ready to give you satisfaction according to the laws of knighthood.“ So saying he drew his sword, and prepared for battle, in the same moment gleamed the black knight's sword and blow succeeded blow. The stranger delivered such a violent stroke on the Emperor's helmet that his blade flew in pieces, and he stood defenceless. But Charles was ashamed to kill the unarmed, and said to him: I do not wish your blood, but prefer to give you your liberty, if you say who you are, and why you wander about here in the wood.“ „I am Elbegast“, replied he, „since I have lost all my property, and the emperor Charles has driven me out of my country, I procure my subsistence by stealing

and robbery. Till now, no one has vanquished
me, you are my first conqueror. As you act so
magnanimously to me, speak, what I can do for
you to prove my gratitude." „If you", replied
Charles, „are Elbegast the defamed thief, whom
the Emperor already long endeavoured to catch,
so prove your gratitude by helping me to steal.
I came here to rob the king Charles, and for
this business I can use your assistance, come
therefore with me, and let us make common
work." „I will not rob the king", answered Elbegast, „for although he has taken my property,
and banished me, he did so from evil council,
and far be it from me to hurt my sovereign.
I only rob those who have amassed treasure
unjustly. Do you know Count Eggerich of Egger-
monde? Him we will visit, for he has already
caused much damage to many honest men, and
even he would deprive the Emperor of Life and
Honour if he might." Charles learning such faithful sentiments, and that he intended well towards
himself, was glad in his heart and said: „I will
go with you to Eggerich", and so both went to
the count's castle. Here with uncommon dexterity
Elbegast broke a hole in the thick wall, crept
through, and bade Charles follow him. They
arrived fortunately in the count's rooms; then
Elbegast understood to open locks noiselessly,
and knew to arrange himself everywhere. But
the count who slept lightly, remarked something

and said to his wife: „I hear a noise as of persons creeping obout in my house, perhaps there arc robbers in my castle, I will get up and see.“ He really rose, lit a torch, and lighted about in all passages and rooms. But because Charles and Elbegast had already slipped under the count's bed where nobody supposed; he found nothing, extiugnished the torch and went to bed again. Then the countess said to Eggerich: „My dear husband certainly no robber has entered our castle, but rather I believe that the inquietude of your mind does not allow you to enjoy sleep, and excites your head with imaginary things and dangers. Confess, they are particular plans which keep you awake; confide them to me, so that I can advise you, and reflect for your advantage.“ „Well!“ replied the count, „because the execution of my intention is decided for to morrow I will not longer conceal it from you. Know then, that I have sworn with 12 equally disposed knights, to murder the Emperor, who has forbidden us encampments on the roads, and take toll from travelling merchants and other wanderers. Nobody knows of our Confederacy, and I forbid you on pain of death to mention a word of it to whomsoever it may be.“

Not a word of this conversation escaped Charles. Then he slipped, as they were again fallen asleep, away with Elbegast after leaving to him the found valuables, he hastened home, where he arrived before day-break, took his charger into the stable, and gained his sleeping apartment as unremarked as he had left it.

In the morning he summoned his council and said to them: „I dreamt this night that count Eggerich with 12 allies would come here for an evil purpose, he has no less an intention than murdering me on account of the hated peace of the country, which I endeavour to sustain and which does not please the robber-knights. Take care therefore, that a sufficient troop of armed men will be kept concealed to appear at the first signal, and seize the crafty ones."

About noon Eggerich came trotting with his accomplices, and demanded to be conducted to the Emperor. As soon as they had ridden into the court of the castle, the doors were closed upon them, the armed men surrounded them, and in tearing open their clothes discovered the hidden arms. Convicted and incapable of denying; the conspirators suffered a shameful death by the hand of the Executioner. But Elbegast, whom Gharles had induced to come to court under the promise of complete pardon, he richly rewarded, and insured him subsistence for life by for ever renouncing the profession of a thief.

But in grateful recognition how well he had done in obeying the angel's warning, and how good it is to submit implicitly even to the most obscure dispensations of Providence, the emperor named the residence where the angel appeared to him „Engelheim“ i. e. in the present day „Ingelheim“ by the so celebrated palace of Charlemagne on the Rhine.

Eginhard and Emma.

Of several children which the wife of Charlemagne bore him not one stood higher in his favour than his youngest daughter Emma. Not only by great beauty, but excellent understanding, with childish grace, and the softest most attractive manners, she made herself worthy of her father's preference, and the emperor always used when he passed a short time in his family-circle seeking recreation from the heavy cares of his government, to call the girl his dear Imme. In the palace at Ingelheim his council assembled almost daily. They were the wisest most tried men that he honoured with his confidence, he esteemed and respected them. Several indeed enjoyed his especial affection to such a degree that they inhabited the palace with him, could be called his friends, and were his daily guests. Almost all were in an advanced age, because Charles confided in the quiet reflection of riper years a more extended regard, and a more decided wise judgment in state affairs than is to be found in younger men. However the emperor made one exception, regarding age with the young Eginhard who on

account of his extraordinary talents and know
ledge, had been early chosen not only as councillor, but also private secretary to the monarch.

Educated at the court, and of fine pleasing
manners Eginhard was a favourite of the ladies,
and the object of many secret wishes; but he
made the deepest impression on the emperor's
daughter Emma. The private secretary, constant
companion of his monarch, ofteñ passed days
near Emma, could not fail to observe the still
attention with which the high lady favoured him,
and he soon discovered that she entertained a
secret inclination for him. How could Eginhard,
the feeling youth, remain indifferent to this discovery, how could he remain cold and without
to return her love? He struggled violently to
suppress his rising passion, and reminded himself
of his duty not to abuse his sovereign and emperor's confidence; but it was this which rendered
more difficult the struggle of duty in charging
him to teach his daughter music. The oft undisturbed society of the two lovers soon led to
a mutual understanding, and the oath of eternal
fidelity sealed the heart-band.

For a long time the veil of secrecy concealed
their quiet happiness, it was not seen and betrayed by any listener, but not satisfied with the
hours of day when they were allowed to see
each other they claimed soon those of night, and
Eginhard clandestinely visited Emma's sleeping

apartment, and enjoyed there the blissful hours of Love.

The spring had been the witness of their first confession, and the beautiful summer-nights disappeared only too quickly for the lovers. To the summer succeeded the autumn, with its rough November storms; but foolish enough, the lovers anticipated the longer darkness of the coming winter-nights, which should also lengthen and embellish their interviews.

So sat they once confidentially talking in Emma's small room. The stormy winter-night had been almost passed in conversation, as the sand-glass showed it was the highest time for Eginhard to return to his apartment. She went with her lover to open and shut the court-door, but who can imagine-their terror, as they found the court covered with snow. It was impossible for Eginhard to pass through the snow without his footsteps betraying him, impossible for him to risk the good reputation of the beloved, or her father's anger. Emma recovered herself first. „I know an expedient“, whispered she, „to free us from the embarassment, it is the only one, and at the same time the most secure. Place yourself on my shoulders dear one, I will carry you over, then only the steps of a woman's feet will be seen, and no suspicion excited.“ „Oh artifices of women!“ langhingly answered Eginhard, „it is only a pity, that for the execution

your strength fails", and fearing she was not
equal to the heavy load, he at first refused to
agree to the proposal. However Emma's persuasion, and the impossibility in any other manner
to secure themselves against detection, overcame
in him the feeling of delicacy, and he allowed
himself to be carried over to his lodging on the
beloved one's shoulders.

But unfortunately these nocturnal visits did
not remain unperceived. By cares, as they easily
visit the sovereign of an immense Empire, extremely excited, the Emperor could not, just in
this night find the desired sleep, and unquiet as
he was, he rose from his bed, and stepped from
his sleeping apartment into the adjoining saloon,
where a balcony allowed an open view into the
court. There he saw a female figure carrying
a man through the snow; and urged by curiosity
he went to the balcony. How great was his
astonishment as he recognized in them, Emma
and Eginhard. Not without great exertion, did
Charles master the violent agitation which this
unexpected sight caused him, and just as unremarked as he stepped to the balcony, he returned to his apartment.

The next day he called his council, with whom
also Eginhard appeared, and laid before them
the significant question? what a king's daughter
had deserved, who clandestinely and by nightly
leisure had received a paramour into her room?

The council reflected a time, then they decided,
that in love affairs the best — was pardon,
Charles did not make any opposition, but asked
further, what a low nobleman deserved who ·
entertained a secret love-intrigue with a king's
daughter, and indeed nightly slipped into her
apartment? Again the council decided, with the
exception of the youngest, for pardon, and only
this youngest, it was Eginhard, who had hitherto
remained dumb and pale, spoke for punishment.
„He deserves Death!“ said he loud and emphat-
ically, and surprised by this verdict, the Emperor stepped before him and answered: „Death
would be too severe a punishment; but banishment becomes such a transgressor, as well as
the duty-forgetting daughter; deprived of her
exalted rank, and live with her paramour distant
from her home, forgotten by her dear relatives.“

Silently and in deep meditation wandered,
early the next morning two pilgrims along the
road to Mainz. From there they walked to the
other bank, then they left the public road, and
the density of the wood hid them. Towards
evening, tired with wandering about, both requiring night-quarters, they came to a Charcoal-
burner's hut, in which they received refreshment
and shelter. The next morning, after they had
gone a good distance, they arrived at an open
place in the wood, which afforded a most charming prospect and therefore especially pleased them.

A murmuring brook sprang from the earth, and a flourishing willow plantation extended to the near bank of a river. Here the lovers rested a time, and here first loosened the anxious timidity, in which both had remained since their exile. In lamentable tenderness they accused each other, of being the cause of such a hard destiny, and they swore, by double tenderness to make each other forget the harshness of their lot. Then they resolved, to remain in this lovely vale and build themselves a cottage. With near dwelling shepherds Eginhard exchanged some of the valuables, which he had brought with him, for cows, sheep, and the most necessary farming utensils, and he hired rooms in a habitable, spacious cottage, in which love sweetened the meal and did not allow them to miss any of those splendours, by which they had been surrounded at court. Six years passed in this solitude like so many months, and the lovers bliss was still increased by the growing up of 2 boys, which Emma had presented to her Eginhard.

But Emperor Charles grieved meanwhile the loss of the beloved daughter: his hair whitened, his cheeks fell in, and his sad look said distinctly enough that he was not happy. He did not more pass his time in his family circle when the affairs of his government allowed him leisure; but rather hastened with his suite from the castle, to range the woods for game because hunting

better suited his state of mind. Once he undertook an extended hunting excursion to the forests
of the Odenwald. In the pursuit of a splendid
stag, he lost himself, and too late he learned that
none of his hunting - companions had remained
with him. He sounded his horn, but no answer
hailed him in return, and discouraged, that he
had mistaken his way so much, he dismounted
from his horse, bound it to a tree, and seated
himself in a shady spot. While reflecting, which
direction he should take, to return to his people,
sprang a lively boy, attracted by the call of the
horn, out of the bushes, and with childlike astonishment he regarded the strange man and the stately
charger. Charles, glad to see a human being,
beckoned friendly to the boy, to approach, and
made him soon so confidential, that he played
with his weapons. Questioned the boy related,
that his father and mother lived in the neighbourhood, and he offered to show the way there.
Wishing to make the acquaintance of the inhabitants of this wilderness, who according to the
appearance and conduct of the child could not
be without education, the Emperor followed, and
soon found himself before a fine, ornamental
cottage, in which was a beautiful young wife
busied in preparing the supper. Emma — for
it was his daughter — received the stranger with
courtesy and offered him a night's lodging, as
good as the mean shelter could afford; then she

told him, that her husband was hunting, but must soon return, and that he would certainly be glad, to take supper with a doubtless noble knight. Charles could not turn his eyes from the charming wife. Although she was not known to him, yet the sight of her filled him with an inexplicable interest, and the question was at his tongue'send, how it happened, that they had chosen such a remote solitude for their residence? In this moment the husband appeared. Heartily and friendly he saluted the unexpected guest; however the young man in a singular manner, seemed to be known by his exterior, so that Charles could scarcely conceal his astonishment. At last they seated themselves at the table, and the hostess placed, after a simple soup, a dish of venison. Scarcely had the monarch tasted it, when overcome by sad remembrance he called out: „Ah, just such a dish my Emma used often to prepare me, as she was still with me and was my favourite!" At these words Emma and Eginhard sprang from their seats and looked fixedly at their guest. At if waking from a dream she cried: „Yes, it is my father!" fell at his feet sobbing: „Your daughter, your Emma is at your feet! it is she, who fled here, who far from the noise of the world, has passed her days here with the loved one, and blesses the moment, which is allowed her to see still once the author of her life." Then Eginhard fell at the Emperor's feet supplicating pardon and reconciliation. A long pause ensued; on the sovereign's face was reflected an internal struggle; but then succeeded a scene of love, rich in embraces and expression of childlike tenderness.

Before Emma's tears of joy melted all the rancour of the severe father; he fully pardoned her and Eginhard, and passed the happy hours of the night with them in their cottage, as he passed them in the splendour of his court.

Meanwhile his hunting companions, full of anxiety for the missing, had searched through the forest the whole night, and only by daylight they came near the valley, where the three happy ones tarried. The horn signal, constantly blown by the searchers, was at last answered and soon the whole suite stood before the cottage.

Holding Emma by one hand and Eginhard by the other, and accompanied by the two little ones, the Emperor stepped out: „Look here“, said he, „while you sought me, I have made a precious hunting-discovery. I found in this solitude my expelled daughter and my friend Eginhard again, bitterly wanted by my heart during six long years. They are my children; they shall henceforth not more be separated from me. Hasten and let us return to Ingelheim, so that we can there celebrate the feast of reunion and alliance, which I herewith bless. Eginhard my son-in-law shall from now again be my councillor; but on the

place, where my Imme passed so many happy
years and I enjoyed the blissful hours of refind-
ing, she shall build a convent „Happy-place."

And so it happened, and at the place, where
the convent was erected stood formerly a town,
which after the name of the founder was called
„Happy place" still existing on the Maine. In
the churh is still shown the tomb of the couple,
whose bones are inclosed in one coffin; bnt this
coffin the grand-duke of Hessen has lately presented to the Count of Erbach, who as some
assert, is a descendant from a branch of Eginhard's lineage.

Queen Hildegard.

When the Emperor Charles marched out, to
punish the frequent irruptions of the Saxons into
the French empire, and at the same time to
spread Christianity among them, he confided his
favourite residence, the castle at Ingelheim, and
all it contained, to the protection of his half-
brother, the knight Taland. But quite particularly
Charles recommended to him the safety of the
Empress Hildegard, who remained at Ingelheim,
and at the same time he charged the knight, to
report, to him after his return, of all that had
occurred in the palace.

Taland was educated at the court of the
Grecian emperor, and unhappily his otherwise

good character, there spoiled by the dominating
loose morals, so that among other things he had
lost all belief in female virtue, and entertained
the opinion of being able to seduce every wife.

But since he had lived at Charles court, he
seemed to have renounced the art of seduction,
and none of the ladies to have charm for him;
for his eye quietly aimed at one, who outshone
all other beauties, but for him unattainable, the
Queen Hildegard. By the monarch's earnestness
and severity retained in the strictest limits of
respect, Taland took care, not to betray his passion; but as Charles' departure for the army had
taken place, the infamous Taland projected plans
to satisfy his illicit inclination, and the charge
of a Protector and Commander of the castle gave
him sufficient means.

He began manifesting his love to the high
lady opportunely, by glances and mien, and these
remaining without success by impudent indications. As Hildegard allowed these to pass unobserved, the seducer even ventured, to declare
himself distinctly when once together, and to
assert with the most passionate oaths that he
would rather die, than renounce the return of
love from the Queen. With astonishment and
aversion the high lady had listened to him, and
with the dignity and pride of offended virtue she
refused him in the most decided manner; but
Taland considered this refusal only as a mask,

and therefore repeated the next day his shameful courting, even more pressing, passionate, menacing. The noble queen, to avert misfortune and to debarass herself of the troublesome knight, contrived a trick. She acted, as if she were affected by the violence of his love, and appointed to meet him on the following evening in a distant wing of the castle, where, as she said, their meeting could take place without disturbance. Highly delighted the knight was at the agreed hour at the indicated place; also Hildegard appeared there and she opened the door of a retired apartment, into which she begged the knight to step. But he had scarcely crossed the threshold, as the door was closed and bolted. „There", called the Queen to him, „there you may be, honour-forgetting dissolute, brood over your foolish love, till my husband returns and withdraws you for merited punishment!"

The outwitted was almost stiffened with fright. He found himself in a small, very remote chamber scarcely provided with the most necessary furniture, could only afford him a sad lodging, and there was no possible delivery from this dungeon, than by the clemency of the offended Hildegard. Daily he received very frugal food, which a very discreet chambermaid pushed through a narrow grated door, and as often as the servant appeared, the captive begged her to assure the Queen of his deep, most sincere repentance, and his most

supplicating entreaty, to be freed from his ignominious imprisonment. Hildegard refused a long
time, distrusting the assurances of the imprisoned;
but as she received the news, that her husband
would soon return from Saxony, and Taland's
entreaties were always more urgent, she released
him on the day of Charles's entry into the castle,
in pretending, the knight was just returned from
a secret embassy.

.Raging and revengeful the released reflected
now on the ruin of te Queen. He hastened to
meet the Emperor, and under the appearance of
the most zealons devotion he lied to him, that
Hildegard had broken the oath of marriage fidelity,
that she entertained intercourse with a stranger
knight, and even had been surprised by him,
the Protector; he added that not longer to be
witness of such shameful infidelity, which to
punish belonged to the husband and king, con-
sequently had gone to another district of the
Empire, till he heard of the Emperor's arrival.

The more Charles loved his wife, so much
the more was he inclined to jealousy and the
more easily he believed the words of the calum-
niator. Beside himself with anger, he commanded
the Queen to be seized conducted into the wood
and there decapitated. Taland willingly undertook the execution of this command; he informed
the court of the king's will, and surrendered the
innocent Queen to two of his minions. These

roughs dragged her into the forest during the
night, and had already raised the murderous
sword, already would Hildegard offer up her last
prayer to the Creator, as from the bushes, a white
closely veiled figure advanced and in a hollow
voice cried out: „Stop, wicked wretches! do not
finish the work of Hell, fly, that the vengeance
of Heaven does not annihilate you!" The super-
stitions minious fled, and nevertheless informed
their master that his orders had been punctually
executed.

Hildegard found herself again in the arms of
her faithful waiting-woman, for it was she who
had chased the murderers, fearing that she too,
the confident of the Queen could be the object
of Taland's revenge, and inspirited with the wish
to save her mistress, she had secretly followed
the minions from the Castle and had rigthly calculated on their superstition for the success of
her plan. But there was no security for the two
women in the whole neighbourhood; they were
obliged to seek safety at a distance, and after much
wandering they came to the hut of an old hermit
who received them hospitably. Here Hildegard
dwelt a long time with her faithful servant.
The queen soon confided in the pious old man,
and he offered with her the most fervent prayers
to Heaven for the safety and manifestation of her
innocence. In this wilderness she learned from
the old man the curative effect of different herbs

and roots, all well as their application, and collected
a treasure of beneficent knowledge, which had
a decided influence on her later destiny. By the
advice of the pious man the two women in disguise
at last made a pilgrimage to Rome, where they
maintained themselves by means of the learned
medical science, and Hildegard was soon very
renowned. The Holy Father himself consulted
her in an illness and recovered by the employed
remedies. Hildegard's assumed name Arabella
was everywhere mentioned with respect, and even
to Germany echoed the news of the almost miraculous cures of the enigmatical woman. But
from the moment however, that Thaland informed
him of the pretended execution of the Queen, he
had no more peace. He was gloomy and taciturn,
avoided intercourse with men, as much as he could,
and not seldom hid himself for days in the thickets
of the woods. Repentance for the rashly ordered
act, the thought, that his wife was not guilty, or
perhaps had not been guilty tortured him unceasingly, and he prayed to Heaven, to allow
him to find a means for the quieting of his soul.
The occasion of a campaign against the Longo-
barden was welcome to him; he intended, after
it was finished to visit the holy Father in Rome,
to disclose the him his sad state of mind, and
thereby to obtain perhaps alleviation for his tormented conscience. Aalland begged to be allowed
to accompany him for since his misdeed, the

infamous, had been effected, as if for punishment
by a consuming malady, and he hoped for recov-
ery from the milder air of Italy. His request
was allowed, and so left, after victoriously ended
war, Charles with Taland for Rome.

The reception of the Emperor there was pomp-
ous. Among the people concealed and unremarked,
Hildegard saw with a beating heart and the most
painful emotion the solemn entry of her husband ;
but with horror and terror she perceived the traitorous Taland at his side. It could not fail, that
the with fever seized wicked wretch should soon
apply to the renowned Arabella. Already the
day after his arrival he visited her, and after
Hildegard had heard of his lamentable condition,
she said: „Knight, I shall be able to cure you with
the help of God and my art, if you are free from
the guilt of a crime, or in case you have committed one, declared and confessed to a priest
what deception you have done. If you omit such
penitence, your death is certain. Alarmed Taland
hastened away; but tortured by accusing conscience and fear of death, he confessed. But as
he feared the revenge of Charles, he could not
resolve to acknowledge his misdeed, he did not
confess it, and deferred the declaration from day
to day, so that he became worse and he was
soon near death. At last he sent for the Emperor
to his sickbed and at the same time Arabella, to
declare to the former what he had sinned against

the innocent Hildegard, and to demand from the latter, if possible remedy for his sickness, in hoping his present condition would effect pardon from his royal brother. Great was Charles's emotion, as he disclosed the net of the lowest wickedness, and pain and repentance almost broke his heart. Yet he soon became consolation and all absorbing joy; for as Hildegard, the called cure-assistant, appeared, she was not able to restrain herself at the sight of her husband. She threw away her disguise and with the words: „Oh my royal master and husband“, she fell at his feet.

Surprised and deeply moved, Charles raised Hildegard, in whom he again recognised his wife, and both were united in a long embrace, shedding tears of sadness, joy and thanks to the righteous disposer of Destiny. But deadly pale Taland regarded what passed, inmovably sitting in an armchair in which, lamed by surprise he sank down, and as Charles would loudly demand explanation, he found him a corpse. The powerful impression of the moment had killed the wretch.

But Rome celebrated a feast, as none had ever been kept, the festival of the reuniting of the excellent pair; the Pope blessed the new bond, and with a more joyful heart than he had ever felt, he returned with his Queen to the Rhine. And also the faithful waiting woman, who continually had remained inseparable from her mistress, saw her Rhine home, and the palace at Ingelheim, and

honored by the Empress, as one only can honor a
friend, she was long witness of the happy days
which the Queen passed with her beloved King.
As thanks for her preservation, and proof of her
innocence, which the Heaven had so wonderfully
permitted, Hildegard founded the Abbey of Kemp-
ten, and the records of this foundation have preserved the intelligence of the miraculous event.

Rudesheim.

Gisela.

In the agitated times of the Crusades, when from
nearly all Christian countries numerous knights
and horsemen streamed to the Holy Land, to obtain possession of the Holy Grave from the Saracens,
to establish a kingdom there, and as fanatical
priests of all places demanded for this, as they said,
God-pleasing work, preached also in the Rhine-
countries Bernhard of Clairvoux. Energetically he
exhorted, to devote themselves to the great cause
of Christianity and to join an army, that was about
to set out for Palestine. Among those who obeyed
this summons was the Knight Brömser of Rudesheim. Already a widower and father of an only
blooming daughter, to him very dear, and possessor
of a splendid castle in the charming Rhine-valley,
the paradise of Germany, had the Knight, rich and

much esteemed more cause to remain at home, than leave his Gisela, and expose her to the danger, of early becoming an orphan. But the desire of action and unceasing exhortation, to fight for the honor of the Redeemer, overcame every other regard, and Brömser left the castle of his ancestors, accompanied by the tears and blessings of his daughter, and set out with his many similarly disposed Knights and their men for the Holy Land. After many adventures and difficulties he arrived there, and soon distinguished himself by extreme bravery. His name in the Christian camp was mentioned with renown, his sword feared by the Infidels, and it was always the knight Brömser who was charged with the execution of such enterprises, requiring presence of mind and intrepidity. In a rocky mountainous country, not far from the camp, was the sources, which provided the necessary water; but all at once it was impossible to use it, because a terrible dragon had chosen this rocky ravine for its place of residence. The monster was of a remarkable size, coated with scales, legs with sharp claws, its wide jaws armed with a double row of thorny-like teeth. Quick in movement every knight unguardedly approaching it became its prey. The news of the appearance of this dragon set the whole camp in dismay. In vain the commencing want of water demanded the conquering of this new enemy, in vain the Emperor Conrad himself who conducted the army, solicited the knights; fear rendered every arm powerless. Many regarded the dragon as a punishment of Heaven, sent as chastisement for the outbroken discords between the Christian combattants and for many occured crimes, and this opinion was the cause that even the bravest retired from the jeopardy.

The knight Brömser pitied the general misery. He stood before the Emperor, and offered, to stand the combat in God's name. After having armed himself, he rode, accompained by the blessing of all, to the cavern, where the monster couched. Soon it darted on its newly hoped prey; the knight's horse pranced at the sight of the terrific figure, and Brömser was obliged to dismount, in order to master its movements. Directly the monster was near him, fortunately however he regarded the charger as the first object of its attack, and in precipitating itself on it, it wound the poor animal with its scaly tail and crushed it. The valiant knight profited of this moment, to cut through the tail with a powerful stroke of his sharp sword, before the dragon could uncoil itself from the horse, and so broke the strength of the dragon, and then, as raging with pain, it snapped at Brömser with distended jaws, the resolute knight threw his shield into the monster's mouth, and while it endeavoured to break it to pieces, the fortunate combattant thrust his sword to the hilt into its loins, a stream of blood issued from the wound causing the monster to fall to the ground and die.

Glad of the acquired victory, the knight began to return. He had already made the half of his way, when suddenty a number of Saracens precipitated themselves on him from an ambuscade, and made him a prisoner. With bound hands the noble knight, the deliverer of his colleagues, was dragged into the enemy's camp, exposed to the mockery of the wild hordes, and at last surrendered as property to an Emir. This sent him to a fortified castle carefully guarded. Here in the seclusion of the solitary dungeon, in terrible almost hopeless imprisonment, he was seized with a longing for his dearly beloved native country. He thought on his beautiful domain, his left Gisela with melancholy, and in the despondency of his heart, he made a still solemn now, that, if he was allowed to return home, he would found a convent, and would dedicate his daughter as its first nun. He felt himself consoled and quieted by the vow, and indeed his deliverance was not far distant. On a dark night the Christian army surprised and attacked the castle, in its victorious course took the knight, and led him triumphantly into the camp. He remained only a few months with his comrades, then with the Emperor's permission he returned to Germany. His journey home was fatiguing and dangerous, however he at last arrived well at Rudesheim. He was received with jubilation, and Gisela wept tears of joy in embracing him, as she had tears of sorrow at his departure.

On the day after his arrival a young knight appeared at the castle, and presented himself to Brömser as Kurt of Falkenstein. With candour and confidence he related how he had become attached to Gisela, as well as that she loved him, and that therefore they only required the father's blessing to make them the happiest couple. Brömser seemed in deep thought, and then regarded his daughter in whose countenance was to be read a confirmation of Falkenstein's words and said, in seizing their hands, wtih tender sad tones: „How willingly I would accord your wishes and bless you as my son, for I knew you father: in the East he often spoke of you, the valiant one, who fell at Edessa fighting against the enemies of our faith — he was my favourite companion-in-arms; but a vow binds my will, and you may never belong to each other. In ignominious captivity with the Saracens, loaded with chains, I vowed, in case I returned home safely, to found a convent to the honour of the Virgin Mary, and that Gisela should be the first nun in it. By the intercession of the Blessed, I was soon after in liberty, it is therefore my duty to fulfill my vow, and, as truly as God helps me! I will earnestly accomplish, what I vowed, therefore in future may no earthly love find place in Gisela's breast."

As soon as Falkenstein understood this. he rushed, like a madman, out of the saloon, mounted

his charger, and galloped away, but Gisela fell
insensible to the ground, and from that hour she
was deranged. She wandered through, like a
spirit, the wide corridors of the castle, and once
as a raging storm ploughed through the waves
of the Rhine at the midnight hour, and the howling tempest broke the oaks of the near forest,
the unfortunate one crept to her father's bed,
whimpered him farewell, hastened then to the
balcony, and precipitated herself into the Rhine
The hastening after father came too late, to be
able to restrain her; he only saw her waving
garments disappear in the profound depths.

Grief and remorse now embittered the life
of the childless old man. It is true he omitted
nothing, to restore his diseased mind, and he not
only accomplished the building of the convent to
calm his conscience, but also tried by other means,
indeed even by mixing himself in quarrels, and
the pleasures of hunting to procure himself dis-
traction; but neither private warfare nor hunting,
could deafen the torment of his conscience. One
day a farm servant brought him an insignificant,
wooden figure of the crucified, which the plough-
ing oxen had turned-up, and Brömser regarded
this finding, as a sign from Heaven, to build a
church, on the spot where the figure had been
found. This he did, and had the figure placed in
the temple, and soon it became praised as working
miracles, so that pilgrims from far and near visited

in. In the same year that he completed the church,
which he named the Need of God, the knight died,
and strangers, uo sympathising relatives, accompanied him to his grave.

Bingen.

The Mouse-tower.

Hatto, bishop of Fulda, wished to obtain the
vacant archbishopric of Mayence, and employed by the Emperor all passible means, to attain the accomplishment of his wish. He knew how
to arrange by bribery and other means, that the
choice fell upon him although there were more
worthy candidates.

This advancement stamped still more his ambition, pride, and inhumanity. Principally he let the
poor subjects feel his oppression. High taxes were
extorted from them, so that he could execute large
buildings and satisfy his love of splendour; tolls
were imposed and new burdens invented, as if the
country was only therefore destined to satisfy the
ruler's whims. Below Bingen, but near Bingen
loch, he had built a strong tower, opposite the banks
of which stand the ruins of Ehrenfels and castle
Rhine-stone, in the middle of the foaming waves,
so that all passing ships could be easily stopped

at this narrow passage, to oblige them to pay toll.
Soon after the building of this custom-house, it
happened, that a general scarcity visited the Rhine
country, and particularly the Bishopric. A terrible
drought parched the fields; vermin and hail-storms
destroyed the little that was germinated, and a
general Famine was the more threatened, because
Hatto had almost bought-up all that was left of the
last harvest, and securely locked in his granaries.
The feared misfortune occurred in all its terrors,
very soon over the whole country, and spread inexpressible misery among the poorer population.
It is true the Bishop allowed his stores to be sold,
but at such high prices, that the exorbitant demands
could not be satisfied by the greater part of his
subjects. The poor were therefore obliged to have
recourse to means, which produced maladies, and
so increased the general misery. In this necessity
the unhappy people stormed the prince with the
most supplicating and touching prayers. Even his
council and friends urged him to pity the deplorable
condition of the poor, and to be for them a suc-
couring sovereign, instead of an oppressor; but all
representations and requests remained useless.
The tyrant still continued, to sell his corn only for
the highest price, for he was wishing, to build a
splendid castle of extraordinary size, for which he
required large sums of money.

But the increasing distress, and the severity of
the archbishop increased the dissatisfaction to

exasperation, and as this at last threatened to pass to acts of violence, Hatto opposed with mockery and cruelty.

One day the hungry crowd of men, women, and children, after vainly soliciting bread before the Bishop's palace, forced themselves violently into the apartment, where the Prince and his guests sat at a luxurious banquet. Hatto received the intruders with mocking condescension, promised them corn, and begged them to go to a large barn where they should receive the mentioned food. Glad to receive this promise the unfortunates retired; but scarcely were they in the barn, as the Barbarian ordered the doors to be fastened, and, oh the inhumanity! set fire to the building, and as the burning sacrifices supplicated lamentably for commiseration and the flames forced their howling cries of pain, Hatto spoke to those surrounding him: „Hear how the corn-mice squeak! I do not do anything else with the rebels, than with other mice, which I catch; I burn them."

But this terrible act called down the vengeance of Heaven on the infamous author. Out of the ashes of the burned barn crept thousands upon thousands of mice, and as a devastating stream took their way to the palace, filling all apartments, and fell even upon the bishop with bold avidity. However he tried to defend himself, and his servants kill thousands, there was no end of them, and the wretch began to recognise, that a higher

Judge had undertaken to revenge his crime. Left
by his suite, who fled from terror, Hatto hastened
to a ship, to escape the pursuers; but in vain. By
legions they swam after him, as he was ferried
over the Rhine: and as he, in despair landed at
the Custom-house near Bingen in thinking there
to be protected, his innumerable enemies pursued
him still, gnawed and perforated the tower with
incredible quickness, dug themselves entrances
through the thick walls, and at last reached him
whom they sought.

Hatto succumbed to the mice, which fell upon
him by troops, and hundreds of thousands, and
after consuming him they disappeared entirely. —
The tower is still called the Mouse-tower. Nobody
inhabits, or uses it: its gloomy, half dilapidated
walls stand there, as the monumental column of a
black, terrible act, haunted, as a warning against
such similar crimes to suffering men.

The legend appears in a milder light, if one
refers to History concerning Hatto, according to
which he appears to have been a clever regent,
but imperious Prelate. The emperor Ludwig and
the duke Otto then held the regency of the kingdom, and Hatto was the emperor's confident, so
that he was called the Heart of the King. A re-
presentant of the German clergy and first admin-
istrator of 12 rich and powerful abbeys, he was at
the same time the principal founder of that tem-

peroral power, which the seat of Mayence obtained
for itself. Without doubt, his proud despotical
character, by which the people were obliged to
suffer much, as well as many inventions of his
powerful rivals, assisted in producing that terrible
legend of the Mouse-tower.

The holy Rupert.

Under the government of Ludwig the pious,
Duke Robolaus dominated in the country of the
Saxons. He was not favourable to the Christian
religion, besides being of a wild impetuous character, he was also courageous and skilled in arms.
Bertha, the daughter of a powerful duke, on the
Rhine excited in him a violent passion, and the
soft amiable maiden, and pious, devout Christian,
was not averse to him, partly because she admired
his heroical actions, and also hoped to couvert
the future husband to Christianity.

Unfortunately this hope was not fulfilled. The
rough warrior did not regard Bertha's gracious representations, and at last he forbad them entirely,
and was of so sulky a temperament, that the poor
suffering wife was obliged to separate from him,
and to reside at a distant castle. Here she gave
birth to a son, who was named Rupert, and was
her only consolation and favourite. Bertha wished
to educate him as a pious Christian, because she

regarded the predilection of her husband for warlike life as the cause of their misfortune. She
therefore endeavoured, above all things to incul-
cate in the young heart mild virtues, and an inclination for a quiet domestic life.

By an invasion, which Robolaus undertook
against a neighbouring race, he was in a bloody
battle the sacrifice of his temerarious courage.
As Bertha heard of his death, she was much
afflicted, for then she thought only of his good
qualities. She resolved, to leave her present sojourn, and to remove to her parents who inhabited
the ducal palace at Bingen.

Here many nobles of the country solicited the
hand of the beautiful young princess; but she declined all, even the most brilliant offers, in wishing
to devote her life to the education of her beloved
son. He also rewarded her trouble and care in the
most beautiful manner. Fortunately he had not
inherited from his father the wild pride, but the
mother's meekness and piety, and soon developed
a spirit of charity, and this increased with his
years to the great joy of Bertha and her parents.
Rupert tarried willingly among the poor children
of the place; he shared with them what he had,
gave to the poorly clad, even of what he himself
wore, and once as a troop of half naked, hungry
boys were assembled around him, for which his
gifts were not sufficient, he conducted them to his
mother saying: „Take care of them, dear mother,

for they are also your children." Just so showed
itself, as Bertha would erect a splendid building,
the charitable feeling of the pious boy, in opposing
this intention with the words: „First feed the
hungry and clothe the naked, those who are in
need and are our brethren."

By such charity Rupert was soon the object
of universal love, of which with increasing years
he made himself more worthy. All he had and
could beg from his mother, he gave away without
any regard for himself. Grown to a young man,
representations were made to him from all sides,
not only on account of his generosity, but his
neglect in the practice of knightly arms, it was
more suitable to his high position, it was said, to
accomplish himself in combatting and exercising
his charger, than constant intecrourse with beggars,
and cripples. But neither representations nor
mockery could make any impression on Rupert;
he continued indefatigable in charitableness, and
found his reward in the blessing of the necessitous.

Once, on a beautiful Spring morning, Rupert
slumbered on the banks of the Rhine, where he
had lain himself in the shade of a tree, tired from
a walk; he saw in a dream a venerable old man
in a long robe standing at the stream, surrounded
by a troop of friendly playing boys, the old man
took them one after the other, and dipped them
into the river, whence they reappeared finer and
more lovely. At the same time there rose in the

Rhine an island, charming and splendid as a Fairy-
land, full of sweet paradisiacal fruits; a many
colored plumaged choir enlivened the fields, and
an abundance of delicious blossom-perfume filled
the air. To this islet the old man led the boys, and
clothed them in snow white garments. Full of desire for the wonderful islet, Rupert hastened to the
old man, with the request to allow him to share
in the charming retreat. But he replied in solemn
tones: „Here is not a retreat for you Rupert, your
charity and pure pious sense, render you worthy
to enjoy the higher delights of Heaven, and to regard the face of the Transfigured." And behold at
these words arose from the flowery fields of the
islet a rainbow in thousand coloured beauty, and
as Rupert regarded upwards, he saw a number of
angels with golden wings, in their midst the Child-
Christ in indescribable brilliancy. At his side knelt
respectfully the holy John, and 2 angels soared
above, holding a garment which Rupert had lately
presented to a poor boy. With the garment they
clothed the Redeemer-child, and the latter said:
„The clothes you have given to the naked, and fed
the hungry; for such works belong the higher reward in the splendour of eternal glory." In blissful delight Rupert would stretch out his arms to
the lovely Christ-child, as the charming figure disappeared and — he awoke.

From this day Rupert wandered about, like one
transfigured. He took the resolution, to make a

pilgrimage to Rome, and from there to visit the
Holy repulchre, and then end his days in the capital town of Christianity. All representations of
his mother, although she had educated him as a
pious Christian, had however as princess destined
him for a knight, obtained from him, nothing else
than the promise, to return to her from Rome for
a short time; and with that he renounced the
princely dignity, and instead of the Purple, he
took the pilgrim's staff.

On returning after a year, from his wanderings,
the fatigues and privations had completely under-
mined his, without these, weak bodily health. He
died, a youth of scarcely twenty years, in the
arms of his mother, who soon followed him.

Rupert was later accepted among the number
of the saints, and the convent at Eubingen, is said
to possess still the garment which he once presented to a poor child, and seen in a dream.

The prophetess Hildegard.

After the death of holy Rupert and his mother,
the possessions of the Duke of Bingen fell to several
relatives, on which the, not far from Creuznach situated, castle Sponheim was built. At the castle
lived the knight of Bökelheim with his wife Mathilde, who presented him only one child, a daughter, baptized by the name of Hildegard. This child

was very early intrusted for her education to an abbess to the convent Dissibodenberg, and so Hildegard passed her youthful days in a convent.

She very soon displayed a predilection for reading pious books and legends; but particularly remarkable were her frequent visions, by means of which, according to her assertion, she could predict future events; and indeed not unlike our modern time is the picture, that at that time, she sketched of the future, in the obscurity of her cell.

The immorality and wickedness, in which the powerful ones, but especially the priesthood of that time were sunk, found in Hildegard a severe, judge, and she relentlessly exposed shameful deeds and vices.

As on the Rhine the holy Bernhard preached the crusade, he visited Hildegard and induced her, to support him by her voice. On leaving he presented her a ring with the motto: „I suffer willingly", and this ring is still shown in Wiesbaden. Later Hildegard was abbess of the already mentioned convent, and her reputation increased to such a degree, that troops of believing pilgrims arranged themselves about her and solicited her blessing.

Hildegard has left behind her many works written in Latin, which testify of her learning and much knowledge. Although she was bitterly zealous against the priesthood, yet she was later pronounced holy by the Pope.

Rheinstein.

The Ride to the Wedding.

In the beginning of the thirteenth century inhabited the castle Rheinstein a knight named Sifrid, just as rich and powerful, as he was defamed for his robberies and wicked actions.

Once returning home heavily laden with booty, from one of his incursions, he brought a female of extraordinary beauty, whom he had taken away from Frankenland. But however he as victor triumphed over the captured, he soon felt himself conquered by the gentleness of the beautiful female.

The noble Jutta's arrival at the Rheinstein effected a surprising changement in the knight's character. From then no acts of violence, no more robberies: quietly the merchant passed the, at other times feared castle, and fearlessly the shipper steered past the walls of the rampart. — Jutta's flattering voice had persuaded the knight to renounce entirely his former manner of life; so much can Love do!

Formerly the noisy residence of bold highwaymen. Rheinstein was now the cordial habitation of peace and harmless enjoyment. The wild guests gradually left it, and the rough war comrades, covetous for booty and licence, sought other service; in the service of Sifrid there was no more booty to be gained. since the happiness of quiet housekeeping dominated there — Jutta had wished it so, and Sifrid highly esteemed her, as beauty and virtue are honored.

But this quiet happiness was not to remain long undisturbed. After a year's household management, Jutta died in giving birth to a daughter. The loss of the beloved wife threw the knight in a deep melancholy, which gradually became gloomy misanthropy. Only the consolation, to have in the child a dear remembrance, and the care for this precious pledge alone bound him to life, and he devoted his days to the welfare and education of his daughter.

Gerda, the child's name, soon displayed those excellent qualities, the inheritance of her noble mother; as a tender flower gradually develops its beauty, she grew in grace and loveliness under the protecting care of her father.

However as retired as Sifrid had lived hitherto, he could not refuse hospitality to tired wanderers, or pious pilgrims, who rested at the foot of the castle, and so the treasure which the castle hid, was soon known, and the report of Gerda's beauty was soon spread in the whole valley and neighbourhood. It was not long, before a number of knights of high and low nobility, found themselves at the castle, all wishing to conclude a marriage, which promised a double gain, the charms of the splendid maiden with the great riches of the father. In order to keep off the suitors, which daily in-

creased, the old master of Rheinstein appointed to
meet them at Mayence at a Tournament, at which
he with Gerda would assist : the hand of the beautiful heiress should be the prize of the bravest.

Not easily could a tournament number more
participators than this, and the knights showy re-
tinues and splendid accoutrements increased the
magnificence of the festival; but the finest was
thought by all to be Gerda, whom to win, many
now entered the lists, while from a high balcony
she regarded the combattants.

Among the knights present two distinguished
themselves, Kurt of Ehrenfels, possessor of the
same named castle, and Kuno of Reichenstein, of
the castle, near Rheinstein, so that both seemed
one castle. Both knights were renowned combatants and if Kuno, younger than his opponent the
prerogatives of a finer education and a nobler
character, so overbid him the rough Kurt, who had
the surname of the Bad, in riches and extensive
possessions. Sifrid wished from avarice, Kurt to
be the gainer, but Gerda however had long had an
inclination for the amiable Kuno; but as the cap-
rice of Fortune often decides, so it decided this
time in favor of those who had willingly seen the
victory wrested from love. After Kuno had vanquished all other rivals, and dismounted several,
he was obliged to succumb to the superior strength
of Kurt, and gladly Sifrid saluted Kurt the wicked,
as his future son-in-law.

And so the destined marriage day arrived without Gerda's supplications and tears being able to shake her father's resolution. With pale cheeks and inflamed eyes, she appeared in costly garments and splendid wedding ornaments, not a happy bride, but like a sacrifice to whom one dedicated a solemn death. But before she became an offering to the inflexible will of her father, before one forced her to the altar, she would seek consolation and assistance of the mighty protectress of suffering maidens, of her, the Queen of Heaven, throw herself at her feet and pray to her in the chapel of the castle. And so she hastened to the chapel and threw herself before the figure of the Holy-Virgin. „Without your help, oh Mary full of grace, am I eternally lost, grief and sorrow will kill me! O protect me, save thy child from such misery!" So she supplicated the Holy Virgin, and long lay she there at her feet, when at last impatient, Kurt hastened and impetuously demanded of her to join the marriage procession. But the devout Prayer had marvellously strengthened Gerda's courage, and with a placid mien she advanced to the knight, glanced still once to the side where on the pinnacle of Reichenstein Kuno gloomy and sad regarded the castle Rheinstein, and followed, full of confidence in the mother of the Redeemer, the preceding Kurt.

Arrived to the expectant guests of the Feast, she begged, in order to ride to church, they would

allow her grey ambler to be saddled. which Kuno
of Reichenstein had presented her on her 18th birth-
day. One did, as she wished, and now the procession went down the mountain to St. Clement's
church, the ruins of which are again replaced.

Kuno saw the procession from his castle, and
irresolute, whether he should revenge himself on
his rival or bury himself in a cloister, he regarded,
abstractedly sunk in grief, when suddenly an extraordinary sight roused him out of his sadness. Just
in the moment, as the procession had arrived at
the church, Gerda's horse, which till now had kept
quiet step, began to prance, and overthrowing all
who approached, it broke away furiously. Directly
the knights rode after to bring it back: but in vain,
it galloped to the Rhine, in which to throw itself
Gerda not regarding Kurt's calling. drove it on. for
death in the cold stream had been desired by her;
however on the banks of the river the faithful
animal turned, and quick as an arrow it fled up the
steep rock, on the summit of which Reichenstein
was with its massive walls; scarcely quick enough
could Kuno let down the drawbridge to receive
the beloved, who was in so wonderful a manner
led to his arms.

Then after resigning themselves to the most
lively pleasure, he ordered, the doors to be immediately closed, care for the embrasures and altogether put all in the most defensive condition, —
unnecessary trouble however. the Heaven had

already spoken its judgment. A few minutes after
Gerda's arrival, Sifrid her father, was severely
wounded by the stumbling of his horse, brought
on a bier to the door of Reichenstein; he requested
friendly admittance, and blessed, from free inclination a union which, to accomplish, God un-
mistakeably had determined. The given promise
to the knight of Ehrenfels had already been discharged by Death; for in the same boat, in which
some hours before Kurt exulting was conducted
to the Rheinstein, one now carried back to Ehrenfels a wedding dressed corpse: chasing in blind
rage after the ambler running away with Gerda,
the unfortunate had fallen with his charger on a
rock of the bank, and had broken his skull.

Lorch.

The Devil's ladder.

On a castle at Lorch, the ruins of which one sees
not far from Assmannshausen, once sat knight
Gilgen silent and absorbed. Almost an old
man, he reviewed his past stirring life and the un-
success of his hitherto exertions and actions.

As a young man he had been with Brömser of
Rüdesheim in the Holy Land, and had been a
valiant combatant for the conquering of the Holy

Sepulchre. After his return he had married a beautiful, although poor maiden, an orphan, to whom he was most devotedly attached. But after a year's domestic felicity, he lost his wife by the birth of a daughter named Gerlinde.

In order to stun the pain of that loss, and if possible forget it, he had mixed himself in the disputes and affairs of the neighbourhood, and so defended several years a number of quarrels in the interests of his friends. The consequences were unfortunately the loss of his possessions, and the necessity to satisfy himself with the small income of his family-castle Morosely he retired therefore from every intercourse, and only the dear child, to which he applied all love and care, held him to this world. In such a monotonous life he had passed many years. He was visited by a hermit, whose cell was in the near mountains, and who was recognised every where as a magician. He understood to awaken in the morose knight the taste for palmistry, astrology and other secrets arts, and after repeated visits, won his interest so much for these things, that instruction in the same formed Gilgens favourite occupation. The knight had the hope by the black-art to open a connection with the world of spirits, and thereby obtain knowledge of hidden treasure, as well as the possibility, to raise them, — an endeavour, which in those times was not unusual, and as the legend was, had already often been richly rewarded.

Gerlinde was and remained her father's favourite, and his highest joy. For her principally it was that he strove for money and property, so that once, a rich heiress she might be the wish of all knights, not only for her fortune as she promised to be, but by her beauty and grace. Her bodily charms began to develope themselves in a surprising manner, already with her thirteenth year, and as well proportioned as her mother, she appeared to have inherited fortunately her virtues, and a quiet almost melancholy manner rendered her tender traits still more interesting.

It was on a spring-evening, that the knight silent and absorbed sat in his armchair. The hermit had just left him, and his exertions, by all magical operations to find out, according to tradition, an immense treasure in the mountain, had remained without effect. However the chiromancer had left him with the assurance, that he would certainly succeed in pointing out the place, latest in seven days, by the beginning of a complete eclipse of the moon; but the knight doubted so much the more of the success, because already many similar assertions of the magician had proved themselves false.

The weather was rough and uncomfortable; the wind howled round the towers and bastions of the castle, the weather-vane creaked, and the clouds hurried past. All nature seemed to be in revolution, and only with attention, could one hear, the watcher's horn at such an unusual hour. Scarcely had these tones ceased, as a groom entered to announce, there was a strange little man standing before the door who demanded a night's-lodging. His appearance was so singular and strange, that the porter hesitated to open, and therefore had sent to learn the knight's wishes. The knight, inquisitive to see the guest, went to the door, and perceived by the pale light of the moon, momentarily shining through the clouds, —

A dwarf scarcely six span tall,
In scarlet coloured garment,
Flowing over his shoulders as a pall,
The grey-locked hair seemed to torment.

A small yellow cap, in tassels rich,
First narrow then wide, as a pear,
Ascended almost like a crown, which,
The deeply feared-brow seemed to bear.

He twirled a small staff in the air
And unintelligibly talked —
Appearing a Being of precipice rare
As if from deep ravine he walked.

The hermit had already warned the knight against an inimical gnome-tribe; he therefore called rudely and indignantly to the dwarf: „What is your wish?" „Let me enter", it echoed, „I wish

refreshment and lodging for the night; to-morrow
I shall travel father, and will reward you for the
service of love." „With nothing", replied Gilgen,
whom the deep bass of the stranger highly dis
pleased, „such rascality does not come into my
castle. You were the right one, to bewitch my
cattle, and corn and eggs carry away through the
air, and as reward to trouble me in some manner.
March off, to your equals, and do not trouble me
any longer." So calling out, he shut the window
and hastened back; the dwarf murmured something to himself, and disappeared in the bushes.

The next morning Gilgen went hunting and
only returned late in the afternoon, and then
learned to his great astonishment that Gerlinde
had disappeared. She had not returned from a
promenade, which she had taken alone, and notwithstanding all the searchings of the servants, she
could not be found. Immediately all the men-
servants were obliged to mount and rummage the
country in all directons. The knight himself did
not regard fatigue and weakness; he mounted his
best charger and searched through mountain and
valley, forest and field, in calling out the name of
his loved child. Coming to a mountain, called the
Kedrich, he met a shepherd boy of whom he inquired concerning his daughter. The boy informed
him, that at noon he had seen three dwarfs in red
mantles, who had led-away on horseback, a
beautiful maiden of about fourteen years, and they

had disappeared under the alder trees of the mountain. Beside himself with grief Gilgen rode as near as possible to the Kedrich, and there called-out three times: „Gerlinde, where are you?" Scarcely had he done so, as he perceived on the summit of the inaccessible mountain-cone his child, that longingly stretched out her arms towards him. But behind the maiden stood the same gnome, who yesterday had demanded admittance to the castle, and mockingly the dwarf called to him: „That is the reward for your Hospitality."

What was to be done? To climb the rocky mountain was impossible: Hitherto nobody had ventured, to make the trial, for it was known. the crevices could not be hewn Yet the knight would make himself a road. A number of workmen appeared the next day with chisels, axes, and hammers; but they could not work the hard rock, and after fatiguing themselves the whole day, a shower of stones fell upon them from the height and drove them away. Despairing of all, the knight hastened, although the night had already commenced, to the hermit's hut. He related to him. what had occurred, and the old man sank into a deep meditation, then he lit a fire, boiled a beverage from all sorts of herbs, in stirring which sparks crackled. and he muttered unintelligible words, then he poured the fluid into a hole in the wall. where they sparkled in a thousand flames and thereby spoke loudly:

„Regard here from your flaming throne
On your servant and faithful son,
Hear my deep, profound request
And, be executed my behest.

The on Kedrich, living gnomen,
A knight's child have stolen;
The father is in pitiful distress
For his child, his heart's mistress.

Oh! help with your whole might,
You master of the midnight,
Thee a pair of owls bring I you
And a goat as sacrifice true."

As soon as he had spoken these conjuring
words, there began a fearful noise in the chimney;
the wind whistled through doors and windows with
cutting tones, so that the knight was overcome
with horror and anxiety. After a time the magician
murmured articulate sounds, and directly it was
again still. Then he said to Gilgen: „Return home,
knight, and hope for the best. On the very same
day, that I will deliver you a treasure, I hope
also, to free your daughter from the malicious
power of the dwarf."

Somewhat quieted Gilgen returned to his castle,
and the next morning the Hermit announced to
him, that the subterranean prince, to whom he
called, had given the following answer:

„A black knight, and horse as black,
With fine arms for attack,
In dream, he the maid already saw.
Whom to save, Kedrich will draw."

The denoted black knight must also be waited
for. On the third day towards evening a black
knight really appeared at the castle, in black armour, and on black charger, and inquired after
a very young maiden who had in a dream appeared
to him, and whom he was destined to save from
some great danger. Who was happier than Gilgen?
The guest, who namend himself R u t h e l m, was
heartily welcomed, and the next morning early
saw the two knights riding to the Hermit, where
further proceedings were spoken about and directly commenced.

All three went to a height opposite Kedrich,
and crept into a cavern at its base. Here the magician lit a large fire and threw a quantity of magical perfume into the flame, in murmuring the
form of incantation. The knight Ruthelm was obliged to place himself in a circle, which the magician designated on the ground, and before long,
it began to be animated in the depths of the cavern.
By the light of the clear flaring fire the astonished
knight saw a most wonderful apparition:

From dark rocky lap well'd
Of dwarfs a great multitude bow'd.
Soon was the wide cavern held,
By the cries of the lamenting crowd.

It was their chalk-like faces
In colour like their clothes,
Creeping about as twilight graces
Filling the cavern with living throes.

The chief and tallest of them advanced to
Ruthelm, bowed seven times to the earth and said:

„Are you the selected knight,
The noble maiden's bold adder,
So speak if it please your might,
We begin to build the ladder."

The knight consented and directly the dwarfs
hastened into the wood. Then began carpenting,
hammering, sawing, and cutting which lasted till
evening. Then the dwarf-king again stepped before the knight and repeated:

„What us the master of the depths found,
Of water-abyss and fire-gulf bound.
Commanded, is before dark night
Completed by diligence of our might.

Then ascend, fighter, plead
By seven hundred steps not fatigued
The ladder to the mountains rally,
To be the tender maiden's ally.

There above, are star'd
To you cunningness sped;
Therefore be on your guard,
Else they will strike you dead.

Consider are they
The known red gnomes
Secure on Kederich's stones
Destine you their prey."

Scarcely had he said this, so the whole swarm
of dwarfish carpenters passed quickly into the
cavern and disappeared; but their work, the gigantic ladder, stood leaning against the steep wall
of the rock. The knight Ruthelm prepared himself,
to commence the dangerous ascent; the Hermit
put a miraculous ring on his finger, and recommended, to turn the Talisman in the moment of
danger. The twilight had meanwhile begun, and
the party remaining behind passed the night in the
wood, curious to learn the success of the ladder-way.

Nothwithstanding the severe climbing, the
knight could not reach the height before day-break.
Firstly, as the morning fog from the valley dissipated itself, he saw that he was on a wide plain, on
which the most luxuriant landscape, and a charming garden was spread before him. He could
scarcely believe in his eyes; and his astonishment
increased as he wandered through the garden; for
all the fruits of the tropics grew here in abundance
and in incomparable beauty. Soon the adventurer
saw a crystal palace, before which two red gnomes,
evidently should have stood as sentinels, but fortunately had fallen asleep. Without much reflection, he cut off their heads, then forced his way

into the castle, and here he met the ravisher of
Gerlinde. Immediately they seized their swords,
and began a violent struggle. The little one fought
quickly and cleverly, he was obliged to avoid
Ruthelm's heavy blows; but as he could do nothing against his bravery, he had recourse to magic,
and suddenly he sat heavily on the knight's neck.
He did not neglect, to turn the ring, and in consequence he was able to rid himself of his enemy,
and throw him to the ground. He then threw himself on the sorcerer, and in threatening him with
a dagger, he extorted the confession of Gerlinde's
place of concealment. Then he stabbed the gnome,
and hastened to the place, where he hoped to find
the imprisoned.

After having wandered through the magical
apartments of the miraculous palace, he found the
hiding place of Gerlinde. She reposed in an agreeable morning slumber, and the knight thought
never to have seen a more charming creature. For
a time he stood surprised and dazzled by so much
beauty, and he could not resolve, to disturb her
sweet sleep. At last he awoke the beauty with a
kiss, and in begging her not to be frightened, he
told her, he was come, to free her and to conduct
her to her father's arms. The dear child believed
to dream, as she heard such words from an unknown person; however she willingly resigned
herself to the guidance of the knight. Both now
traversed the long row of apartments, and after

they had loaded themselves with the valuable jewels, which had been employed for ornamenting the rooms, they entered the garden. Scarcely had they passed through it, when it, with castle and beautiful environs, sank into the earth with a terrible crash, so that nothing remained but the bare rocks. Horrified they hastened to the ladder, and with great difficulty they descended it; however they fortunately succeeded, and with indescribable joy father and daughter embraced each other.

Some weeks afterwards the knight Ruthelm led Gerlinde as his wife to a fine castle, which he possessed in Lower - Franken, the father sold his, and not to live alone, left with his children. As the jewels which they had brought from the magic castle were of immense value, the knight Gilgen with his family possessed riches in abundance, and also the Hermit received a large share of the treasure. But in the neighbourhood of Lorch one has since heard nothing more of the malicious gnomes of the Kederich, who had done so much evil to the inhabitants of the vicinity.

The Archer.

Near Lorch, on the boundary of the Rhine-valley stand the ruins of the former castle Fürsteneck. Knight Oswald, owner of this castle, an excellent archer, lived in bitter enmity with Wilm von Saneck, a neighbouring nobleman, who attempted by all sorts of cunning snares to get him in his power. He succeeded in doing this, in attacking Oswald from an ambush, as accompanied by a groom he was returning home. The prisoner was dragged to Saneck, and thrown into the depths of a tower, and soon afterwards cruelly deprived of his sight.

At Fürsteneck it was at first believed he, had been killed by robbers; but as there were no indications of such an act, so Edwin, Oswald's only son, knowing the malice and cunning of Saneck, had the suspicion, his father could have fallen into his power.

Resolved, to venture all to procure certitude upon this point, Edwin disguised himself as an itinerant singer, in which he was assisted by his dexterity in playing the harp, and wandered towards Saneck. Near the castle he rested under a tree, and directed his regards principally to a large tower of the castle, where as a foreboding told him, was his father's prison.

He had not long lain there, as a man joined him, who seemed to be a peasant from the neighbourhood and accosted him in these terms: „Why do you regard so particularly that strong tower? that is a cage, in which they confine birds after they have well plucked off their feathers.“ „Is it a prison then?“ asked Edwin. „Certainly“, he replied, and made confidential by the young man's friendly conversation, and more so by a touching song which he sung, the unknown related, how he had been an unseen spectator, that in that tower a knight and his servant had been imprisoned. Edwin had much trouble, to repress and hide the impression, which this assertion made on him, and tried to learn other particulars, but all, he could learn was, that in some days there would be a grand banquet at Saneck. He determined, to use this circumstance in order to examine the place, to visit the castle disguised as a singer. On the mentioned day he repaired thither. Jubilation and noisy joy echoed from the saloons, and as he entered, the heads of the persons present were already much heated by wine. They welcomed the strange singer, and readily listened to his songs; but after drinking so much that they were partly intoxicated, they paid no more attention to him, and he remained unnoticed. More excited by wine than his table-companion, the knight Wilm talked in a very lively manner with him; and the masked singer neared to overhear their conversation.

„Do you know too", said the neighbour to Saneck, „one suspects you of capturing the knight Oswald of Fürsteneck, and of having imprisoned him." „Hum", answered the other, „all tales are not lies." „One asserts too", continued the other, „you have even blinded him." „Well", answered the other, „what does it signify if a candle is blown out, or goes out, that is the same thing." „But it

is a pity", said a third, who heard the conversation,
„for the art of archery which Oswald possessed in
so high a degree."

„I will wager, he will still hit his object if one
makes it known to him", said another knight.
„Done, I will wager that he will not", called out in
arrogant inebriation Saneck, and ordered the prisoner to be brought before him. Edwin who had
heard all, could scarcely restrain himself, for grief
and anger almost made him mad, as his father's
pity exciting figure entered the saloon. All present
sprang to their feet, to be spectators of the result
of the quickly known wager. As Wilm made the
unfortunate prisoner acquainted with the wager,
and ordered bow and arrows to be given to him,
a sudden thought seemed to penetrate through the
blind knight; convulsively he seized the weapons,
and said : „Knight Saneck give me a sign where
you place the object?" „Here", he answered, „on
this table, I place the cup which you are to hit."

„I shall hit my object", said in the same moment Oswald, the arrow flew deep into — the heart
of Saneck. A wild cry arose; but Edwin sprang
forward, stepped before his father, and called
loudly: „I am the son of this poor, against all laws
of chivalry, imprisoned and blinded man! Which-
ever of you who loves honour and right, will approve of his act, whoever thinks otherwise, I will
answer with my sword." All were astonished, but
most of the knights present declared themselves

for Oswald and Edwin, who, crying with sadness and joy embraced each other. Free, Edwin conducted his father to his castle, near Lorch; and although he could not restore his lost sight; he sweetened his last days by filial tenderness.

Bacharach.

Palatine Count Hermann of Stahleck.

In the wildly romantic country of Bacharach, equally charming and engaging for eye, and feeling, is also to be found, as particularly memorable, the so called B a c h u s - A l ta r. It stands just below the town, between an islet, and the right bank of the Rhine, but unfortunately it is only possible to see it, and read the inscription, now by time become illegible, when the water is very low. This altar is generally considered to be a Memorial of the Romans, who had placed it here to their wine-god, on a later supposed inundated island, and from which, without doubt, the name of the town must have been derived.

Above Bacharach, lies picturesquely on the summit of a mountain, the ruin Stahleck. This castle was inhabited, in the middle of the 12th century, by Hermann of Stahleck, nephew of the Emperor Conrad 3rd. equally brave and wise, but

an avaricious knight. With his young amiable wife
he could have enjoyed a peaceful existence, if his
inquiet spirit, and longing for action had not prevented him. It is true, the gentle supplication of
his wife exercised so much influence over him,
that he did not take the cross and seek danger in
the distant Eastern countries; but so much the
more was he occupied at home with the execution
of a long entertained plan. He wished to obtain a
great part of the country subject to the Arch-
bishoprics of Mayence and Trier, to which from
more than one reason he believed to have a right
of possession.

His hatred against every spiritual domination,
and particularly to that of the mentioned bishops,
excited him still more to put his plan into execu-
tion, with the assistance of the faithful ally necessity, and many other knights of the same opinion
as himself. He began the war by storming the
castle Treis, which, belonging to the diocese of
Trier, and situated on the Mosel, was an important
and strong place.

Adelbert of Monstreil, Archbishop of Metz and
Trier, thereupon collected his men, to obtain again
the lost castle. But not believing himself sufficiently
strong against Hermann's united power, he sought
his refuge in spiritual weapons. As a battle was
about to take place between the two armies, Adelbert with a crucifix in his hand, made a speech to
his companions-in-arms, in which he said, the angel

Michael had appeared to him the night before, had handed him the held crucifix, and promised him certain victory, if the same combatant in firm belief on an invisible higher power, would attack the enemy courageously. The speech had the best results; Hermann's troops, perceived the advancing bishop with the crucifix, and the fanatical courage of their opponents, did not remain firm, and fled, without having fought. This unfortunate commencement of his enterprise however, did not deter the Palatinate Count, he continued the war with renewed vigor, also against the Archbishop of Mayence, Arnold of Selnhofen, and would have completely carried out his intentions, if the spiritual gentlemen had not found, and used, another very wonderful party to free themselves from their indefatigable and dangerous enemy.

The chaplain of the castle Stahleck was won by them, and seduced by splendid promises to Intrigue and Treachery. At first he refused absolution, by confession, to the wife of Stahleck, because her husband was unjustly warring against high dignitaries of the Church; and because it was the duty of the wife to use all means in her power, viz: persuasion and supplication, against such crimes; then as in this embarassment the anxious wife did not know how to act; the chaplain urged her to write a letter to Hermann, to conjure him to cease the struggle, and as this remained without success, he proceeded to the forcible shameful

means which he had already long since prepared.
Two discharged criminals, unprincipled villains,
were hired by him to ride into the camp of Hermann, announce themselves as soldiers seeking
service, and allow themselves to be enlisted. Then
they should seize a suitable opportunity to murder
the enemy of the hishop, and then return to receive the rich reward of their action, and absolution for past and future sins.

Only too well the hardened villains executed
their detestable commission. They forced themselves into the count's tent as the watch was confided to them, struck off his head, with which they
fled to the Traitor, as proof of their obedience.

This offering was however remarked by a servant of the countess who was immediately informed.
Beside herself with anger and pain, she forced
herself, with dagger in hand, into the chaplain's
chamber, and there seeing her dear husband's head
on the table, she threw herself, with heart-rending
cry: „You are the murderer of my husband“ upon
the wretch and stabbed him. Then she seized the
dear head, and covered it with innumerable kisses,
and suddenly changing her conduct, she ran like
one insane about the castle. She raved against all
who approached her, in a manner, that left no
doubt of her insanity, at last fled to the highest
garret of the castle and precipitated herself,
smashing her bones to pieces.

Later a coffin united the rests of the unfortunate

loving wife. The revenging Nemesis however soon overtook the principal planner of the abominable murder, the Archbishop Arnold of Mainz. By op- pressions of all kinds he was since a long time ex- tremely hated by his subjects who forced them- selves, in public revolt, into his palace, destroyed all with fire and sword and chased the tyrant. Not- withstanding he returned, to exercise terrible vengeance on the guilty. In vain his friends warned him, uselessly wrote to him the prophetess Hilde- garde: „Turn to the Lord whom you have forsaken; it is high time, for the hour of your death is near." He paid no attention to it, and took, the castle being destroyed, his seat in the abbey of Jakobsberg, outside the town. This circumstance hastened his ruin. The abbot, a secret enemy of the Archbishop, betrayed him, in giving opportunity to the enraged citizens, wo forcibly entered the abbey by night. They overpowered and cut down the garrison, and at last murdered Arnold himself, who had done them so much injury.

Kaub.

Castle Gutenfels.

In the middle of the 13th century the castle at
Kaub was inhabited by Count Philipp of Falkenstein with his extremely beautiful sister Guta. A
number of young knights from far and near courted
the maiden: however none could boast of the least
success. for the countess was insensible to all
suitors and refused all decidedly.

At that time there was held at Cologne a
magnificent Tournament, to which knights from
the farthest districts of Germany were invited, and
a great multitude of spectators were attracted.
Among the nobles present at the diversion, was a
knight from England. Nobody besides the Archbishop of Cologne knew him; but the Bishop assured that the foreigner was fit for the Tournament.
He was of the Britons a man of the handsomest,
most powerful figure, of the most engaging, finest
manners, and therefore for the assembled ladies
an object of particular attention. The truly royal
accoutrement, in which he strode about, the golden
lion on his shield, and the excellent charger, which
carried him, increased the interest for him. Besides
he obtained the most brilliant victories, and the
most valiant knight lowered his lance before him.

Also the Falkensteiner and his sister were present. and Guta, who did not remain an uninterested

spectator of the acts of the foreigner, wished the
time of the Festival past, so that she could regard
his face. This good fortune she enjoyed in the
highest degree; but from this moment she lost her
peace of mind. She felt an unconquerable passion
for the handsome Englishman; she longed for an
opportunity, to speak with him and win his regard.

But the enigmatical knight appeared to have
regarded Guta and to feel for her —and as she was
destined, whether by her own arrangement or by
chance, to hand the prize to the Victor, he clearly
made the maiden understand his feelings. In the
surprise of the moment she dropped her glove, of
which the foreigner took quickly possession, in
begging her to allow him, to keep it as a remembrance of that fine hour. He expressed himself more
explicitly the same evening, in the banquetting
saloon while the music resounded and he was
Guta's inseparable companion. He begged secretly
for her love, swore to be hers, and in three months
return from his country, where duty now called
him, and to come to her brother's castle. Then he
would publicly sue for her and declare his name,
which circumstances bade him still keep secret.
Guta could scarcely reply, but her glances were
sufficiently eloquent. With secret pressure of the
hands the lovers separated.

Five months were already passed, and the
Briton had not yet fulfilled his promise. Germany
was at that time (the house of Hohenstauf being

extinct), more than ever the battle-field of the party-
struggles for the election of the Emperor. Alphons
of Castile, and Richard of Cornwallis, brother of
Henry 3:rd king of England, were at last proposed,
and Richard having received the most influential
votes, chosen for Emperor. After he had been
solemnly crowned at Aix-la-chapelle, he began his
journey into the interior of the country, subject
to his sceptre.

On a beautiful spring morning, Guta sat solitary
and sad in her chamber. She thought of the
foreign knight, whom she believed never to see
again, and whom she now accused of the most
culpable imprudence, now fancied fallen in battle,
and as all hope to possess him, disappeared, she
renounced the joys of this life and took the firm
resolution, to retire to a convent. Trumpets
sounded from the high road, and a splendid procession stopped before the castle. Guta concealed
herself, not to be obliged to show her weeping face.
But count Falkenstein received the brilliant visit
with hospitable kindness and conducted it into the
state-room. Here he recognised on entering the
English knight, and was much astonished as he
addressed him thus: „I am Richard of Cornwallis
chosen German Emperor, and come to solicit the
hand of your sister, the countess Guta, of whom I
became enamoured by the Tournament at Cologne,
and with whom I am now resolved to share my
throne. I beg you, let her be called, so that she

can decide concerning my demand.“ „My Imperial
Master“, replied the knight, „my sister Guta has
been ill since mouths; a secret grief seems to afflict
her, threatening to wither her youthful bloom, and
she appears most unwillingly before strangers.“
„Bring her“, added the Emperor, „this glove, and
say, the bearer wishes to speak with her.“

This surprising message and the sight of her
glove changed Guta's mourning into the most lively
joy. Impetuously she hastened to the beloved, and
not yet knowing his high title, she flew to his arms.
But after the first moments of this happy saluta-
tion, she remembered that the knight had not once
mentioned his name or country, and indescribable
was her astonishment, as her brother told her
whom she embraced as her futere husband. She
regarded this declaration as joking, and even when
Richard assured her, that her brother had spoken
the truth, she still doubted, till finally the splendour
of the numerous and noble retinue, and the honours
which were shown to the beloved, fully convinced
her. With imperial pomp the wedding-festival
was célebrated after a few weeks, and the highly
blessed Count Falkenstein from that time named
his castle near Kaub, in honour of his beloved
sister, Gutenfels.

Palatinate near Kaub.

Palatinate Count stone.

Konrad of Staufen, Emperor Friedrich's 1st half brother, was possessor of the Palatinate Count stone, that beautiful, firm castle known by the name of the Palatinate, built on a rocky island, below Kaub, seems to meet surprisingly the view.

In possession of all riches Konrad only wanted one thing, a son, that could continue his race, and inherit his estates. All the descendants of the knight was a daughter, Agnes, just as gentle as she was charming and sensible, who was beloved by her parents with the greatest tenderness. Powerful Princes solicited her hand, among whom were the Dukes of Bavaria and Brunswick, and even the King of France. But Agnes had already chosen. Henry of Brunswick alone, distinguished by chivalry and a handsome person, had found favour with Agnes, and both resolved to confirm their bond of love by the favor of Agnes' mother. The Count, ignorant of this, had at the same time received news of Henry's exertions for the beautiful Agnes, and knowing the Emperor's, his brother's intention, to keep the Palatinate in the family and to marry the maiden to one of their relatives, so he reflected how he could, the best, guard her from the snares of the Brunswicker. For the purpose of effecting this object, to properly finish and

strengthen the Rhine-palatinate, so that it could
serve the mother and daughter, as a not very
accessible, and yet well guarded dwelling. This
plan he carried out. But love found in what was
intended as an obstacle, exactly a welcome assistance. Henry succeeded in entering, disguised as
a Pilgrim, and Agnes' clever mother, who had favoured his entrance, took care, that the band of
love was sanctified by priestly blessing. The
united then enjoyed the whole bliss of their first,
fiery love.

However the consequences of the, in quietude,
effected connexion began to show themselves, and
as it would be impossible, ever to conceal them
from the Count, Agnes' mother undertook to disclose it to the father. It is true on being made
acquainted with the circumstances that Agnes'
father fell into a terrible rage, however he reflected,
what had occurred could not be changed, and he
therefore resolved to go to the Imperial residence,
which then was at Worms and inform the Emperor
of all that had happened. Friedrich 1st reflected
that a marriage, between a scion of the Welf and
a daughter of the Hohenstaufen, concluded, could
reconcile the traditional hatred of these races, gave
his consent, and the Palatine saw a grand festival
that in splendour and magnificence was never
equalled.

The Palatinate Count who had made the experience, how necessary it was, to guard daughters,

and to render it easier to his descendants, had the Palatine still more strengthened, and decided that in one of its chambers Agnes should keep her first child-bed, and that it should serve for the same purpose to all future Palatine countesses. This chamber is still shown to all visitors in memory of that event.

Oberwesel.

The seven Virgins.

Near Oberwesel, on a height, since long in ruins was the castle Schöneberg, once the seat of a family of the same name. Here resided a knight with seven daughters. Because destiny had not presented him with a son, and anticipating the extinction of his race, he grieved extremely and thereby fell into a severe illness, which prematurely tore him from his children. Unfortunately their education was very defective, their father, early a widow, scarcely troubled himself about them, and a distant relative, who ought to have replaced their mother, had developed in them more vanity and coquetry than domestic virtues. After the death of this relative, the already grown-up daughters were left to themselves, and as they all shone in youthful beauty, to their castle belonged rich estates, they did not want suitors, who an-

nounced themselves to try their fortune. But it
seemed, as if the hearts of the Orphans were incapable of feeling the tender passion. Every guest
was received most hospitably, and he could remain,
as long as he pleased at the castle, however when
he thought of making his wooing effective, instead
of promises, he found only mockery and sneers.
Therefore many left the castle and its inhabitants
in justifiable contempt, however the beauty and
riches of the maidens always attracted new suitors,
so that there was always present no inconsiderable
number, and a gay and joyous life was led there.

Several years the castle maidens had continued
this certainly egotistical, but dangerous and con-
temptible life, and many knights from far and near,
effected by love, sojourned still with the seducing
syrens, flattering themselves with hopes, and
troubling themselves to supplant their rivals.

By a grand banquet two knights fell into a
jealous dispute concerning their mistresses, which
threatened to end in a bloody duel. Both were too
popular not to excite general attention to this disturbance, and endeavors to reconcile them. By this
occasion several expressed themselves loudly, that
one should urge a final decision on the castle-
maidens, so that no further discord could happen,
and each could know to what he had to trust. This
proposal pleased so much the more, because every
one believed, to be the favored of her whose love
he had troubled himself to win. Urgently therefore

the seven charmers were requested, to declare themselves decidedly, and make a choice for marriage.

Against this demand was no refuge, and the maidens saw themselves obliged, the next day to note those whom Destiny determined their wooers.

At the destined hour the suitors appeared in the roomy State-saloon, where they were assigned, and full of expectation they riveted their eyes on the door, through which the Graces, announcing Fortune and Misfortune, were to enter. A servant appeared, to announce to the waiting knights, that the Virgins expected them in an arbor, on the Rhine. Quickly all the marriage candidates hastened there, but how astonished were they, to see their fair ones in a boat, already distant from the bank, on the raised stern of the boat the eldest Prude stood. From where she made the following speech to the Candidates: „It has never been our intention, to love one of you, or indeed to take as husband. We only love our liberty too much, to like to sacrifice it for any man to be his Slave. With the Confession that we have treated you as fools, we connect the announcement that we leave our castle for a long time, to go to an Aunt in the Netherlands, where we intend to continue the same game with the knights of that Country, that we have played with you. Therefore good-bye, sweet gentlemen, good-bye and do not fret too much.“

This speech was accompanied by loud laughter

from the sisters, and the boat continued its course. But what happened! While the ashamed and deceived knights followed the mockers with inflamed looks, a sudden storm arose, the boat rocked more and more, struck violently on a hidden rock, and was wrecked, so that the collective Transgressors were drowned.

On the spot, where this occurred, there soon arose above the surface of the water seven rocks, which to the present day, are called the seven sisters, there stand all the Prudes as warning and terror to all Navigators.

L u r l e i.

Lorelei.

As Antiquity willingly peopled its mountains and castles its fields and rivers with fairies and magical-beings, and to these ascribed benevolent or pernicious influence on Men, so it has been especially to the Rhine to which are connected many a fine and romantic legend of Water-witches, Nymphs and Gnomes, recited from father to son, and so preserved to our Times.

But no country of our fatherland is more adapted to give a certain consistence and color to narrations, of which the foundation is partly historical,

than the sometimes uncommonly lovely, occasionally terribly wild banks of the Middle and Upper
Rhine. By regarding the heaven - aspiring as it
were out of the stream rising rocks with their per-
pendicular, oft projecting walls, by the singular
formation of the mountains, by the noise, with
which the waves force their way through rocky
passages, and rush through the once precipitated
stone-mass, one easily believes himself placed in
a Fairy-land, and if anywhere, so was here the
favourite place of that Being, with which the
Imagination occupied itself so willingly.

One of the most known and charming Legends
is that of the Water-nymph Lore, which at Ley, a
rock situated above St. Goarshausen, had her residence, from which therefore she was called the
Lorelei. To the shippers she appeared on the top
of this rock, in the loveliest most charming figure.
Picturesquely flowing Garments and Veil of the
color of the green waves surrounded her tenderly
formed limbs; long blond hair waved from her
shoulders, and who regarded her face could never
more forget the glance of her animated eyes.

As benevolent Fairy she gave favor and happiness to all the good inhabitants of the country,
but to the evil-doers she showed herself inimical,
and many who pertly rowed to the foot of the rock,
and ventured to mock her power were seized by
the raging waves and drawn into the abyss. Who
impudently climbed to her favorite place, were

cast into the shallows, or were seduced by her and lost themselves in thorns and bushes, where all paths disappeared, so that only after several days exertions could they find their right way.

In those times lived in the Rhin-palatinate, the near magnificent island-castle, Palatinate Count Bruno and his only son Hermann, a handsome young man of twenty years, who was the flower of Chivalry and the delight of his father. Often and much the young knight had heard of the enchanting Lore at Lei, and every time, when he perceived the projecting rocks, he wished, to see the water-nymph, to whom he felt himself drawn by an irresistible power. Scarcely a day passed, that he had not this inexplicable feeling when near the mysterious Ley, he wished to be able to announce the feelings of his heart in an affecting manner, in hunting through the neighbourhood, or with his Zither seek out a quiet concealed place.

Once already very late in the evening, nearer, than he had ever ventured to the foot of the mountain, in a grotto, he expressed his Longing in low singing, and casting his glances to the height, suddenly there hovered round the top of the rock a brightness of unequalled clearness and color, which, in increasingly smaller circles thickened, was the enchanting figure of the beautiful Lore. An unintentional cry of joy escaped the youth, he let his Zither fall, and with extended arms he called out the name of the enigmatical Being, who seemed

to stoop lovingly to him, and beckon to him in a
friendly manner; indeed, if his ear did not deceive
him, she called his name with unutterable sweet
whispers, proper to love. Beside himself with
delight the youth lost his senses and sank senseless
to the earth. Only with the morning-dawn did he
recover his senses, and in feverish excitement he
hastened to his father's castle.

From this moment Hermann was as if changed.
Like a dreamer he wandered about, only thinking
on the beautiful fairy. He directed, as often as he
left his father's dwelling, his steps only to Lei, and
if the pleasures of the chase sometimes led him to
a distance from the eastern woods, so in returning
he was magically drawn to the vicinity, and he
never approached, without saluting the place, where
she had appeared to him and had since occupied
all his thoughts.

The old count saw with affliction this changement in his son. He did not know the cause, but
he concluded it was some unhappy passion, and
therefore resolved to distract the inexperienced
youth by serious occupation, and to open to him
an active future. For this purpose he wished to
send him to the Imperial-camp where the youth
could win his knight's spurs.

Herman was obliged, however unwillingly, to ·
obey his father's commands; for it would have been a
disgrace to him to withdraw from a struggle, which
every knight zealously wished and obliged to

undergo manfully. It was on the evening before
his departure, as he wished still once to visit the
grotto, and offer to the Nymph of the Rhine his
sighs, the tones of his Zither, and his songs. He
went, this time accompanied by a faithful squire,
whom he had let into the secret, down the stream.
The moon shed her silvery light over the whole
country; the steep bank mountains appeared in
the most fantastical shapes, and the high oaks on
either side bowed their branches on Hermann's
passing. As soon as he approached the Lei, and
was aware of the surf-waves, his attendant was
seized with an inexpressible anxiety and he begged
permission to land; but the knight swept the
strings of his guitar, directed his looks to the
rocky summit and sang:

> Once I saw thee in dark night,
> In supernatural Beauty bright;
> Of Light-rays, was the Figure wove,
> To share its light locked-hair strove.

> Thy Garment color wave-dove,
> By thy hand the sign of love.
> Thy eyes sweet enchantment,
> Raying to me, oh! entrancement.

> Oh wert thou but my sweetheart
> How willingly thy love to part!
> With delight I should be bound
> To thy rocky house in deep ground.

Scarcely had these tones sounded, everywhere there began, tumult and sound, as if of voices above and below the water. On the Lei rose flames, the Fairy stood above, as that time, and beckoned with her right hand clearly and urgently to the infatuated knight, while with a staff in her left she called the waves to her service. They began to mount heavenward; the boat was upset, mocking every exertion; the waves rose to the gunwale, and splitting on the hard stones, the boat broke into pieces. The youth sank into the depths, but the squire was thrown on shore by a powerful wave.

As he, pale with anxiety and terror brought the strange narrative to the unhappy father, the old Count was overpowered with grief and anger. He swore, to be revenged on the Fairy, to seize her if possible with his own hands, and to deliver her to death by fire. For this purpose he hastened, the following night, with some bold comrades to Lei, surrounded and ascended the mountain, to search through it. There he saw, not without terror, the nymph on the top, standing perpendicularly above the water, plaiting her long tresses, the stranger regarded the Fairy with gloomy looks.

„Where is my son?“ cried the Count beside himself. Lore pointed to the dephts, in singing with low, scarcely audible tones, like the sound of a distant Aeolian-harp:

There below stands in the wave's womb
Crystal-clear my fine castle tomb,
There conducted I my darling expected,
Whom already long since I have selected.

When she had finished she threw a glittering
stone into the waves; immediately a wave rose
and received the Fairy and conducted her below
into the stream, where she disappeared to the eyes
of the astonished pursuer.

The Fairy was never more seen; but her enchanting tones have often been heard. In the
beautiful, refreshing, still nights of spring, when
the moon pours her silver light over the country,
the listening shipmen hear from the rushing of the
waves, the echoing clang of a wonderfully charming
voice, which sings a song from the crystal castle,
and with sorrow and fear he thinks on the young
count Herman, seduced by the nymph.

But the rock of the water nymph, formerly
Lorelei, now named Lurlei, yields since that event,
a beautifully repeating echo which is ever admired
and praised as a gift of the Fairy.

The Lore-Lei.

I do not known what it signifies,
That I am so sorrowful?
A fable of old Times so terrifies,
Leaves my heart so thoughtful.

The air is cool and it darkens,
And calmly flows the Rhine;
The summit of the mountain hearkens
In evening sunshine line.

The most beautiful Maiden entrances
Above wonderfully there,
Her beautiful golden attire glances,
She combs her golden hair.

With golden comb so lustrous,
And thereby a song sings,
It has a tone so wondrous,
That powerful melody rings.

The shipper in the little ship
It effects with woes sad might;
He does not see the rocky clip,
He only regards dreaded height.

I believe the turbulent waves
Swallow at last shipper and boat;
She with her singing craves
All to visit her magic moat.

H. Heine.

St. Goar and St. Goarshausen.

Towards the middle of the 16th century of the Christian era arrived in the then deserted, little inhabited valleys of the Rhine a pious, zealous Believer, the holy Goar. He built himself a hut in the wildly romantic country below Lurlei, where the stream, forced into a narrow rocky bed noisily rushes through.

He not only communicated to the poor fishermen of the country the mild tenets of Christianity, but he taught these simple folks many useful things, such as the cultivation of the vine and other garden products, as well as a better construction for their vessels, so that the renown of the honored man was very extended.

Siegebert, the Frankenking, a pious christian sovereign, heard the praise of the holy Goar and w ished to make his acquaintance. Accordigly he was called to the Court, and he pleased the King so much, that he named him his friend and raised him to the dignity of Bishop of Trier. However this title did not suit the unassuming, modest man of God; he preferred, to still live among the fishers and be their benefactor. And that he remained, till he was called in a high age, to a better life.

The great Reverence and Love, which he so extensively enjoyed, built over his hut an oratory, which was visited by Pilgrims from far and near,

who came to pray at his grave; the religions belief
of that time ascribed to his Bones, the power of
miraculously healing all sorts of maladies. Later
this oratory was so enriched by pious gifts, that it
was changed into a convent; no Pilgrim travelling
along the Rhine, left it unfrequented, and the
Legend was indeed spread, that to those who disregarded it, some misfortune happened. Even
Charles the Great, as he once descended the Rhine,
without visiting and praying at the shrine, is said
to have experienced the truth of this Legend, in a
thick fog suddenly covering the surface of the
water and rendering his further travelling dangerous. Only after the mighty sovereign had repaired
his neglect, and performed his devotions at the
grave of the holy man, was it again clear and the
continuation of his journey possible.

Among the many miraculous cures, which took
place through the healing powers of Goar's grave,
one mentions also the remarkable convalescence
of the wife of Charles namely Fastrada, who seeking relief here from a dangerous malady found
perfect health. And just on this grave too the sons
of Louis were reconciled, their father having divided the kingdom between them, bloody hate had
separated.

The continually increasing riches of the convent
allured later a numerous band of robbers, to obtain
mastery of all its treasures. The fiends then set
the convent on fire, and yielded all contained

documents and relics to the flames. But the pious
feeling of the Middle-ages rebuilt the church and
the continual pilgrimages caused many families to
settle around it. Thus gradually rose the friendly
small town, which bears the name of the miraculous
solitary, as well as the opposite lying St. Gours-
hausen.

Sternberg and Liebenstein.

The brothers.

On his old ancestral castle Liebenstein near
Hirzenach lived Kurt, a knight of that name. He
had already experienced many bloody combats,
protected the good right of his Emperor in many
a bloody battle, and now thought, of passing his
days in quietude and in the joys of his two blooming excellent sons.

Heinrich and Conrad deserved to be called the
father's pride; bot were equally inspired with
genuine chivalrous feeling, a profound feeling for
right, and a great predilection for arms; but in
every thing else they were very dissimilar.
Heinrich, the elder, earnest, still and reserved, was
more a friend of domestic joys, as soon as Peace
allowed them; while Conrad more lively, more
ardent, allowed himself to be dominated by the
impulse of the moment, but was also engaging from

his candid, natural nature. At the same time grew
up with them Hildegarde, of the family Brömser,
a relative and an orphan. The brothers loved her
as a sister, because she, from childhood was regarded so by them. But when they had attained
the age of manhood, Kurt considered it necessary,
to inform the sons of the true connection, at the
same time expressing the wish, one of them would
become Hildegarde's husband. From this moment
the brothers regarded Hildegarde with other sentiments; another Love replaced their former affection, and both wooed for the maiden's favour.

Heinrich esteemed her with profound sincere
feeling, which he seldom expressed, Conrad with
the light impetuous sentiment of first youth, less
profound, and therefore richer in expressions. He
was preferred by Hildegarde; but Heinrich buried
in generous self-denial the infinite grief of his heart
and was noble enough, to participate openly in his
brother's happiness. It is true, the old knight
knowing the character of his sons, had preferred
to have seen, Heinrich and Hildegarde become a
pair, but he did not wish to make any obstacles to
her free choice; therefore he did not delay with
his consent, and allowed all preparations to be
made for a splendid marriage-festival.

This however should only take place after the
completion of a new castle to be called Sternberg;
and that the Families could enjoy uninterrupted
intercourse, he had the castle built near his own.

But Destiny had not decided for the wished for happiness. As little as Heinrich envied his brother the joy, he felt however, that it would be impossible for him to be the constantly quiet witness of it; he therefore longed for an excitable, active life, in which he could forget his unhappy inclination, per- haps could find an heroical death.

With such feelings nothing could have been more welcome to him, than the holy Bernhard of Clairvaux' appeal for Crusade to the Holy Land. With general inspiration this challenge was an- swered, troops of knights and combatants armed themselves; the crusade flag waved on all castles, and thousands of brave heroic hearts beat with the hope to free and keep the Holy Sepulchre. Heinrich declared to his father he would go to Palestine, and would join the army of the Crusaders. Kurt knew the reasons of his son, and silently approved of them. Before the castle was finished, before the brother's marriage could be celebrated, the youth left his home and marched to the East with a chosen company of combatants.

With him marched from that valley of the Rhine knightly youths, and young men of nearly all noble families, Brömser of Rüdesheim, Friedrich of Schwaben, Gilgen of Lorch, and many other friends, inspired like himself with pious zeal.

Soon after Heinrich's departure, the knight Kurt became dangerously ill, and on the same day that the castle was finished, he departed this life. This death did not allow the marriage of the engaged till after the expiration of a year, a circumstance, which, as unwished for to Conrad as it first came, was however the cause of a complete changement of ideas. In company with some wild spirits of the neighbourhood, who, incapable of tender feelings, described the marriage-state to him as a troublesome, restricting band, and defamed the weaker sex, the young knight learned to regard Hildegarde with indifference, and his love for her decreased so much, as his friends knew to make him more sensitive for the noisy pleasures of the chase and drinking-feasts.

After several months, news was heard of Heinrich from the Holy Land. On different occasions he had distinguished himself, and his name was mentioned with admiration in the Christian army, his sword feared by the Enemy. Conrad heard this news with the most eager participation, and with those feelings, that without to be envious, but rather with reluctance, that he could obtain the same renown and the same honor for his arms, instead of passing his days in inactivity and senseless occupations. His resolution equally to join the Crusaders was as quickly resolved on, as executed, and after a hurried farewell from his bride, who melted in tears, he departed.

His journey was fortunate; but as he did not possess his brother's despairing bravery, he could not obtain his renown, he was therefore soon tired of the tedious campaign, the fatigues and privations, and left Palestine after a short sojourn, to return to Europe. But before he embarked at Constantinople, he made the acquaintance of an exceedingly beautiful Greek lady of whom he became passionately amorous. Zealously he sued for her favor; with his agreeable figure and vivacious engaging manners he soon obtained it, and so he committed the folly, of wedding a lady little known to himself, and of a strange nation, and, notwithstanding the tender engagement at home, he conducted his wife there.

Meditating and sorrowful Hildegarde sat in her chamber and reflected on her unfortunate destiny, and as she regarded the beautiful, but uninhabited, and apparently, uselessly built Sternberg, she saw to her astonishment travellers with beasts of burden and baggage moving to that castle. Who could take for his residence her Foster father's castle, belonging to the two absent brothers, without her being informed a word about it? She called her waiting-maid, and ordered, that inquiries should be made; she received a message, the more unexpectedly it came, cut her so much the more to the heart, a news, filling her with terror and endless sorrow. Conrad it was said had returned from the war against the Infidels, he had connected himself with a most beautiful Greek-lady, and to-morrow would make his entry into Sternberg, which he had chosen for his residence.

So it happened. The abandoned Hildegarde saw
the Faithless, saw her engaged, with the stranger
wife enter in the most splendid manner. The
shameless did not throw one glance across; he
avoided intentionally, to look at Liebenstein, not
to disturb the bliss of his happiness which he felt
at the side of his beautiful wife. Feast succeeded
feast. Music and jubilee sounded daily till midnight
across from Sternberg, and its hospitable halls
were never empty of visiting, congratulating friends,
who found themselves very comfortable at the
richly appointed luxurious tables. But so much
the quieter was it at Liebenstein. Hildegarde
avoided the rooms, which looked towards the
neighbouring castle, and removed to the most retired part of the castle. She passed her solitary
hours in diligent occupation for the household and
in praying.

Late one evening, as all were already in deep
sleep at Liebenstein a strange knight with his
squire demanded admittance and lodging. Both
were already granted by the castle-steward, the
strange knight conducted to his apartments and
attended to, without Hildegarde's being acquainted
of the arrival till the next morning. How astonished
was she, as the knight quite unexpectedly appeared
before her, to see the knight Heinrich. He was now
returned home; but not because he was tired of
war, but because he had heard of his brother's
strange marriage, and only the thought of Hilde-

garde's sorrow and abandonment did not allow
him to remain at a distance from her.

With sadness and reluctance he saw Hildegarde's
pale, suffering figure, learned the, oft interrupted
by tears, story of her misfortune and the outpour-
ing of her grief. Without speaking a word of his
intentions, he begged her to be composed, and hope
for a happier future, then rested a day from his
fatiguing journey, without any one at Sternberg
knowing of his return.

But on the fourth day he sent a confidant over
to his brother, and had him challenged to mortal
combat, on account of his unknightly behaviour,
and faithlessness to Hildegarde. The challenge
was accepted by Conrad, and the following day-
break was to witness the terrible spectacle of a
brother-duel. On the narrow way separating the
two castles, stood, already by day-break the combatants (who were by Nature destined to the most
sincere Love and Concord), opposite each other
with drawn Swords, and already had sounded the
signal for the beginning of the decisive God's
judgment, as a thickly veiled female figure stepped
between the brothers and ordered peace. „What
do you wish to do?“ said she with respect inspir-
ing words, „do you wish to plunge your fratricidal
steel into each other's bosom on my account? I
forbid this abominable sinful struggle. It would
be also useless; for my decision is taken. Still to-
day a convent will receive me, where I can pass

my days in quiet and prayer, in praying God that
he will pardon your Conrad's falseness to me, as I
also pardon you, and that he on you Heinrich may
be pleased to pour his richest earthly blessings,
as reward for your heroism and your knightly
devotion to me." So she spoke; then ascended the
mountain to the high road, where her attendants
awaited her, and immediately began her way to
a neighbouring convent.

The brothers were reconciled to each other.
Each returned to his castle, and if between both
there was no cordial, sincere connection, because
Heinrich could not approve of the strange sister-
in-law, and fickle temper, with which she accepted
his homage, there was however peace between
them, and Conrad even visited Liebenstein occasionally. But a most unfortunate event for Conrad however brought the brothers again more
together. Already a long time Conrad's wife was
in secret correspondence with a young knight who
enjoyed hospitality at Sternberg, and at last eloped
with her during a dark stormy night. This elope-
ment not only convinced Heinrich of the unworthi-
ness of his wife but also restrained for ever, his
foolish passion for her, and allowed him to recognise in its fullest light, his base conduct to Hildegarde. But with this knowledge and the repentance
caused by it awoke in his heart his love to her,
whom he had forsaken so shamefully, and he felt
himself the more unhappy because the noble one

was now irretrievably lost to him. Only in his brother's affection he found consolation, and both resided in the castle Liebenstein while Sternberg was deserted.

Hildegarde remained faithful to her vow, and bequeathed her rich possessions to the poor of the neighbourhood. Heinrich and Conrad lived together amicably till death separated them; and still now the neighbouring castles, which after the brother's decease fell to Brömser of Rüdesheim, are called the Brothers.

Kreuznach.

The Ebernburg.

Two legends are connected with the name of this castle.

By its siege in the 15th century the provisions of the garrison were almost exhausted. But not to allow the besiegers to remark this, the master of the tower had the last Boar, which they had, bound daily, as if with the intention to slaughter it, but then led into its sty. – The besiegers, by the daily screaming of, according to their opinion, a slaughtered Boar, were deceived in their hopes to overcome the garrison by hunger, raised the siege, and from that time the castle was called Ebernburg.

The second legend is ascribed to the robber-knight Rupert, as possessor of the castle, who soliciting for the hand of the beautiful Countess of Monfort, she refused the solicitation, as she had already chosen a youthful friend of the Count, the Rhine Count Heinrich. Reflecting on revenge for this abasement, the robber-knight withdrew from his former companions, only amusing himself with hunting in his extensive forests. On returning from such a hunt, a very strong boar, stood at bay near the Rheingrafenstein, never before seen of such a size in these woods, all thrown weapons rebounded broken from his sides; already Count Rupert stood unarmed before the monster, which made itself ready for an attack with advanced tusks, as suddenly in this fearful moment the animal lay dead at his feet. It was the Rhine Count Heinrich who had acted so magnanimously towards his adversary. Accidentally coming to the spot, he no sooner saw the despairing condition of the Count, than he directly forgot all animosity, and by a fortunate blow killed the animal. Reconciliation and re-established friendship between the two Counts were the consequences of this noble action, and soon the Rhine Count Heinrich soon led the amiable Monfort to the Altar. In memory of this event, a carved boars-head ornaments the door of the castle (still visible) which received the name „Ebernburg.“

The Ebernburg was in the 11th century possessed by the Salic Emperor, from it descended

1394 to the Sponheim-Kreuznach line; 1448 Rein-
hard of Sickingen obtained it. 1481 Franz of Sickingen was born, through whom the Ebernburg re-
ceivid its historical mention. 1515 Franz of Sickingen was outlawed, and retired to his Ebernburg,
at that time as place of Refuge for many pursued
named „the Asylum of Justice.“ By the besieging
of his castle Landstuhl near Kosel in the Rhine-
palatinate, Franz of Sickingen was deadly wounded
by a ball and died on the 7th May 1523. After his
death the Ebernburg was taken and destroyed.
Also Sickingen's wife, the noble and philanthropical
Hedwig, died earlier, leaving 3 sons and 3 daughters.

The descendants of Sickingen later became
Catholics. Charles Ferdinand of Sickingen built
in the 18th century on the declivity of the mountain
above the village a castle, of which are still some
ruins, in 1794 the French destroyed it.

DIE FEINDLICHEN BRÜDER.

Bornhoven.

The inimical Brothers.

ear Bornhoven the rotten ruins of an old castle
frown from the height, and reflect themselves
in the green waves of the stream. But these
remnants are not romantic, they do not salute the
wanderer, like so many, old, dilapidated castles
and ruins of the Rhine by charming environs, and
friendly changeable landscapes; gloomy and sad
the grey stone of the castle regards below surrounded by dry unfruitful fields, bushes and plains,
of miserable huts and the stooping, creeping about
figures of the inhabitants. It is a melancholy picture, to which Nature has denied every ornament
and charm, and this country makes on the wanderer that painful uncomfortable impression, for
which no one can account, and reluctantly exper-
iences, when one unexpectedly sees Prisons and
places of Execution.

And if you ask, who could have chosen those
unfriendly, deserted heights as residences, you are
answered, that the curse of heaven rests upon the
country, since the unholy actions committed by 2
brothers, in unnatural anger destroyed each other.

On that once proud castle lived a powerful, very
rich knight, who left behind him 2 sons and 1
daughter, property, and besides a great quantity
of gold. But all these possessions had been ob-

tained by robbery and oppressions of every kind, and
therefore the knight was cursed by young and old,
and all believed that at his death, the great riches,
obtained unjustly, and kept by avarice, could not
bring blessings.

The brothers possessed the avarice of their
father, the sister on the contrary the softness, piety,
and innocence of a too-early lost mother. The poor
lamentable maiden was therefore by the effected
with shovels, division of the gold most shamefully
cheated, because she was incapable of seeing exposed with her own eyes, the arbitrariness and
cunning of her brothers. She hastened to apply
her share to charitable Institutions, to found religious houses, and then to retire to a convent, to close
her days in quiet retirement.

But the brothers, although enriched by the
cheated part of the sister; were not in agreement
as to sharing the booty. Fields, woods and vine-
yards gave occasion to contention and dispute,
which ended in hatred, animosity and complete
separation. Those, destined by Nature, to live in
peace and happy concord, attacked each other with
unholy blindness, on account of trivial objects of
their inheritance, which by their riches should not
have occurred, and were continually sworn enemies.

There fell at last into the burning mass of their
contention, the terrific spark, which blew it into
consuming flame, and let loose the fury with the
most destructive rage, the spark of Jealousy. Both

loved the daughter of a not far residing knight, who understood to enchain them with coquettish arts. It did not require more to cause the brothers to draw their swords in duel, from which every humane feeling turned with disgust.

As well as by the actions of the brothers, so disaster rested upon this duel. Blind with rage, they attacked one another in running upon each other's sword, and both ended their wicked life in the same hour.

Boppard.

Convent Marienburg.

The knight Bayer of Boppard was a scion of one of the noblest families of the Rhine-country; a young, it is true somewhat wild fighter yet not bad-natured, and capable of tender feelings. He loved Maria, a neighbouring castle maiden of great beauty, found soon return, and was thereupon the engaged and bridegrom of his dear maiden. Passionately devoted to the pleasures of the chase, Konrad often passed a long time with distant friends, having the same inclination, and were collectively bachelors. Whether it was, that these excited in him a repugnance to the marriage-state, or that his sentiments changed, enough, he sent Maria a declaration, that he could

not decide to subject himself to marriage, and
that he relieved her of her given word.

Some time after Konrad rode alone through the
forest. Just arrived at an open place, he saw a
strange knight advancing to him, and as if chal-
lenging stopped close before him. „Who are you?“
asked the surprised, „and what is then your demand, that you so place yourself before me?“
„Regard my shield“, answered the stranger, „and
my arms will be your answer. I am Maria's
brother, returned from the East; and I meet you
here, to demand satisfaction for your shameful
unfaithfulness to my sister. Prepare yourself for
a Life and Death struggle.“

This bold challenge excited Konrad's anger.
He drew his sword from its scabbard and the
struggle began. The opponent's weak arm could
only for a short time resist the strong blows of
knight Bayer, and deadly wounded he sank to
the ground. Konrad now hastened to open his
helmet, and regard the unknown face; but how
great was his terror, as in the pale features he
recognised Maria's traits. „By your hand I wished
to fall“, said she with a dying voice; without you
life would be a burden.“

In vain he strove to restrain the flowing life
of the maiden, but after a few moments she resigned her heroical spirit. Like a madman, he
threw himself upon the deceased, and grief rendered him senseless. So his servants found him

and only with trouble did they restore him and
separate him from the corpse.

Maria was buried in the most splendid manner,
and Konrad whom from this moment repentance
did not allow a moment's rest, had, in a measure
to expiate his guilt a convent built over Maria's
grave, which he named Marienburg and to which
he bequeathed all his property. Then he hastened
to the Crusade-army ot Palestine, to seek for the
death which should unite him to Mary. Long he
sought it in vain; he reaped only Renown and
Victory; but at last by the storming of the Fortress
Ptolomais, he found it fighting without armour,
and being the first to ascend the ladder he received the deady thrust of an enemy's spear.

Rhense.

Emperor Wenzel.

During the Confusion, Disturbances and Quarrels
of every description which afflicted the German
Empire towards the end of the 14th century,
Wenzeslaus of the house of Luxemburg, ascended
the Imperial throne. But he was not the man, to steer
the State-ship with safety, and his mind was not
in accordance with serious occupations, and the
prosperity of the government; an open, joyous

disposition, in enjoyment and pleasure, was much more the object of his wishes, and he soon discovered, that these were not to be found on a throne, that under purple and ermine an ambitious heart could fine contentment, but not his, to whom Splendour and Renown were vain things.

Wenzels favourite sojourn was therefore not the Residence and the Cabinet, his society not that of the Counselors of the Empire; he much more preferred, to sojourn on the smiling banks of the Rhine, and to drink at its source, so to say, its vine-blood. He preferred to dwell at Rhense, where he very often, at the renowned Königstuhle, celebrated a feast, surrounded by equally minded, gay companions, with song and wine. The Elector Ruprecht of the Palatinate, had already long striven for the Imperial crown, and hoped, that there would not be serious difficulties in the way of Wenzels voluntary ceding, and was his constant companion. He seized every opportunity to make the Emperor sensible of the disagreeables and burdens of the high dignity, and to let him know, that it would be better to free himself from them, especially as discontent dominated since a long time amongst the Elector's subjects, and therefore his deposition was to be feared.

Once sat Wenzel again among his friends at Königstuhle, and the fiery juice of the Assmannshauser vine had disposed many to joviality; the goblets crossed, and gay melodies sounded. The Emperor spoke in jovial arrogance to Ruprecht: „You already long aspired to win the Crown, which was put on my head. I cede it to you, in case you are able, to place before us a wine, which by the company is preferred to this.“

Ruprecht rose directly, beckoned to a servant, and gave his orders. A barrel was soon rolled in, from which the cups were directly filled. „That is“, called the Elector, „of my Bacharacher; taste it, my nobles, and say without shyness, if it pleases you.“

The wine found general approval, and all drinkers preferred it to the Assmannshäuser. As proof of such preference they sat longer than ever at the Königstuhle and revelled the whole night in this delicious grape-juice.

Wenzel kept his word, he ceded his Crown to Ruprecht of the Palatinate, for which he gave him 4 waggon-loads of Bacharach wine.

Lahneck.

The twelve Templars.

In the beginning of the 14th century the Order of Temple-knights, which had been founded principally for religious purposes, and defending Christianity in the East, on account of its extended power, was severely persecuted by several Regents. It was principally Philipp the Beautiful King of France, and the Pope Clemens 5th who worked at the annihilation of the Templars. The first had for this purpose allured the Grand-master Molay with 60 knights, from the island Cyprus to France, and had them collectively most cruelly executed in Paris; the latter thereupon dissolved the Order by an Edict, and arbitrarily disposed of its property.

The remaining knights, rendered timorous by such terrible measures, dispersed themselves in other countries, where they were allowed to reside; however as far as the power of the Pope extended, it was used to effect the ruin of the pursued. The Archbishop of Mainz, Peter of Aichspalt, was summoned to exterminate the residing knights in his diocese, and the obedient Bishop resolved to make a commencement with 12 who held possession of the Lahneck-castle.

A strong detachment of the Archbishop's troops suddenly invested the castle, and demanded of the Garrison directly to surrender unconditionally. But the knights recollecting the Fate of their executed brethren, armed themselves for desperate resistance, resolved to sell their lives dearly.

A regular Siege began, and was conducted with all zeal. To the raging attacks of the superior force the Templars opposed the quiet defence which expected nothing than death. Several stormings were repulsed by the heroic-couraged knights, and struck by thrown down stones and shots, many mercenaries fell to rise no more. The Archbishop, inflamed with rage, and stung by shame, that the whole power of the Besiegers could not overcome the 12 knights, ordered a general and last storming. During a dark night the castle was simultaneously attacked on all sides, and although the renown-worthy Templars executed miracles of bravery, their number was too small to render it possible for them to resist the constantly increasing advance of the Besiegers. Soon the principal entrance was in their power, a part of the knights killed, and the rest obliged to retire to the castle-keep. In this unfortunate struggle, encouraging each other hy cries and reminding each other of their murdered brethren, they fell to the last man, who although bleeding from many wounds, still held his sword menac ingly. Meantime the morning had begun, and the sun illuminated with his first rays the bloody scene of the castle-keep. The leader of the Arch-

bishop's mercenary troops effected by involuntary
esteem and admiration for this last combatant,
offered him Liberty and Life, if he would cease
the useless resistance and beg for Grace. But
the Templar without deigning an answer, swung
with remaining strength a spear among the opponents, threw himself on their lances and resigned
his heroical life.

Laach.

Genovefa.

Palatinate Count Siegfried, a noble knight and
vassal of the French King in Austrasien, viz, in
the contry between the Rhine, Maas, and Mosel,
was married with Genovefa a Princess of Brabant.
For several years they resided at the castle
Palatinate, at the embouchure of the Mosel and
Saar; in the most cordial concord, and, although
childless wedlock, in undisturbed happiness; as
the Arabs who had conquered Spain, broke into
France by the Pyrenees.

Quickly all Dukes and Knights of the country
were obliged to join the King's army, in order
to oppose the numerous Barbarians. Also Siegfried
could not forget honor and duty by the appeal,
and not participate in a struggle which should
decide the fate of the whole western Christianity.'

As painful therefore as was to him the parting from his wife, he felt himself bound to quit her, after intrusting to his friend knight G o l o of Drachenfels the administration of his property, particularly recommending the sorrowful wife, house etc. to his protection.

Golo was an honourable, upright, but still very young and impassioned man. He was, for a time, faithful to his trust, and as circumstances caused it, he was almost ever the companion of the Countess, whose esteem and friendship he soon acquired. But just this confidential intimacy with the beautiful, charming wife aroused in his heart a dangerous inclination. It is true that at first he tried to struggle against his love, but by daily seeing the Countess it found fresh nourishment, at last his passion caused him to forget all the duties of friendship, and he only thought on the object of his desire.

Genovefa had not any idea of what moved the feelings of, as she believed, her faithful protector; but by the fine gift of observation, so natural to women, the condition of Golo's mind could not remain long concealed, and inconsiderate expressions, which escaped the knight, left her no scruple that it was herself who had lit the consuming love-flame in him.

Perhaps Golo if he had been left to his own good principles, would have left a place so dangerous to him, and not have discovered his feel-

ings to any one; but unfortunately for him, a not
far residing relative of the Countess, Mathilde of
Strahlen, visited her, and soon discovered what
was passing in the young knight's heart.

Mathilde was artful and envious, imperious
and sly. She knew how to win Golo's confidence,
and as she regarded the beauty of the Countess
the reflection of a beautiful soul, with envious
jealousy, and was penetrated by that hate which
the bad are accustomed to have against the good,
she encouraged the knight to sue for the favour
of the Lady, in awakenning in him false hopes,
which by the virtue and piety of Siegfried's wife
never could be accomplished. The noble Countess
was secretly informed that Mathilde and Golo
plotted something secretly; but she paid little
attention to it; for it is difficult for a pure soul
to believe in the designs of reprobates But she
was soon to experience, how shamefully her
pretended friends could act. Deluded and in-
stigated, driven on the way of the wicked, Golo
became quite another man, as he had been under
the guidance of his worthy friend Siegfried. He
did not more attempt to bridle his consuming
passion; he only thought on its satisfaction, and
every plan that his disreputable friend proposed
to him was agreeable.

At last the Plotters had arranged all, to act
decidedly. Every attempt of Golo's approach to
the Countess had remained fruitless; therefore

Mathilde advised him open and rash procedure. A formal declaration of love, was the first thing that should happen, and if this, as was to be expected remained without result, then force and compulsion should be substituted instead of the hitherto used mild means.

Genovefa heard with astonishment and indignation the bold temerarious love-offer of the knight who, destined as her protector and honored with the confidence of her husband, could so forget his duty and all chivalry; she further forbade his appearing before her, and menaced him with the revenge of Siegfried. The first open step was now done, the return barred, and the once commenced road must be followed. An imitated handwriting of the steward Drogones, containing a confession of his illicit intercourse with Genovefa was sent to Siegfried. By this letter the distant knight was to be filled with hate against his innocent wife, and every possible messenger should be made ineffectual. The apprehension however that such could secretly arrive to the Countess, induced Mathilde and Golo to have her watched most strictly, to send away all attached domestics, and only to retain those persons devoted unconditionally to them; indeed, the shameless pair not however contented with this, carried their wickedness so far, as to imprison the noble lady.

In this prison the unfortunate wife, after 6 months absence of her husband, was confined of a boy, to whom she gave the name of Dolorous, because he was born in such great sufferings.

Meanwhile Siegfried had fought bravely with the army. The Cristians unequal to the numerous swarms of Arabs, were obliged to retire in many bloody conflicts, and a gloomy, misfortune impregnated cloud neared the Infidels from the beautiful banks of the Rhine and Loire. Karl Martell advanced to assist with a newly formed army, and enlivened again the courage of the Christian army. At Tours a decisive battle took place. Whether the Crescent, or the Cross, henceforth should dominate in Europe depended on this battle, which in every case must be a mortal combat.

At Martell's side fought Siegfried with his men, and did miracles of bravery. In the midst of the enemy's masses waved the feather of his helmet, his powerful blade shone, and many saracens fell by his fist. The Victory was long undecided, at last it was wrested by the persevering, not to be resisted courage of the Western countries, and many thousand killed covered the battle-field. Siegfried had remained without wounds almost to the end of the battle; but in the evening, when pursuing he was struck by a lance, so that he was obliged to resign himself to a surgeon's aid, and saw himself condemned to inactivity. Then he thought more than ever on his distant solitary wife and the next day he sent his friend, Karl of Rheingrafenstein to his home, to carry intelligence of his early arrival, and to bring news of Genovefa.

The knight arrived just as Mathilde and Golo laid before, an assembled council of several Nobles and Judges, false proofs of Genovefa's Guilt and Infidelity for Judgment and to pronounce Banishment on the injured. In vain Karl of Rheingrafenstein sought to hinder such a detestable procedure; Bribery and Cabal conquered, the unhappy wife was declared guilty, and for Karl there was nothing else to do, than to throw down his gauntlet as proof of her innocence. Golo knew, that if he would not give up all as lost, he must accept the challenge, and immediately a day was appointed for the duel. This duel ought to have been a Divine-judgment; but Hell gained the Victory. Karl succumbed to the despairing bravery and strength of Golo and with pierced breast yielded up his ghost.

Nothing more was able to avert Genovefa's terrible destiny; after the death of her defender death appeared unavoidable to her; the Tribunal insisted on its verdict, and she would have ended her life on the funeral-pile if a part of her enemies had ventured, to give the Country, where she was honoured and loved, the spectacle of a public execution, on the other side Golo's passion had not resisted the death of the beautiful wife. A secret nightly assassination, in a solitary forest,

distant from all witnesses, by hired servants'
hands, seemed the most advisable to Mathilde.
Two bribed grooms received orders, to conduct,
during the night, the Countess and child away
from there, and as proofs of the accomplished
murder, to bring the tongues of the sacrificed
victims. The commissioned were ready to execute
the fearful deed. Genovefa and her child „Dolorous“ not able to comprehend his misfortune, saw
in the deep wilderness, the daggers pointed at
their breasts; but the melting tenderness, and
assertions of the Countess, that she was innocent,
at last moved the wicked wretches, to spare her
life and that of her child; however they dragged
the unfortunates so far into the forest, that return
was rendered impossible. Then they were left
to their fate, and produced 2 sheeps' tongues as
a proof that the order had been strictly executed.

Siegfried hastened, as soon as his wounds were
healed, to his home. There Mathilde and Golo
laid before him the proofs of Genovefa's guilt,
and as these as well as the termination of the
Divine-judgment only too clearly seemed to fix
Genovefa's guilt, so the shamefully deceived
nourished not a doubt, and he endeavoured, although in vain, to forget the Faithless.

Genovefa had, after wandering a long time,
found a cavern which afforded her shelter; but
deprived of all subsistence, she believed, to be
obliged to die here from misery, and pityingly

she regarded Dolorous, to whom she was not able to give nourishment; at once, there came as if sent by God, a white deer into the cavern, and nestled at the feet of the Forsaken. The deer must have had young ones lately for her udder was swollen, and she willingly offered it as nourishment for mother and child. The tame animal returned daily, and at last remained constantly with them. Roots and herbs were soon found by Genovefa, and so passed her sad days, it is true without Hope, yet confiding in the justice of the Almighty, to whom Dolorous daily learned to pray more fervently.

For Siegfried, who amid his splendid retinue and at his castle still lived solitary, was no more peace. The memory of his wife followed him as a shadow, and whatever he undertook, to distract himself, nothing could extinguish in him the remembrance of past times, and his former happiness. His favourite pastime was the chase, to which he devoted himself so much the more as it seemed more suitable to deaden the grief of his soul.

One day he arranged a grand hunt, in which he participated. The pursuit of the game had conducted the count further into the forest than ever, and he just thought of returning, as a white deer sprang out of a thicket just before him. He would still hunt it, and pursued it through thorn and bush, across plain and moor. He had already wounded the animal with a drawn spear,

and already it seemed as if it could not escape
the hounds, as it fled to a cavern, and with
astonishment he saw a female figure advance
from it, to whose feet as if seeking protection,
it caressingly laid itself.

The presence of a human being in this wilderness appeared most singular to Siegfried; but
how great was his terror and astonishment, as
by approaching nearer, to recognise in the pale
afflicted woman's face the traits of his wife, and
she at the same time called out his name with
the expression of fright and joy. Genovefa fell
at his feet calling on God and all Saints as witnesses, she asserted, that she had ever remained
faithful to him, and related, how, persecuted by
Golo's passion and Mathilde's malice, she only
thanked her preservation to a miracle.

The sight of the wife attenuated by grief and
misery, whose ragged garments scarcely covered
her nakedness, and the words of Genovefa, in
which were expressed the deepest suffering of
abused virtue, made on the Count a terrible effect, and as the little Dolorous, playing about in
the neighbourhood of the cavern, advanced with
bashful curiosity and Genovefa pointed him out
to Siegfried as their son, the knight could not
longer resist the force of the moment, and weeping with grief and joy he pressed wife and son
to his bosom. But then he sounded his hunter's
horn. and his retinue hastened towards him, and

with them also Golo. „Do you know these?"
thundered out the Count to the villain, tearing
him from the throng and conducting to Genovefa.
Golo paled, and all standing round were astonished,
as they saw the wife and boy and learned who
they were. Surprised by the terrible unexpected
accusation, and not prepared with any exculpa-
tion; he confessed all, and in naming Mathilde
as his seducer, he begged for his life. But Siegfried
thought of no grace by such an enormous crime.
Golo was delivered to justice, and suffered, for
his great grievance to the innocent, treachery,
and the disgraceful blindness of an unbridled
passion, by the executioner's hand. Mathilde fled;
pursued however by horsemen, she, on horseback,
plunged into the Mosel, the waves of which buried
her. Genovefa bloomed in her husband's love a
new bliss, and Dolorous, nobly thriving in strength
and virtue, was the joy of his parents. From
gratitude to Heaven which so visibly had watched
over her, the noble lady founded the Frauenkirche
near Laach, in a country, which she preferred
above all, and according to her express wish, she
was interred in this church, where now her
monument is shown to visitors.

Hammerstein.

The Salic blood.

Not far from the friendly, charming Neuwied, rises from steep rocks and surrounded by woody heights, close to the banks of the Rhine, the since long in ruins castle Hammerstein. It is said, according to some chroniclers, to have received its name from its founder, Karl Martell, according to others owes its name from the rock, on which it is built, similar to the form of a hammer.

Here dwelt about the beginning of the 11th century Count Otto of Hammerstein. This knight conducted with Bishop Erkenbold of Mainz a long bloody struggle, and as the spiritual man could not succeed against the brave powerful Count by force of arms, he sought to ruin him in some other manner, and soon a very welcome opportunity offered itself.

Otto had married his beautiful cousin Irmegard. But for such a marriage with so near a relative, was, according to Canon-law, necessary Papal dispensation; but the Count had obstinately refused, to request the permission, and therefore Bishop Erkenbold did not neglect, to pronounce Excommunication against him, and by special Synod verdict to declare his marriage invalid. But as he did not succeed to disturb the happiness of the young couple, as Excommunication and Verdict

remained without the expected effect, he applied
to the reigning Emperor Henry 2nd with unremitting petitions to give weight to the Ecclesiastical-
law by the employment of worldly power for.
the purpose of punishing the incestuous Otto.

The Emperor too much devoted to the Clergy,
was easily won by the Bishop and personally
besieged Hammerstein with a considerable force.
However the garrison defended itself with just
as much courage as cleverness; and it seemed
that the Siege would, if even successful, be a long
one. so that the Emperor tired of this useless
struggle, had willingly seized an opportunity to
finish it by a compromise.

By a sally of the Count, with his heroic wife
at his side, both were wounded by arrows, and
bleeding were obliged to be carried into the castle.
As soon as the Emperor learned this, he said to
the Bishop: „Indeed! methinks almost, we shall
never be able to humble the courage of these lovers.
Therefore and because the blood, against which
they sinned has now flowed, they have atoned
for their guilt, we will finish the feud. I will
have that proposed to the Count, and I think you
should, I wish it, marry the pair with all the
usages and blessings of the Church." And so it
happened. A sincere reconciliation concluded for
ever the dispute, and Otto celebrated with his
noble guests the most splendid feast, that the
halls of Hammerstein had ever witnessed.

Altenaar.

The last knight of Altenaar.

In the rocky and narrow valley, which flows through the Aar, now splashing as a torrent, now foaming and rushing as a wood-stream, lies on the top of one of the many precipitous mountain-cones which wreathe the bank, the ruined remains of the formerly powerful castle Altenaar.

In times of yore the race of the same named possessor and inhabitant of this castle ended by a terrible death, still known by the people, and never since the seat of a noble of the country, although the castle was long stately and inhabitable. Kurt of Altenaar, the last of his race, a liberty-loving courageous knight, who energetically opposed the presumption of the Bishops and Princes of his country, suddenly saw himself inclosed in his castle by enemies. The resistance was courageous, and worthy of an honourable knight, the rocks defied the attacks, and many a mercenary fell by the fists of Kurt and his followers, or was struck by the throw of heavy stones. The Siege however continued, and the want of provisions was at last the most dangerous enemy of the garrison.

Kurt could name the day on which he should be obliged to share his last loaf among his comrades and then surrender or perish. But there occurred

on the side of the besiegers, if not want of provisions still moroseness and discouragement. The
extremity of the garrison was unknown to them,
and they believed, never to be able to become
masters of the castle, the height and resistance
of which mocked their boldest attacks.

Already the Bishops and Princes saw the near
outburst of discontent in their ranks, daily already a number of their servants and vassals
deserted from a dangerous useless struggle, and
already revolt and disobedience threatened a
complete dissolution of the besieging army, as
there appeared on the highest tower of the castle,
irradiated by the first morning rays, in splendid,
complete equipment and mounted, the venerable
Kurt. The tall noble figure, the long silver hair,
the marble paleness of his face, over which waved
the feather of his helmet the white steel armour
on milk coloured charger imparted to the knight
something August, almost Spiritual, and expectat-
ingly every eye, in a large circle was raised to
the tower. The extended right hand of the knight
signified that he wished to speak, and as the
besiegers listened anxiously, he spoke audibly so:
„See here the last man and the last steed of all,
which breathed in the tower. Hunger has snatched
away wife, child, comrades; none is left. But they
died free from hated tyranny and" ignominious
yoke. And so I die as I lived, worthy of a knight,
unconstrained and free." After these words he

spurred his charger to the edge of the rock; the
noble animal reared, but driven by the strength
of its rider, it.made a mighty spring from the
giddy height into the abyss, from rock to rock,
accompanied by rattling stones into the waves
of the Aar, which closed over knight and charger
and buried them for ever.

- Fright and terror overcame all, who witnessed
it, and hastily the besiegers retired; for none of
them wished to enter a castle, which had become
a heap of Dead, nor longer remain in a country,
which appeared to them the home of terror.

Rolandseck.

Count Roland of Angers, contemporary and
nephew of Charles the Great, a worthy, brave
knight and palatin, had distinguished himself
in war expeditions and adventures His name was
become known in the countries, which he passed
through, and in which his sword had chastised
many robbers, served unresisting innocence, or
had carried away the victory in tournament. He
was sojourning in Paris, at his uncle's camp, to
rest from the many expeditions, and try to enjoy
the leisure enjoyment of the court luxury; but
he did not find it to his taste. His inquiet spirit

longed for activity and dangers, for the usual vicissitudes of an adventurous expedition, but not for the comfortable quietude of a constant residence and a regular if also splendid life.

He therefore requested of his Imperial master and relative, to try in unknown countries his knightly wandering life. His request was granted, and the next morning's sun already saw. Roland mount his celebrated and courageous·charger Brilliador, and followed by a faithful, proved squire, leave the splendid residence.

The beautiful plain, through which the Marne flows, and the rough Vosges were the next objects of his journey. Hereupon he turned to Rhein-franken, chastised some robber-knights, and forced them to deliver up their booty: then visited an old friend and companion in-arms, the knight Kurt of Frankenstein, and at last resolved to travel to the beautiful banks of the Rhine, and salute at their castles the resident knights.

So he travelled down the Rhine, just as the Spring had spread her charms over the plain, and had clothed the romantic banks with the ornament of fresh green. The knight seemed never to have enjoyed such a beautiful country so much, and as little as he was accustomed to pay attention to the Beauties of Nature, yet he could not resist to lose himself for hours in contemplating the beautiful vicinity. Many a day's journey had he completed, visited many a stately

castle, and every where found the most hospitable
reception, as one evening the Drachenburg caught
his sight. The walls and pinnacles of the extensive, fine knightly castle glittered in the gold
of the declining sun, and shone with the other
summits of the Siebengebirge over the twilight
valley. The heat of the day had yielded to refreshing coolness; the flocks returned to their
folds, the fatigued vine-dresser to his hut, the
fisherman counting the booty of the day, draws
his boat on to the bank, and not the least air
ruffles the smooth, green crystal-like drops which
fall from its sides.

This beautiful picture of repose, this peace
in Nature, over which the firmament spread its
pure azure, made on Roland an unusual, profound
impression. For the first time in his life came
over him the inexplicable feeling of sweet sadness, and it chained him so much, that, at last,
his squire was obliged to remind him, that it
was the highest time to continue their way, if
they wished to reach night quarters. The paladin
asked a passer-by, who lived at that high tower?
and as he was answered, the knight Heribert,
but the castle was called the Drachenburg, he
recollected, that it was just this knight to whom
he was charged to bring greetings and messages
from friends in France and Upper-Rhine. Roland
therefore did not hesitate to cross the stream.
It was already night, as he arrived at the castle-

door. After mentioning his name, he was bid welcome, and knight Heribert received him heartily, and with all the marks of distinction, befitting such a worthy and high guest.

The next day the Host presented to the Hero his only daughter Hildegundis. By the sight of the beautiful maiden, blooming in youthful charms Roland appeared as if enchanted. The courageous, for combat and hazard longing knight, in whose heart a noble love had never found room, the battle-accustomed warrior found himself seized with a feeling for this lovely maiden, which was quite new to him, and which overpowered him the more irresistably. From then he was as if changed; he did not converse more of adventures and warlike deeds, he praised much more family-life and the delights, which the possession of an affectionate wife must afford; he did not think of proceeding further, for he wanted the strength, to separate from a being whom he adored.

The condition of his heart could not remain concealed from an observer, and therefore was quickly remarked by Heribert. Hildegunde herself saw with maidenly delight, his inclination for her, he had found favour with her from the first moment, and whose renown and heroic feeling was praised in songs and ballads.

Roland could not long restrain the powerful feeling of his heart. He confessed it to the dear object of his wishes and found hearing. Heribert

had not the least objection, to the very renowned
Paladin becoming his son-in-law, and from no
side did there seem to be the least obstacle to
their happiness. Already they thought of building a castle on the beautiful Rhine, near their
parental house, and already Roland wished to
renounce adventurous wandering, and only live
in domestic felicity, when suddenly a message
from his Imperial Uncle changed all.

The Moors devastated northern Spain, and even
France was threatened with their irruptions.
Charles sent an army to repel them, and his
nephew ought not to fail where, in struggle with
the Infidels, Honour and Renown were to be
acquired. An order of the Emperor promptly
recalled Roland, and such a summons every
knight and noble was obliged to obey, if the
World should not doubt of their first virtues
Bravery and Heroism. How could Roland dis-
regard the voice of Honour and Duty? As nameless as was the grief with which he parted
from the adored, however much it affected him,
he yet tore himself away from her embraces.
An indescribable anxiety mastered Hildegunde,
as the day of departure arrived, and Roland
mounted the charger which was to bear him
away in the midst of enemies and battle crowds.
His firm, solemn promise, to return as soon as
possible quieted the anxious girl very little, and
could not scare her secret fears.

After many mutual oaths of eternal Fidelity, which were seldom spoken so candidly and sincerely, and after a sad parting from the knight Heribert, Roland left the castle, become so dear to him, and hastened to the army. After bloody combats, and dangerous struggles in which he sword of the Paladin was victorious verywhere; yet one could not foresee the duration of the war.

A hot battle in the valley of Ronceval should decide, for the whole Christian army stood opposed to the Infidels, and the exertions of both were great. The Victory fluctuated a long time, and late in the evening the French made a furious attack on the enemies lines, and wrested a glorious victory. But this success was dearly bought. Many noble knights were slain, and also Roland struck by the club of a gigantic Arab was severely wounded, and in the confusion sank to the ground. The combatants stormed over the fallen; only his faithful squire remained with him, to protect him if really dead, or bury him if a corpse. The army missed him, for some had seen him fall, considered dead, and the news of his glorious death was spread everywhere.

Even to Drachenburg arrived the announcement that Count Roland, the flower of Chivalry had been killed in the Saracen-battle. With what grief Heribert heard of the sad event, with what heartfelt sorrow Hildegunde heart the intelligence it is impossible to describe. But as the first outburst of grief was past she determined to reflect in her chamber on the memory of the departed, and indulge in her sorrow. Seldom was she seen to pass through the halls of the castle, and some weeks after receiving the terrible news, the convent of the near Rhine-island saw her a devoted and zealous novice. Her fervent request and destiny, determined the Bishop to shorten the novitiate, and after a short time the unhappy maiden was allowed to take her irrevocable vows.

It is true in that battle Roland struck by a heavy blow had fallen senseless to the earth, but not killed. The faithful squire discerned signs of life in him, and with trouble carried him to a shepherd's hut, where, nursed by benevolent men, and supported by his robust nature, the Paladin recovered. But months passed, before he felt himself strong enough, to leave his sick bed, and travel by short journeys to where his heart called him.

It was on a foggy Autumn - evening that he knocked at the door of Drachenburg; full of gladsome expectation and anxiety, which surrounded him as presentiment of his future. Heribert could not believe his eyes, as he saw Roland stand before him, and as the believed to be dead hastily asked after Hildegunde, the stooping father covered his face, and after a long pause only was he able to pronounce that she had become the bride of Heaven. Roland was as if struck by lightning; speechlessly he stared at the mouth announcing the most terrible news, and in the same hour he left the castle.

Opposite the convent, on the left bank of the Rhine is a mountain, seen at a long distance. Here Roland built a castle, ever to be near the beloved, and here he passed days and nights at a window of the castle, affording him a view of the convent.

For many years he lived on this height with his faithful squire, and every morning he had the happiness of seeing Hildegunde at a distance, indeed some times it appeared to him as if she saluted. But this sorrowful pleasure was not long allowed him to enjoy. The adored did not appear one morning, and the following day he saw a funeral procession moving to the church-yard. Who was the nun carried to the grave? was it as foreboding seemed to whisper to him, Hildegunde? had sorrow at last plucked the Rose? What his thoughts indicated was only too early confirmed by his squire.

From that hour Roland did not speak again. Immovable and with pale face he stared at the churchyard of the convent, and so he was found once by his squire, the half closed eyes still directed to the place of repose of the dear departed.

The mountain on which was built the castle is still called Rolandseck. During a stormy night of the winter $18^{39}/_{40}$ fell a projecting arch of the

last ruin of the castle. On the site of the arch
is built a new one, to remind the wanderer of
the most faithful and sincerest Love of chivalrous
antiquity.

Konigswinter.

The Drachenfels.

The western summit of the Siebengebirges which
projects very near to the bank of the Rhine is
called since primeval, antiquated pagan times
the Drachenfels. This name was given it by the inhabitants of that country because once a Dragon
havocked there, on the south-west declivity in
one of the naturally formed Rocky caverns which
is now called the Dragon-hole and where the
Dragon lived. The Monster had a most frightful
figure; an irregularly formed head with jaws,
large enough, to swallow several men at once,
and armed with a triple row of formidable teeth;
a belly of extraordinary length, armed with scales,
which in the sunshine glittered with a thousand
tints; a serpent-like long tail, equally expert in
twisting itself in a thousand curves, as well as
to beat the booty to the ground; the whole body
moved on short sharp clawed legs, so the chro-
nicle describes the Monster which was the terror
of the near and distant neighbourhood. It is not

astonishing that the heathen inhabitants of the
valley of the Rhine not able to resist the frightful
guest, showed it reverence, and regarded it as
a high creature destined for their punishment
and correction. The priests believed to be obliged to reconcile the anger of the Divinity by
sacrifices, and these sacrifices consisted, in those
times of Barbarity and superstition, of men which
had attracted either the hatred of the priests and
people, or had been made prisoners in war. At
the time when Christianity began to spread itself
on the left bank of the Rhine, dominated in the
forests of the right bank Rinbod and Horsrik,
two powerful princes and warriors. Blindly devoted to Paganism, and excited by idol-serving
priests to hatred against those who made themselves acquainted with the mild blessing principles
of the Redeemer, they often undertook bloody
excursions across the Rhine, and never failed to
bring a number of made prisoners to the monster
of Drachenfels. It happened once, that the two
princes returning from such an inroad, as usual,
divided booty and prisoners.

Among the latter was a beautiful Christian
maiden, whom Rinbod charmed by her youth
and grace, demanded for himself, while Horsrik,
who felt not less passion for her, equally demanded, for his share. A serious quarrel broke
out between the two, and the irritable Horsrik
would draw his sword, as the High-priest stepped

between the disputants, prevented the combat
by his authority, and said: „A believer in strange
Gods, a daughter of those Christians which we
detest and hate, shall not disunite our Princes
to our ruin; therefore neither will take any share;
rather a welcome offering to the Dragon, to be
dedicated to-morrow, to the honor of Wodan,
our highest God. Against the decision of the
priest was no objection, however willingly Rinbod
had ventured to save her, for he had felt a more
noble love for the maiden than his rival. With
terror and horror the unfortunate maiden learned
her fate, and only the thought, lent her strength
that it was the will of her God and Redeemer
to whose commands, she as a good, pious Christian
must submit without murmuring.

The day of terror arrived, the maiden with
many prisoners who were to share her lot were
conducted to the summit of the Drachenfels. A
number of warriors, and people, with all priests
of the tribe followed to be witnesses of a tragedy,
that since long had not had this magnitude, and
taken place with so much solemnity. Also Rinbod
stood above, full of grief and sadness, that such
a beautiful holy maiden should be thrown to the
monster, and he believed to be obliged to
die, as she still and resigned, advanced, ornamented with the sacrificial band, already not
more belonging to the earth seemed equal to a
Divine being.

In her hand she held a crucifix, which she had concealed about her; on it the figure of the Redeemer she fixel her eyes, and his sight filled her with confidential hope and salvation. Willingly she allowed herself to be conducted to the place of sacrifice where, bound to a tree, she should wait to be swallowed by the monster. It did not last long before it rose from its place; and scarcely had it seen its prey, it rolled itself nearer, to snap her up. Whoever saw the Dragon in its complete deformity and hideousness, was obliged to tremble and be filled with horror; also the maiden almost lost her senses, as destruction seemed to near her, and in holding, as if for defence the cross before her, she exclaimed in the great anxiety of her soul: „Lord, my God, help me in this great affliction!" And lo, what happened! The monster, that had already opened its jaws, to swallow the bound offering, retired at the sight of the cross as if struck by lightning, and fell, uttering a frightful wide-echoing howl, into the Rhine, the waves of which covered it for ever. With astonishment the encircling collected crowd of heathens had seen this miracle. They believed not to be able to trust their eyes in seeing the feared and Divinely worshipped monster, annihilated by the small figure of the Christian - God; but to all it was clear, that this God must be more powerful, and greater than their heathen idols. Rinbod

was the first to recover from his astonishment.
With loud exultation, he hastened to unloose the
hands of the maiden, and in triumph led her
away. The other captives were freed, and the
folk seeing themselves released from the monster
by the figure of Jesus, already had secretly admired the confidence of the Christians, now demanded loudly to belong to a Religion, whose
God so visibly helped his people.

The maiden undertook, to spread Christianity
by her preaching. Eagerly these heathens learned
the tenets of the Evangelists, and soon thousands
received the holy baptism. But the first and
most zealous Christian was Rinbod, and the maiden
rewarded him with her hand. Then they built
a castle on the same Drachenfels, and he became the founder of the race, of the Drachen-
burgers that flourished about ten centuries.

Heisterbach, in the Siebengebirge.

The converted Sceptic.

Among the monks of the cloister Heisterbach
Aloysius distinguished himself by his learning
and unremitting study of the Holy Scriptures.
To the rich treasure of knowledge of this brother,
every one, and even the Abbot had recourse, if

it concerned enlightenment of obscure passages in the writings of the Holy Fathers, and Holy books; for no other knew, so well as he, how to explain their meaning, and loosen impending scepticism."

But one passage had ever been abstruse to him, and so the constant subject of his thoughts: the words of the Apostle Peter viz: „A thousand years are as a day with the Lord." This passage constantly occupied the thoughts of the monk. Often he sat in his cell reflecting on these words; but the more he meditated, so much the more increased his doubts, and the greater was his unbelief. His ideas were sometimes so confused, that his brethren feared for his senses.

Lost in speculations, he had once reclined under a tree in a near wood, and at last fallen asleep there. The vesper-bell first awoke him, and reminded him that it was high time to return to the cloister. But with astonishment he did not see the serving brother at the door, but another opened to him. However Aloysius did not pay particular attention to this circumstance; for already the brethren's hymns resounded in the church, and he hastened to take his stool. But this stool was already occupied; quite an unknown person had possession of it, and this regarded him with the same astonishment as Aloysius felt. Meantime the singing finished, and he noticed that all the monks were as strange

to him, as he appeared to them; he was asked
his name, and what he requested? He announced
himself, and as he asserted he belonged to the
cloister, he was regarded with more astonishment than before, and all were almost inclined
to think he was a lunatic.

At last one of them remembered to have read
in the annals of the cloister, that several centuries
before, a certain Aloysius who distinguished himself by great learning, had lived in the Abbey,
and by a promenade in the wood had completely
disappeared. Aloysius now mentioned the Abbot,
under whom he had been received in the cloister,
as also the time, he had passed there; the books
were referred to, and it was clearly proved, that
he was a Ressurectionist. During his sleep, appearing to the Sceptic only a few hours, 3 centuries had elapsed; but Heaven had worked this
miracle, to show that men should not meditate
and doubt the words of the Holy scriptures, but
believe with child-like heart.

Bonn.

The Treasure-seeker.

Towards the end of the 17th century, as in Bonn, people began to recover from the oppresions of war, after the raising of the Siege, there lived in the town a young locksmith. He had made his master-piece, and wished to settle at Endenich, where his father performed the duties of a sheriff of the Provost-tribunal. But like many others he had lost his property by the war, his house had been consumed by fire, and he was obliged indeed to live to see, his elder son the lamented sacrifice of excessive zeal in saving his valuables.

In deep affliction the old man resolved to pass his remaining days in peace, and to enjoy the presence of his other son, and to find his happiness in his. His locksmith business maintained Konrad excellently; everywhere was building and repairing, and at places moved diligent hands, to obliterate the traces of destroying war. However the young master's luck did not remain long undisturbed. He became amorous of another sheriff's daughter of the same place, and this passion was soon so violent, that he believed not to be able to live without the possession of the adored object. Unfortunately Gretchen's father, named Heribert, did not allow the hope of a favourable wooing. It is true he had lost much by the war, accord-

ing to appearances indeed all; notwithstanding
one saw with great astonishment his burnt houses
and barns again raise themselves from the ashes;
his mortgaged fields were free, and he showed
riches, which he neither formerly possessed nor
could honestly have obtained. The neighbours
often consulted together, and communicated their
suppositions concerning the enigmatical wealth
of Heribert. Some who judged most indulgently,
believed, he must have gained much by supply-
ing the enemy; others believed he had discovered
buried treasure; still others, and the greater part
asserted, he was in connection with spirits or
goblins, to whom he had sold his soul, or had
made a compact with those, who were the terror
of the country, with the subterranean infernal
Lapp who was contracted to deliver him hidden
treasures. The only thing certain, and undoubted
by all these suppositions was, that the pride of
the sheriff increased with his riches, and that
he regarded his fellow-citizens with that contempt,
from which, unfortunately, so few can restrain
themselves to whom the fickle-goddess turns her
favours. Oft the arrogant had declared, that no
youth of the village could hope for his daughter's
hand: but rather would seek a son-in-law among
the rank of the town, either a rich merchant, or a
high official person. Therefore for Konrad was no
hope by regular means, only rare good fortune could
procure the poor young man a favorable prospect.

True lovers never begin with the endeavour to obtain their parents favor; they apply to the object, and the amorous locksmith did the same. Gretchen was a pure guileless maiden, and Konrad the first who had wooed her love. His agreeable figure, his friendly, kind manner, and the power of persuasion, peculiar to him, easily obtained him the inclination of the maiden. What wonder, that he had soon fully won Gretchen's heart, in spite of all fatherly admonitions and instructions, which were calculated to imprint contempt in her mind, against less wealthy persons.

The veil of secrecy, which long covered the happiness of the lovers was suddenly torn by Heribert's hand. He surprised them once in the midst of their confidential endearments; foaming with rage he fell upon them, like a flash of lightning from a serene sky, struck Konrad so violently on the head with a heavy stick, that he tottered to the ground, and lugged home his trembling daughter.

From that moment he nursed a deadly hate, not only against the lover, but against his father. He laid plans for their ruin, and swore to leave nothing undone, to cause the hated ones to be disgracefully chased from the place and delivered to general scorn.

A rich villain has many ways for the carrying out his shameful intentions, and Heribert understood how to make use of them. Konrad's

father soon saw himself incommoded, creditors
pressed him, the sale of his property was imminent, his ruin unavoidable — all consequences
of his enemy's plans. But as successful as these
intrigues were, he however did not succeed in
destroying the inclination in his daughter's heart,
and just as little in preventing the lovers from
seeing each other. In the darkness of midnight,
when all were slumbering, and the watchers
calling the hour, the lovers used to meet and
exchange vows of mutual love.

Konrad had once climbed to his lover's window by means of the weak spalier of a vine,
and while all around lay in deep silence and
darkness, the lovers complained and embraced
in sweet oblivion. Suddenly another window
opened, and the father called out loudly: „Rogue,
Thief! off instantly, or I shall shoot you dead!"

Surprised and frightened Konrad sprang down,
however he recovered his calmness, and standing fearlessly, he cried out to Heribert: „Although
at night-time you have found me at your window,
yet you know my intentions are honest, and love
to your daughter attracts me here. You hate me,
because I am not rich; but who knows how you
have acquired your riches so quickly and easily.
I too could demand much from the devilish Lapp,
if I would have intercourse with him; for I understand secrecy, as he demands it. Would you not
be willing to give me Gretchen as wife, if I

wooed laden with treasures?" A shot was the answer to this impudent question. The bullet missed its object; but the more terribly did despair strike his heart, for he now saw clearly and distinctly that he could never hope to become happy, if he did not find means to equal the unfeeling old man in money and property.

Lost in gloomy thoughts and reflecting on all kinds of designs, the unhappy young man returned to his home. It struck 12, and it seemed as if the tones awoke thoughts in Konrad's soul which hitherto had remained unknown. „How would it be", whispered his evil genius to him, „if I, who am without hope, ventured the last, the only means, that I still can venture; if I really, even also to the loss of my soul, begged, the terrible Lapp for assistance, who living under the graves of the churchyard hears the cry of midnight? Be it so!" he resolved to himself, and hastened to the fatal place. Thrice he called the dreaded name; hollow frightful it reechoed from the walls, and out of the ground there arose a terrible figure, who standing before him with flaming eyes, asked him with a terrible voice: „What do you wish from me?"

Konrad almost lost his senses; he could only stammer out the words: „I demand Gold! help me to it!" The subterraneous imp beckoned to him to follow, conducted him to the depths of a forest, and in pointing to a spot, with its finger on its

lips in token of silence, the figure disappeared.
As if driven by Furies, Konrad hastened home,
and was in a violent fever during several days.
After recovering, he visited the marked spot in
a dark night; for he did not doubt that a treasure
was buried there, and indeed, after digging a
long time, he found an iron chest full of gold and
silver-coins of different descriptions, both foreign
and domestic. He did not neglect to fill his pockets.
The next day he went to Bonn, and bought a
house there, conducting his business on a larger
scale and living there. Almost every evening he
wandered out of the town-door to fetch the other
gold, and the dug hole he covered so carefully,
that nobody could remark anything particular.

As there had been war just previously, it did
not surprise anyone, that Konrad had suddenly,
become wealthy. Hazardous speculations, dangerous service, were largely rewarded during
the unquiet times, and many had, fortunately or
not, exposed Life and Honor to become rich.
The repeated nocturnal visits of the young master
had now and then excited attention, and given
occasion to ill-natured suppositions.

When Konrad had furnished his house, paid
his father's debts, released his mortgaged property, and done all by which he was equal in
riches to Heribert, but in splendour and luxury
surpassed him, he hastened, to repeat his wooing
for the beloved. He found her father now inclined;

for the future son - in - law had become another
man, namely rich. The marriage took place, and
the happy pair saw their wishes fulfilled.

But the obstacles against which Konrad had
to contend were not yet finished. The young wife,
not less inquisitive than other daughters of Eve,
desired to know how her husband had succeeded
to acquire his present wealth. She teased and
tormented him therefore in confidential hours
with unceasing questions, and employed all possible means at the disposal of a beautiful wife
during the honeymoon to obtain her object. He
was about to confide everything to her, as suddenly one evening, beadles and officers of justice
forced themselves into the house, and arrested
Konrad, without any reason, and threw him into
prison. He was to give judicial satisfaction as
to his wealth, and as he refused every explanation, torture was immediately applied. The in-
tolerable pain caused him to confess he had found
a treasure; the tribunal seemed satisfied with
this assertion, and allowed the prisoner some
days repose. During this time his deeply afflicted
wife visited him, she had been allowed to visit
him, so that their conversation could be overheard.
Here in the prison, in the brief hour of a painfully sweet interview, Konrad confessed all to
his beloved wife, of the manner by which he
had acquired his wealth, and the listeners hastened
to inform the judges of all they had heard.

However for the moment this had no disagreeable results; for although, under the discovered
circumstances the treasury could make claim on
the taken treasure, yet the treasure-seeker must
be set at liberty, and Konrad was directly released — indeed still more, the Elector was
pleased to consider the whole affair during the
process, and determined that if the young man
could prove his assertion he should retain all the
obtained gold. But just as Konrad was reflecting on the proof, the Jews in Bonn raised a great
cry, that one of their people, the rich Abraham
who had served as a spy to many war parties, and
had thereby collected immense sums, had suddenly disappeared during a journey, and most
probably been murdered. It was clearly to be
seen that the suspicion rested on the already
under examination locksmith, and at that time
it did not require more, to arrest again the tormented man and torture applied for the accused
crime. A higher degree of torture extorted a
confession from the unhappy prisoner, that he
later recalled, but unfortunately could not weaken.
Even those secret nocturnal walks of Konrad,
which had formerly induced suspicion, seemed
now sufficient witness against him, and according to the opinion of the judge, it was now only
necessary for him to name his accomplice. He
said, after repeated applications of the torture,
that he had an accomplice by the murder, and

that this assistant had been his father-in-law, who had killed Abraham by shooting. But he made this assertion preferring to ruin Heribert, the cause of his misfortunes, than an innocent person. The result of this confession was the arresting of the frightened sheriff, who after repeated torturings confessed all that was desired of him, and both were immediately condemned to be hanged.

The day appointed for the execution had already arrived, and both criminals dragged to the place of execution to be a spectacle for the people, as a most unexpected appearance demonstrated Konrad's innocence.

A Jew just returned from a long wandering, had entered the town-door, and hearing of the intended execution, hastened with the cry: „Stop! Stop!" to the place of execution, and forced his way through the crowd to the judges, — it was the dead believed Abraham. Like lightning, the news spread of the return of the Jew among the assembled crowd, and with great exultation the two condemned were conducted to their homes.

But as gratifying as was the satisfaction of the saved, yet the fear of death, as well as the suffered torture and disgrace, had made an indelible impression on Konrad. He was incapable of all work and every enjoyment, and his wife had been ever since melancholy. Both left the town removing to Endenich, where their father

now lived in the strictest retirement. Konrad's
married-life was childless; therefore he bequeathed,
to reconcile by a pious service his crime of having obtained treasure by the help of an evil spirit,
all his gold and property to churches and charitable institutions.

Aix-la-Chapelle.

The foundation of the town.

The Emperor Charles the Great had his residence
now here, now there in his immense empire, once
he held his court in Zurich, on the lovely banks
of the lake the natural beauties of which ever
charm and enchain the traveller. The monarch
loving justice, and accessible to all his subjects,
had erected, not far from his residence, on a steep
place of the bank, where formerly 2 martyrs Felix
and Regula had been decapitated, a column, upon
which he had fastened a small bell. Every one
who had a request of the emperor, only required
to toll the bell, and directly the monarch himself
appeared, and with all affability listened to the
complaints and representations of his subjects,
and then decided upon them. One day the bell
tolled without any one being found at the Place.
The following day the same, and the Emperor

therefore commanded a page, to hide himself near the column the next day, to discover the cause of the tolling. The servant saw with terror, a huge serpent crawl out of a cavern on the bank, and to his great astonishment set the bell in motion. Directly Charles, who sat at table, was informed of this strange occurrence, he rose to go to the serpent.

„Be it animal or man“, said he, „I will have justice done to every one who demands it from me.“ As soon as the serpent saw him, it bowed thrice before him; then returned slowly to its cavern. But the Emperor and his suite followed it, desirous to discover the wishes of the animal. They found before the cavern an immensely large toad, and it seemed as if it wished to be freed from this animal which stopped up the entrance to its cavern. The monarch ordered the toad to be seized and killed, in order to render justice.

Some days after this remarkable event, the serpent came, to the great astonishment of all present, into the Emperors banquetting saloon, just as they were about to sit at table, and after bowing thrice respectfully, it crawled to one of the standing drinking cups, dropped in it a jewel of unusual size and beauty, and then disappeared, before the Emperor and his quests could recover from their astonishment.

Charles presented the jewel to the Empress and she used to wear it as an ornament for her hair. But this jewel possessed the wonderful property of obtaining the Imperial favor by whoever wore it, and so from this moment the Emperor became so tenderly attached to his wife that he did not wish to leave her at all.

But the Empress very soon discovered the reason of the increased attachment of her husband, and therefore never allowed the stone to be separated from her. Feeling in her last illness the approach of death, and fearing it might get into the possession of some person unworthy of the Emperor's love, she hid it under her tongue, where it remained till after her death. Charles' attachment for his deceased wife was also even then not extinguished; he had her corpse embalmed, and carried her in all his travels with him. This devotion, so singular, awoke in the mind of the Archbishop Turpinus, his companion, at last the suspicion, that it must have a supernatural connection. He took therefore a proper opportunity, to search for a hidden talisman, and soon found the miraculous jewel on the corpse. He appropriated it directly, and continually, wearing it, the Emperor's devotion then passed to the Archbishop from his wife, whom he had interred with suitable splendour. He became so attached to the Archbishop, that he was not allowed to leave his Imperial master, and at last was tired of such a troublesome attachment. On a journey through the western part of Germany he rid himself of it, in a fit of ill-humor at that incon-venient love, by throwing the jewel into the water, where it could not be found again. The magic however continued to work, and if Türpinus was not more the object of the Emperor's love, it was the country which hid the wonderful jewel. Charles felt since so attached to the place, that he had a palace built there and a town founded. But this town is Aix-la-chapelle, still to-day testified by the Cathedral of Charles the Great. Most pref-erably Charles sojourned at the charming Mead-ows, in the still waters of which the Arch-bishop had thrown the ring. Here he often sat long hours in thoughtful melancholy, and regarded the small charming sea, the concealed jewel of which seemed to enchain him with magical power. To this magic the popular superstition ascribes the salutary power of the warm baths of Aix-la-chapelle, which since, for the health of men, bubble from the bosom of the earth.

The Cathedral.

As one in Aix-la-chapelle, more than a thou-sand years ago, built the still now celebrated, magnificent Cathedral, the elders of the town had so much miscalculated the costs, that, before half the temple was finished the destined money began to fail. This was so much the more critical as

repeated demands of further pious offerings only
yielded an insignificant amount, and no other
means to supply the necessary funds. During
the senate, although complete in number was
unable to come to a decision concerning this important affair, so that the cessation of the building seemed imminent a stranger had himself announced, with the remark, he wished to propose
something important to the full senate. The
strange and certainly singular costume of this
man, the strongly stamped repulsive features,
which allowed one to perceive cold calculation
and something mocking, would have made a most
unfavorable impression on the meeting, if the
unknown had not understood to gain its favor by
his fine courtly address.

„Venerable and sage senators,“ began he:
„I have heard, in what a disagreeable position
the town finds itself, in wanting money for the
completion of the Cathedral. I am the man, to
assist you in this emergency, and I am before
you, for negociating the terms on which I am
ready to pay the failing money in full weighted,
ringing Gold.“ General and great astonishment
followed the speech of the stranger. Who was
the man speaking of millions, as of hollow nuts?
Was it a Nabob from India, who converted to
Christianity would employ his means for the
building of a Temple? Was it a King, or a
mountain spirit, in possession of subterranean

treasures ? or had he indeed, as his appearance
almost allowed one to suppose, mocked the whole
assembly ? — The senators asked one another
but nobody could give a satisfactory answer.
The mayor first recovered from the general surprise; he addressed questions concerning condition and whereabouts to the generous stranger,
and this explained himself as follows: „Of what
family and condition I am, your wisdom may
guess or not; but so much I can say to my
complete legitimation, all necessary funds I will
advance, not as a loan but as a present for all
times, and I have no other condition to propose
than that after the completion of the edifice, and
on the day of the dedication of the church, the
first entering by the opened door belongs to me
skin and hair, body and soul.“

If before the astonishment of the sages was
great, now their terror was indescribable. All
sprang off their easy-chairs, and fled to the remotest corner of the saloon; for now they understood with whom they had to do. After a
long pause of dumb terror the mayor first recovered. „Remove yourself from here!“ He
called out repeatedly. But unfortunately this banishment summons remained useless. The dreaded
stepped nearer, and said carelessly: „Why do
you conduct yourselves so singularly and anxiously?
Are not my proposals acceptable and advantageous?
Consider only one I demand, while without thought,

and often indeed thousands are uselessly sacrificed in battle, by Kings and high persons?"
And is it not suitable that one is ceded for the
bénefit of all? Such, and several other produced
very cogent reasons, convinced the councillors
and their fear was gradually less. To this assisted the pressing want of money; after brief
resistance and reluctance the contract was made,
and Master Urian left directly, in recommending
himself to the senators, by the chimney, accompanied by satanical laughter. Before long, he
sent by the same canal, a number of gold-filled
sacks into the council-chamber, and the mayor
after careful examination, found the coins genuine
and the sum perfectly sufficient. After a few
years the edifice was completed but now arrived
the day, on which the dedication of the Cathedral
should solemnly take place. It is true the dignitaries, who had been present at the appearance
of the Apparition had vowed to keep the compact
with the Evil-one as a profound secret, yet some
of them had instrusted it to their wives, so it
was, as easily to be imagined, in everybody's
mouth, and nobody, as it tolled for church, was
willing to pass through the open door. New
embarassment! the mayor did not know what to
do; as a little priest appeared, with the assurance
he had, to cheat the wicked one, reflected on a
plan. It was indeed in the compact, that the
first who should pass through the door, was to

become the devil's property, but not stipulated
what creature it must be and on this defec-
tivenes the little priest arranged his plan. Accidentally a day before, a trapped wolf was put
in a cage, and so placed, that on opening it, the
animal would be obliged to run into the church.
The Evil-one already watched for his prey, and
like lightning he pursued the wolf, as it sprang
out of the cage. But indescribable was Satan's
choler, as he recognized how he had been outwitted and deceived. Spitting fire he broke the
poor wolf's neck, and with terrible howling, and
flying away leaving traces of the smell of
brimstone, he banged the cathedral-door to, with
such force, that it was split. Just on this door
is yet shown the imprint of a wolf in brass,
together with a fir-cone, to represent the lost
soul, and also that crevice is still to be seen, as
sign how a priest once knew to tame the devil.

The hunchbacked Musician.

Formerly there lived in the town of Aix-la-
chapelle. 2 musicians, who obtained their live-
lihood, by violin-playing at dances, festivals, and
other occasions. The one, named Friedel was
a lively, gay fellow, full of gaiety, pleasant,
and love for his art, which at that time was
scarcely above artizan's work, and had such an
agreeably formed face, that he might have been

considered beautiful, if he had not been deformed
by a natural defect — that is to say, he was
hunchbacked, the other Heinz, had singularly the
same defect, but was otherwise deformed. Red
bristly hair, small green eyes, with piercing uncertain glance, a malicious movement around the
large mouth, all made a disagreeable impression,
and it was therefore not astonishing, that in all
circles Friedel's violin hat the preference, while
Heinze's was seldom requested. Besides Friedel
was a better player than Heinz, and the effecting
melodious play, with his fine charming conduct,
caused him to be welcome everywhere, while
his colleague by the discord of his play, as much
offended the ear as his repulsive appearance was
offensive to the fair sex.

As every artist, Friedel's heart soon felt love.
Agathe, the only daughter of a rich wine-merchant, was the tender object of his loving feelings
and to his great joy these, notwithstanding the
deformity of his back, fully reciprocated by the
maiden — a proof, that in love, pleasing manners,
persuasion obtain greater triumphs, than simple
exterior favorable figure.

The lovers could have been happy, if Agathe's
father had not been a proud, tyrannical cit, who
esteemed gold above all things, and, as he had
often expressed, thought of seeking a son in-law
in the noblest families of Aix-la-chapelle. The
prospects of the lovers were discouraging, and

they did not venture on anything decisive till circumstances should compel them, Agathe was to give her hand, according to her father's will, to a young man, who although rich, was known as a dissipated good-for-nothing; in his desperation Friedel ventured to present himself to the merchant, to declare his sentiments, and to beg for the hand of the maiden.

A loud laugh of derision was the answer to the wooing. „Do you think“, cried the arrogant, „I am so embarassed for a son-in-law, that I shall throw my daughter away on a musician, who plays for his subsistence? or do you rather think, to be the more agreeable to me, because you are grown with a little vexation which suits you admirably? No, indeed“, continued he, „so far is it with me not yet, thank Heaven, that I should take a son-in-law, whose deformity would descend to my grand children, and could expose me to the ridicule of the whole town.“ He accompanied these words with a wave of his hand, intimating to Friedel that he was dismissed.

Wounded to the quick, and full of bitter rancour against the man, who had so reproached him on account of his undeserved misfortune, the unhappy youth hastened from the place. He rushed out of the door, and wandered, uncertain where his feet conducted him, about in impassable ways. Only by the beginning of night, he found himself at the foot a tree, bathed in perspiration. The country was unknown to him, and the return to town not so easily discovered; no wonder therefore; if he wandered about a long time, and only reached the town very late. The clock just tolled the hour of midnight, as Friedel walked through the still, deserted streets. Could he have mastered his thoughts and observed what passed around him, he would have remarked much adapted to have excited his horror. A number of owls flew croaking about the old gloomy tower, and the high gable - ended roofs of the town. Daws, and all sorts of nocturnal birds accompanied with disagreeable screamings, and through the air shot pale, ash coloured strips of light, with howling and piercing whistling, while a troop of singular figures moved above the houses. An attentive observer would have easily recognized these figures for a troop of broom - riding witches. Collectively they took their way to the fish-market, which the people of Aix-la-chapelle called Perwisch. Also the love-sick, solitary wanderer, to whom all this had not appeared singular, went his way thither; but scarcely had he entered the place as he was surprised by a wonderful sight. A clear light of numerous lights hovering in the air like flames of phosphorous, gave to the market a peculiar magical illumination, by the shine of which, a crowded throng of female figures, increasing every minute by new arrivals moved noiselessly. As

great as Friedel's astonishment might be, yet
curiosity attracted him nearer, and his natural
courage allowed him to advance so near, that
he could pretty exactly contemplate the strange
company. He was just reflecting that to-day was
quarter-day, on which, according to an old saying a witches picnic was used to be held here
on the fishmarket at midnight; a woman advanced
to him, who as regarded dress and behaviour
appeared to be the noblest of the society, and
had a singular resemblance with the mayoress
of the town, took him by the hand, and led him
to a table heavily laden with all sorts of delicacies
and beverages. She obliged him to refresh himself, which after he had willingly done, she
handed him an excellent violin, with the request,
to play the gay society to dancing. She had
hitherto occupied herself with the served delicacies; but it appeared singular to Friedel, that
although the society consisted of ladies, not a
syllable was spoken.

As soon as he played the first bars a general
rising succeeded; tables and forms were moved
to the sides, and not without uncomfortable feeling saw Friedel, that around him, although no
tone fell upon his ear, the most lively conversation took place.

Meanwhile they placed themselves for dancing the lady-president gave a signal to begin the
improvised ball. Friedel who represented the

orchestra, played gay airs; but certainly the violin was bewitched, for without his will the tact was always quicker, the couples turned faster, till all was in a confused racing dance. The violinist at last fell exhausted on a chair, the music ceased and the dancing finished. The same lady who had demanded Friedel to play stepped forward again, and in expressing her satisfaction with his playing, she whispered so as scarcely to be heard: „Kneèl and receive the thanks of us all, for the pleasure you have caused us." Then she whispered strange words over the stooping Friedel, laid her left hand exorcisingly on the excrescence of his back, took away with admirable ease this step-mother gift of Nature, and placed it on an empty dish, which she directly closed. This operation was scarcely ended, as the clock struck a loud 1, and in a moment, disappeared the whole society and all provisions, with tables, forms, and Friedel found himself alone on the market place.

Confused by the singular experience, and very excited, he hastened to his lodging, to enjoy quietude; but strange dreams tormented him. Sometimes he fancied himself eloping with Agathe, and the wine-merchant as long legged dwarf pursuing; then as lover in the figure of the mayoress; then he saw this lady being wedded to Heinz, who had taken the growth of an Adonis.

So he dreamed till the clear morning, and the forms he had seen in sleep, only inclined him to consider what had passed during the preceding night as a juggling trick of his fantasy. But a glance at the looking glass showed him, that he was freed from his hump, and was become a slender youth, and to his astonishment he found in his flannel jacket a considerable sum of money, which sufficed to place him equal to the wealthiest men of the town.

The joy at this transformation, and his riches drove him to his Agathe's house. Here he met her father, who regarded him doubtfully, not knowing, whether a stranger or the musician stood before him, who the day before, still provided with a hump, had humbly stammered his marriage-petition.

After the astonished father was certain there was no doubt, the youth repeated his wooing, and this time with success. However he owed his success not so much to his fine figure, as to the displayed gold, and he promised the marriage should take place in 3 months. Who were now happier than the lovers? But the nightly adventure, although Friedel had confided it to his future father-in-law under the promise of strict silence, had not remained a secret, and among others, had reached the ears of the redhaired, hunchbacked Heinz. If Heinz had hitherto hated and envied Friedel as the more clever and popular

musician, so he felt now spite and ill-will in the
highest degree. Everywhere he endeavoured to
spread the most hateful things concerning the
happy lover, related whence he had become well-
formed and rich, and in ornamenting these reports with calumnies, he did not spare allusions
which could make the young man be suspected
of immoral intercourse with witches. But in his
heart Heinz determined to try his fortune in the
same manner next quarter-day. He flattered himself with the hope, just so as his art colleague,
to be bodily ennobled and rewarded.

As the quarter-day arrived on which Friedel's
marriage was celebrated, Heinz hastened with
his violin to the fish-market, resolved not only
to free himself from his natural burden, but also,
if possible, to be more richly rewarded.

Quite true, it was the witches feast on the
Perwisch. The lights flamed, the dressed wives
ate and drank from finely served tables, and
everywhere reigned a lively crowd, however
without sound and noise. Heinz boldly stepped
nearer, and made known by signs his readiness
to play the violin. Directly place was made,
and as before, the dance began; but as the musician avariciously regarded the golden vessels,
which stood around, and avarice caused him to
think more on his gain than on his playing with
tact and melody, so he played more discordantly,
and at last scratched so miserably on the, without

this, not very musical violin, that the dancers, to whose lusty figures such discord was distasteful, raced about wildly. This strange confusion, the violinist considered as a proof of his excellent playing, and in his vanity, he was so foolish as to call the names of several wives of the town whom he believed to recognize. But now the indignation of the dancers had reached its highest degree, darting glances of rage, they showed him their fists, and gave him to understand by unmistakeable signs, that he should cease. Then the lady-president of the feast commanded him to kneel, to receive his reward. This command let Heinz suppose his music had very much pleased, and that it was only the manner of the witches to conduct themselves wrathfully. He therefore considered it time, to request very much, and therefore demanded the valuable drinking-cup, and already stretched out his hand to take it, as a violent blow on his ear punished him. Then the lady took out of a well covered dish, the taken away hump from the good Friedel, and fixed it on the breast of the violinist, before he was aware of the action. In the same moment, the tower clock struck a loud 1, and the frightened saw all disappear from his eyes, and found himself alone on the still, deserted market-place.

Who can paint the poor man's rage and despair, as he saw himself charged with the double burden of two humps? Unfortunately he was foolish enough, to relate the affair, and naturally, the object of mockery and laughter everywhere. Friedel alone, felt pity for the mocked and forsaken, and maintained him for the rest of his days.

Königsdorf near Cologne.

The Bishop election.

In Cologne there was once a gread·dispute for the vacant bishops stool. The clergy and citizens were divided into several parties, who favored their particular candidates and wished to have elected.

As the Emperor Charles the Great, then residing in Aix-la-Chapelle heard of this increasing dispute, he resolved to destroy the discontent by his presence, and if necessary, himself seat a bishop. Quite unexpectedly, and without retinue, he rode along the road to Cologne, and thoughtful, as he was, he had without remarking it reached Königsdorf, as the clear tones of a small bell awoke him from his meditations. A number of people were about entering the chapel to hear mass, and the pious Emperor did not neglect to tie his horse to a tree, and unknown mix with the crowd of devout persons. After Divine-service had been ended, he advanced to

the priest, and wished to offer him, as offering
a gold piece. But to his great astonishment the
priest refused it. „One does not offer“, said the
pious man „here so; keep your gold, which I do
not require. If you wish to do a good work for
this church, so present it with the hide of the
first stag or roe you shoot; for my massbook
requires a new binding, and as it seems to me
you are a hunter.“ The truly pious and disin-
terested wish, expressed in these words, made
a deep impression on Charles, and he determined in his heart to think of the worthy priest.
Meanwhile he continued his journey to Cologne.
Arrived there, he directly summoned the high
clergy and the representatives of the people before him, and gave them to understand, he would
personally direct the election of bishop, if they
could not agree, he would decide. The different
parties tried by all sorts of ways, and by large
sums of money to make him favorable for their
purpose; Charles however ordered that all the
gold offered to him should be used to pay the
debts of the bishopric. Then he spoke to them
who waited inquisitively for his decision: „In
vain you have wished to bribe me with thousands,
in order to gain the bishopric; but none of you
do I consider so worthy of it, as the priest in
that forest chapel near Königsdorf, who despised
my gold, and thinking on his mass-book not on
himself, begged no other gift than the hide of

a roe or stag for a new binding. Go and fetch this worthy man, he shall be your Bishop."

The plain priest could scarcely recover from his astonishment, in arriving to such a high dignity. But as the Grace of God rested on him, he knew how to conduct himself in his new position, and even yet he is not forgotten; it was the Bishop Hildebold, Founder of that St. Peter's dome, on the site of which stands the present cathedral in Cologne.

Cologne.

Ursula and the 11000 Virgins.

In the 13th century King Vionetus governed over Britain. Although extreme Heathenism ruled in his kingdom, he had however turned to Christianity with his wife and only daughter, because an angel had appeared to the latter with the command to accept the blessing principles of the Redeemer. The same angel also admonished the king's daughter, to prepare herself to suffer for the honor of Christ, and to die by martyrdom. Ursula had taken the firm resolution, with enthusiasm, to obey this admonition, and as a German prince, Agrippinus, sent an ambassador to her father's court, in order to solicit the hand

of the equally pious and beautiful virgin, as wife
for his son, she refused decidedly, to marry this
or any other king's son; but would rather devote
her life entirely to the recognized true God, and
his offering for us by Crucifixion. But the angel
that had already once appeared to her, intimated
to her again to accept the German prince's proposal, because she would be able to save his
soul by conversion, and to complete a work
agreeable to God. The angel further commanded
her, to request from her father a retinue of
virgins, as numerous as it could be accomplished,
to induce all these virgins to adopt Christianity,
and take them with her to Cologne to the residence of her future husband. As soon as she was
arrived there, she should, before being married,
begin, with her whole retinue, a pilgrimage to
Rome, but then return to Cologne.

Ursula departed soon afterwards with 11000
virgins and 11 ships across the sea, and then
up the Rhine to Cologne. Here she was the
object of all sorts of honour, but she continued
her journey to Basel, where the Romish governor
assisted her further pilgrimage over the Alps.
In Rome Pope Cyriakus gave his blessing to
Ursula and her attendants, and, as if he knew
what would happen to them, he accompanied
them on their return, to be near them with his
spiritual advice and protection. In Mayence,
Coman, son of Agrippinus, waited for his wife.

Her appearance, the reverential presence of the Pope, the splendid suite, and the truth of the new doctrine soon made him a Christian, and after the marriage had been festively completed, they descended the Rhine to Cologne. •

Just at this time the Huns overran the beautiful fields of Germany. Also they appeared before Cologne with a large army, and notwithstanding the most valiant resistance, the town was stormed. All persons were massacred by these inimical barbarians to Christianity; especially they permitted the Pope as well as Ursula and her attendants feel the particular rage of the Cannibals. They were all martyred with fearful torments, Ursula and her husband were the last objects of their rage; but devoutly resigned they retained their constancy, and fearlessness of death, which even astonished the Heathens. A single virgin, so is related, named Cordula, had found an opportunity to escape the general massacre, and remain concealed.

But in imagination she saw her companions participating in eternal happiness, and delivered herself, excited by this vision, equally to the Barbarians. On account of her pious life and martyrdom Ursula is honoured as a saint. In Cologne is the church dedicated to her, which bears her name, and in this rest even to the present day the rests of herself and her 11000 virgins. The monument of the saint stands there

to the left of the choir; she reposes formed in
Alabaster on Marble, a white pigeon sits at her
feet, because such a pigeon is said to have indicated the place of the grave on which the church
was built.

The Building of the Cathedral.

It was about the middle of the 13th century
as the then Archbishop of Cologne, Conrad of
Hochsteden, took the resolution, to build a
Cathedral in this town, which should be larger
and more magnificent, than any other temple of
Christianity.

As Conrad himself possessed great riches,
which he was ready to sacrifice for religious
purposes, and as one could expect, that not only
from the town, which the building was to ennoble,
but also from far and near great contributions
would be made, so there was, concerning the
money means no obstacles to oppose the great
work; but the great difficulty was to find an
architect capable of fully comprehending the sublime object and to form a suitable plan. However
the architect was found and even in Cologne itself, where he enjoyed a great reputation, and
already had given proofs of his art, which allowed not the least doubt, of his capability to

succeed in what to others might seem unattainable.

The Archbishop sent for this architect, and requested him to sketch a plan for the Cathedral, the plan to be delivered within a year; the Archbishop undertaking to prepare all necessary materials for the proposed building.

The commission extremely flattered the ambition of the architect, Full of desire for the renown, which the execution of such a gigantic work must prepare him and be retained for ever, he promised, to reflect on a sketch, and to draw on parchment a work not existing, and with difficulty would ever be made in size and sublimity of style, splendour and ornament.

From the moment of the Archbishop's relying on this promise, and graciously dismissing the Master, he thought of nothing else but the grand plan. Every other work and every other gain he renounced, to devote himself entirely and alone to the thought, how the grand building was to be arranged, how connected, how the corridors were to be vaulted, and his columns placed, so that the Temple, a monument of the Piety of its time, would also be so for him, the Master, and hand his name to posterity. But as zealously as he reflected and meditated; the many sketches, he had already finished in 10 months, satisfied the expectations of the Bishop just as little as they did himself. He had an

Ideal in his soul, which in imagination he often
saw realized, but which he could not seize, and
actually produce on parchment. As the reflection of a mirror it disappeared again, as soon as
in early morning he tried to produce the repre-
sentation seen in the excitement of his dreamy
night, and it was, as if a malicious demon showed
him the noble picture in order not to allow of
its being realized.

Meantime the period advanced when Conrad
of Hochsteden expected the drawings and plans
of the Cathedral as the Master had promised him.
But out of humor, and absorbed in his own thoughts,
he wandered often through field and forest, and the
sadness and inquietude of his mind increased
continually; for not having yet sketched any plan,
he feared to be disregarded both by his Patron
and fellow-citizens.

He had once — only 3 days before the appointed time — wandered far into the forest of
the Siebengebirges. The night had begun, and
a fearful tempest poured the rain in streams.
No object could be perceived in the thick darkness; only when it lightened for a moment could
he see the nearest group of trees; but the large
trunks appeared like giants menacingly throwing
their arms towards him. The lightning and excitement in Nature accorded with his feelings so
much as not to be frightened by any figure; he
reflected only on the hour, which was to cover

him with shame and mockery, thought with de
spairing ill-humor, that another would share the
renown, of being the builder of the new Cathedral.

As he so, as if seized with the fever of madness, cursed his destiny and himself, and all,
that shall complete the work, the lightning struck
an oak near him and a fearful thunder-clap accompanied the burning flash. The trunk burnt
brightly, and the terrified saw a man step out
of the flames, and quietly advance towards him.

The man's appearance was that of a poacher,
although his red mantle and the feather of the
broad brimmed hat contrasted strangely with the
costume of a hunter. „A terrible storm Dom-
architect“, ejaculated he, in limping still nearer;
„possible you are more fatigued than I, as I have
till now rested behind that tree. How could you
wander through the wood in such a fearful night!
If you will follow me, I will conduct you by a
short way out of the wood and tempest. This
speech appeared like bitter mockery to the despairing. Did he not name him Dom-architect,
and yet it seemed as if at this title a mocking
smile was on his lips. Without answering a word
the Master turned away from the singular stanger.
This however did not daunt him; he beckoned
him, to come nearer, sat himself, as if expecting
him to do the same for a long conversation, under
the protecting branch of a thickly leaved tree,
at the same time carefully covering his cloven

feet, and producing a bottle he continued: „Drink once, Master, to our better acquaintance! there is no bad juice in this vessel, and if you have a sorrow, or reflect about anything, you will experience the advantageous effect of the beverage.“ „My grief“, answered the invited, „is not effaced by any drink, and no juice gives me insight into that, which to discover I vainly endeavour. Therefore spare the contents of your bottle, and leave me alone with your speech.“ „You are an unsociable fellow“, said the stranger; „but that does not frighten me from offering my services and to be complaisant to you, as I have already been to others. Still once, drink! and forget your chagrins.“ With that the importunate held the bottler under his nose, and the Master, at last wishing to be rid of the too tiresome, took it, and made a hearty draught. Like fire it ran through his veins; he felt himself transformed and strangely strengthened. A never experienced feeling of self-confidence came over him, so that he involuntary called out: „Really a genuine Nectar, which you have there, an incomparable cordial!“ and in saying this, he seated himself, returning the flask, beside the stranger. „Ah!“ answered the singular benefactor, „my beverage is good and may convince you, that I am capable of other things; I know indeed — but do not be frightened — that you reflect on the plan of a splendid church; but you will not succeed in

either plan or building, if I do not assist you.“
Astonished at these words the Master regarded
the unknown with staring eyes. He believed to
remark in his traits a grinning malicious laugh,
which he did not understand, and the exhilarating
drink made incomprehensible. „I see you have
not perfect confidence in me“, continued the
stranger, and yet I am the only one, who can
and will help you. Gay, Comrade! still a draught
and you will see, that the best you can do, is
to attach yourself to me. My conditions are easy,
and I keep my word as faithfully as the most
honourable earthly children their oath.“ The
Master had meanwhile again tasted the seductive
potion: it began to make him hot and he would
just ask, how it was to be done, to complete a
plan in 3 days? as the stranger laughing loudly
drew a parchment from his pocket, unrolled it
before the eyes of the highly astonished and with
flaming eyes showed the figure of the Dome that
had so long hovered before the Master's eyes,
and which to draw he had long so vainly attempted. „Yes, that is it“, he exclaimed, „that
beautiful complete picture, which I constantly
saw in my mind, and which has always escaped
me as if by magic; that is it of which I dreamed
waking, confusing my senses pursued me and
each time escaped, when I believed to have it
in my possession.“ „Well then“, said the other,
„I will cede this plan to you, it shall be yours

One thing only I condition — — a trifle; you must sign this bond with a little of your blood. There read!" continued he, in presenting him a small table, on which in a few words the bond was written, „I have a number of similar contracts, and it is my hobby to increase the collection." The Master was almost overpowered with terror; for he had read with horror, to whom he should engage himself. But the thought on renown and shame deprived him of reflection; he signed. Again the lightning struck a near oak; the fiend disappeared and raven-black darkness sourrounded the unfortunate.

Unconscious he left the place. Gradually however the rain had ceased, and by the light of the dawning morning the Master at last found his way out of the wood to the banks of the Rhine. Here a shipper took him on board who had sheltered himself in a creek during the whole night, and was just preparing to sail to Cologne.

Now was the day for delivering the plan. An indescribable melancholy was on the traits of the Master, as he appeared before the Bishop and unfolded the drawing. But full of joyful surprise he exclaimed: „What a splendid Cathedral! that will be a Temple to which no church in all countries where the Cross is honoured can bear comparison. You are an excellent Master, and your renown will reach to remote times, as long as the walls stand, which we will now

strongly build to the honour of the Lord."
The building began with all forces. Thousands
of diligent hands were actively employed from
morning till evening, and after a few months,
one saw here and there the foundations rising
from their depths. But as zealously as the Master
continued the work, and as quickly as the works.
proceeded, he was however not in a joyful disposition. Often he stood gloomy and absorbed,
and seemed as if his soul was distant. The Bishop
had ordered that the Master's name should be
engraved on a brazen plate and walled-in on a
suitable place of the Dome, and so it occurred;
but thereby just as little as by other favors of
the Bishop. was the melancholy conquered which
sadness daily increased. The Master only reflected on the loss of his soul on Hell and Dam-
nation, and with Anxiety and Terror he saw the
quick completion of his building.

Incapable of longer supporting the soul torment, he confided it to his confessor. This promised to assist him by prayer and pious atonement exercises, but at the same time advised
him to visit a hermit in the Eifel-mountains, who
had exorcised many evil spirits, and therefore.
enjoyed a great celebrity.

The tormented Master soon went there, and
the hermit consoled him with the promise of
delivering his soul by continuous mutual prayer,
and with the assurance that by pious atonement

the great crime which he had contracted with the Fiend could be annulled.

Weeks passed, in which the repentant sinner mortified himself, in hair garments subjected himself to the most severe chastisements, and patiently fulfilled all commanded by the holy hermit. This at last told him, that he might return home, and continue his great work as long as possible, and if he continued to live a pious repentant life, Satan would have no power over him.

With the hermit's blessing the Master returned to Cologne; but he was not allowed to complete his work. Disputes of the Town with the Elector interrupted the building. Full of chagrin and grief at this obstacle, the Master buried himself in the strictest retirement, and after a few years he died without being further recollected.

In the same night that he died, disappeared also the tablet from the Cathedral-wall on which his name had been placed. Soon afterwards the disputes became so violent, that the building was discontinued and completely stopped.

The great work began with the assistance of the Fiend, should, after the escape of his booty, not be ended. By dispute, envy, hatred and discord, the plotter of which was the Evil-one, he had succeeded, to interrupt the building of a Temple, which had become the finest and most sublime monument of active and persevering piety of its century.

Only in our times has it become possible, to undertake the completion.

May the demon of Mankind never again succeed, to disturb the work and to sow the seeds, as here and there one fears, of discord in the hearts of those united to complete the sublime Temple.

The wife, Richmodis of Aducht.

In the middle of the 14ᵗʰ century lived on the New-market in Cologne a certain Mr. Aducht, rich and esteemed, with his wife Richmodis. The most tender love with which these persons were united, the never disturbed peace of their house, and their exemplary lives, had acquired them general estimation, and everybody praised them as models of conjugal happiness.

But this happiness was to be painfully disturbed. As namely in the year 1357 the Plague raged here and snatched away a number of the inhabitants, Richmodis suddenly became ill, and after a few days the noble lady died. On a solemn burial was not to be thought of, in such terrible times when hundreds were dying daily; but on the contrary every one hastened as quickly as possible to rid the houses of the corpses, and so Mr. Aducht, as painful as was the separation from the beloved deceased, allowed his departed wife to be interred in all quietude in the churchyard of St. Aposteln. However he had in a certain degree, to honor the wife in death given her a costly ornament, and a brilliant ring.

This circumstance had not escaped the notice of the grave-diggers; they resolved to open the grave, and get possession of the jewellry. At midnight they descended into the grave. Already they had robbed the corpse of almost all its ornaments, and were just endeavouring to draw the ring from the finger, as the lady opened her eyes, and sat upright — Richmodis had only been in a state of apparent death. The thieves in fancy, believed the spirit of the deceased would punish the crime, took to flight and hastened so quickly away, that they left behind the ornament, as well as a lantern, which they had brought with them. Not less great was the out of her lethargy awakened woman, on finding herself in the coffin, and only with great exertion, was she able, to calm herself, and by the light of the lantern, leave the vault, and return to her home. There all was in deep sleep, and Richmodis was obliged to knock long at the door, before one of the servants awoke, and from the window demanded, who requested admittance at such an unusual hour? As she gave her name to the questioner, and he recognized her voice, he hastened, full of terror, to his master, and informed him of the terrible apparition. But Aducht

would not believe him, scolded him as a mad
fool, tormented by the fear of ghosts, and cried
at last, as he affirmed the truth of his assertion
with the most energetic oaths: My wife can just
as little be risen, and now stand before my house,
as it is possible that my horse breaks loose from
its stable mounts to the garret, and looks out
of the window." However he had scarcely spoken
these words, as one heard a violent bumping on
the stairs, and with astonishment and fright Aducht
saw, that his two grey horses were actually about
to climb up to the garret.   Taking courage, he
himself hastened to open the house-door, and the
sight of his entering wife convinced him of the
truth of his servant's assertions.

The most tender nursing procured Richmodis
strength and health again. · She lived happily
with her husband a number of years, and presented him with 3 sons; however since her res-
urrection ever serious and thoughtful.

One showed the house of Aducht during many
years, which led to the name of the Parrot, and
although another house stands on the site, there
is, however in a double manner the remembrance
of the event retained; viz in that new building
are 2 greys represented on wood, looking to the
market from the garret, and to the adjoining street
one has given the name of Richmodis.

Hermann Joseph.

Near the church St. Maria in the Capitol, so named, because on the same spot stood the Capitol of the Romans, lived a poor shoemaker, who by his handwork supported his family and himself with difficulty. Notwithstanding his needy condition the man felt himself happy; for he had a hopeful son increasing his pleasure daily. Hermann Joseph the name of the boy, distinguished himself from all others of his age by diligence and morality, and especially by his childlike piety. When he went to school, which was near the church, or even, when he played on the church place, he used to step to the, so called three King's door, and direct a prayer to the Holy Virgin with the infant Jesus there sculptored in stone. The prayer of a pious child becomes easily a confidential conversation, and so he entertained himself, with the Mother of God and the child Jesus, which more than the former occupied his child-like mind. Often, as he related to them, what he had learned and what otherwise had happened to him, and begged the boy Jesus, to descend once and play with him, he believed the stone figures participated in his wish and friendly nodded to him; even it appeared to him once, as if they beckoned to him to come to them, and then he was very afflicted, for the height of the Niche made it im-

possible, to obey this invitation. „Perhaps“, thought
Hermann Joseph, the dear child Jesus will at
last come down to me. if you give him something
„In this pious simplicity one day he offered a
fine apple to the figure which his father had
given him, and lo! the holy child bent lowly to
him, and took the apple. From then, the boy
thought of nothing more zealously, than to procure presents which he gave to the figure, whether
they consisted of victuals or flowers, and as
the child Jesus accepted them most friendly,
Hermann soon felt himself very intimate with the
object of his love and reverence, which brought
him protection, and felicity, in all his actions,
and daily life. Hermann Joseph when grown
up, had gladly devoted himself to the study of
theology but the limited resources of his parents
did not allow it. Concerning this the disconso-
late youth once complained before the stone
figure of the Mother of God, and directly after
she bowed with charming words of consolation
to him, and notified to him a place in the cross-
way of the Church, where under a stone, he
would find what he required. In fact a small
treasure was hidden there, which enabled him
to apply himself to his favourite study, and after
making quick progress in it, he resolved to enter
the Order of Benedictines, and had himself accepted in the cloister of Steinfeld. There he
devoted himself unceasingly to the Sciences, but

this study zeal was detrimental to his piety, by which alone all hitherto had succeeded and so his scientific studies produced no satisfactory results. Then he applied again in pious prayer to the Holy Virgin, and she showed herself to him in a dream exactly as her figure in stone over the 3 kings'door. With friendly earnestness she admonished him not to neglect Belief and Love to Her, and her Divine Son for the vain sciences, and not further to devote his time too much to study.

He awoke and the dream seemed as a wink from Heaven, which he believed to be obliged to obey, and by which he must now regulate his life. Hermann Joseph died at an advanced age, honoured and loved on account of his piety and extensive knowledge. Later times have pronounced him holy by the mouth of the Pope. His grave is still shewn in the cloister Steinfeld, and in the church St. Maria in the Capitol his figure in stone is placed, as he offers an apple to the child Jesus.

The Mayor Gryn.

At the time when Engelberg of Falkenburg was Archbishop of Cologne, the disputes between this spiritual prince and the town had reached their highest degree. On the one side showed itself the persevering, powerful endeavour to bend the obstinate Citizens under a hated domination, on the other side a stubborn, defiant resistance which asserted the good obtained rights of the town, and knew no yielding. It therefore could not fail, that hatred got the upperhand, and both parties welcomed the opportunity to annoy and damage each other.

The Archbishop exerted himself to influence the government to compel the town to subject itself to his will. For this purpose he built among others the Bayentower with strong walls and battlements as a solid castle; but the courageous Citizens did not allow themselves to be frightened; they stormed shortly afterwards the erected fortress and chased the inimical mercenaries. Among the Mayors of Cologne who particularly took part in the then excitable times in defending the rich trading town, and the rights of the people shone especially the family Overstolz, and with it, not less, the old Cologne family Hermann Gryn. The courageous opposition of this brave man against the Bishop's public and secret plans, drew on him the hate of the opposite party, and the clergy of the Bishopric. No intrigue was spared, to attach something to the honourable man, and as this for a long time was not successful, a devilish plan was arranged for his ruin.

Two canons endeavoured, under the mask of

hypocritical friendship to be on intimate terms
with the Mayor, and with his unsuspicious Character it succeeded only too well. Under all
kinds of pretences they had intercourse with
him, till their intention was ripe for execution.
One day the knight Hermann received an invitation, from his mutual friends, to a banquet
which was to be held in the Dome-cloister. At
the appointed hour he repaired there, and as of
the pretended guests none had yet appeard, one
of the canons made the proposal, meantime, to
inspect the rooms of the large, seldom visited
Foundation building. Gryn was accompanied by
his Hosts. He had already passed through several apartments, when at the extreme end of
a corridor a door was opened, through which,
by invitation of the Canons, the unsuspicious
knight entered a tolerably dark chamber.

He was scarcely there, as the heavy door
was suddenly closed and bolted behind him, at
the same a roaring lion sprang from a corner,
and regarded the entered with flaming eyes. By
this unexpected sight the Mayor at first lost his
presence of mind, but a moment's consideration,
which allowed him to reflect on the cunning of
his enemies, and his danger, yielded him perfect consciousness. Quickly he bound his left
arm with his mantle, leaned against the wall,
and drew his sword. As soon as the, by several
days fasting, excited lion made its spring at the

knight he thrust his protected left arm into its jaws, while his sharp steel pierced its breast, In a few moments the lion was stretched dead. Meantime the traitors, not doubting on the success of their plan, had called for help with hypocritical anxiety for the Mayor, who had been attacked by the Archbishop's lion. At their cry, soon ran together a crowd of persons; the door of the room was forced open, and to the great astonishment of all, they found the master of the town unhurt, and the lifeless animal at his feet. But amidst the exultation, the traitors paled, for their shameful crime was publicly announced by the mouth of the saved knight, and too late they sought their safety in flight. Seized by the raging people, they were without preceding judical verdict, and without regard to their vocation immediately hanged near the Cathedral cloister, there, where from that time stood the so called priest door.

But Gryn's action, on which the Citizens of Cologne think with pride, is represented in bas-relief, still to be seen on the portal of the Town-hall.

The three Kings at Cologne.

The Emperor Frederic (Barbarossa) besieging the beautiful and grand City of Milan, the principal citizens concealed the bodies of the 3 Kings sent formerly by the bishop Eustorgius of Constantinople. But the City was taken. In the retinue of the Emperor was the bishop Reinold of Cologne whom a knight of high rank urgently requested to intercede for him with the Emperor so that he might regain his former favour. The knight engaged in case he did so, to show him the place where the 3 magi were concealed. Reinold promised to accede to his wishes, and kept his word, and the knight indicated the secret place.

·The bishop having had the precious relics disinterred, sent them to Cologne; then he requested possession of the treasure from the Emperor, who granted his wishes. Reinold afterwards had the 3 kings transported into his Cathedral, and the inhabitants of Cologne were very delighted at this event. From that time they have not ceased to regard the 3 kings as protectors and patrons of the City, which since has had 3 Crowns in its arms.

God permitted that a number of miracles were effected by the intercession of the Saints whose glory extended to great distances. Pilgrims came from all countries bringing rich offerings. The precious remains of the 3 Kings are still in the Cathedral; and they will be venerated to the end of centuries.

Dünwald near Mühlheim.

The Oak-seed.

The monks at Dünwald directed all their meditations and endeavours to increase their, without this, very wealthy cloister, so that it might never fail on means to satisfy their inclination for luxury and good cheer.

Once they reflected on annexing a whole district of more than 100 acres, belonging to the neighbouring young nobleman of Schlebusch, and they did not want pretences, both in their archives and old parchments, by which they tried to substantiate their claim.

But the young nobleman was so much the less inclined to recognize this right, because the coveted property, from immemorial time, had been the undisputed property of his ancestors; he therefore believed to be obliged to oppose in every manner, the unjust demands of the covetous monks. The affair was to be decided by the law; but unfortunately the then being sheriffs ventured, (fearing the influence and spiritual power of the cloister) no decided judgment; rather they deferred the judicial dispute, so that there was no prospect of a decision.

The young nobleman made anxious in every possible way by his powerful opponents, even threatened with outlawry and excommunication, let them know, he was not disinclined to end the long dispute by ceding the claimed premises, conditionally only that he would be allowed to cultivate still one sowing on the disputed land and to let it ripen. The very delighted monks did not reflect a long time; they consented, and there was directly a binding well - claused contract planned concerning this compromise, and completed with all necessary formalities. The seed was consigned to the lap of the earth. When the spring was arrived the monks in expectation of early possession regarded the field, in order to see what sort of corn the young nobleman would harvest for the last time. But neither Wheat nor Rye, Barley, or other corn sprouted, but rather gradually budded tender leaves from the earth. At first the monks could not properly distinguish what sort of a plant it might be; but soon they recognized, to their consternation, the budding shoots of young oaks.

The avidity of the monks the young nobleman had deservedly, and to the satisfaction of all right minded persons, fortunately outwitted. Meanwhile the oak seeds grew to fine trunks.

When the tops af the oaks looked over the
cloister its inhabitants had long slept the Eternal
sleep, and before even, in course of time the
trees of the wood dried and rotted, the high
cloister-walls were already in rubbish and dust.

Solingen.

The Solinger blades.

The art to forge blades of a goodness and
excellence approaching the world renowned
Damascenes was not yet known in Solingen
in the 10th century. There was not a want of
good forgers, who endeavoured to imitate the
skilled Orientals; but none of these had succeeded and many Masters had, by fruitless
attempts, prepared their ruin.

Among these was also the old Ruthard an experienced man, become grey in the practice of
his trade; his favourite idea, the wish, to which
he had already sacrificed a year, the estab-
lishment of the art to fabricate Damascene
blades, seemed not to succeed with him. Anxiously he saw his wealth gradually decreasing
by the unremitting, tear-time occupying trials,
and just an unsuccessful attempt had prepared

him new grief, as he left his workshop in the worst humour and entered his sitting room. His only daughter, Martha, far from knowing the cause of his grief shown on the wrinkled forehead of the old man tried in vain to enliven him; for all her friendly questions he had no answer, not once a regard for the favourite dish with which the careful Martha hoped to surprise him, on the holy Christmas-eve. „Thou ought not to have worked on so holy an evening my father" said she, such work never brings luck and blessing. You hammer and fatigue yourself, as if you worked for to-morrow's bread, and yet, I should think, you had gained enough to care for your age, and make yourself happy days." A deep sigh was all the Master answered, then he took dumb and melancholy some bits of victuals, and went out of the house.

„The father is ill", said discouraged Martha to herself, and certainly little inclined to hear my request, that becomes daily heavier and completely oppresses my heart, William is indeed a diligent, orderly young man, the father's stoutest and most zealous workman, therefore to him before all dear and worthy — and ought indeed his poverty be a sufficient reason for me to renounce him?"

Just then William entered the room, but not gaily as is customary to Youth, he was pale and disturbed. „Martha", said he, „we have

no more hope." I have just ventured, to beg
the Master for your hand, doubting indeed on
account of his inexplicable, gloomy mind, taken
since some time, yet in full confidence in his
love and inclination, of which he has already
given me more than one proof, what do you think
he replied? „As long as you", drawing out a blade
of foreign, white, and singularly veined appearance out of the chest, „as long as you do not
understand to forge such a master-work, your
wooing is useless; only he who can do that
will be my son-in-law." And in speaking so,
he cut, as proof of the extraordinary hardness of
this steel, a nail from the wall, without its
receiving the least gap. „Go", continued he,
almost mockingly, pushed me out of the door,
and learn in foreign countries the art, after
which I have vainly endeavoured; through yourself alone can you attain the object of your
wishes; and nothing: I swear will change my
will."

This report caused the loving girl the deepest grief; she hung with all the fervour of
first love to the chosen of her heart and burst
into tears. My happiness is for ever destroyed
she said; for it is not possible, that you travel
to the distant Damascus and return happily from
the war excited country of the Infidels. I should
never be able to support the thoughts of knowing you in constant danger, and should die

prematurely. And yet, said William, what other means have we left? This journey as dangerous as it may be, allows us at least a slight hope, and the sight of your tears, Martha, confirms my determination, to venture all, and without delay I shall prepare myself for the great undertaking. Either you will see me again in a year or never. With these words the young man left the house hastily, and the next morning, without taking leave, he had departed. On the 10th day of his travelling he entered the solitary mountain of the Spessart, and unacquainted with the labyrinths of the road, he lost himself in the forest.

Already he had given up all hope to find a lodging for the night, as he saw, late at night the light of a solitary hut. Advancing quickly he had soon reached it; he knocked, an old ugly woman opened the door. „Good evening", said he, can a poor wanderer find a lodging here? A scanty supper, and a straw-bed is all I want, and I will reward you well for the accomodation." Step nearer my fine fellow, shrieked the old woman in contracting her face in a most ugly manner, and squinting with her red eyes most disagreeably. I will lodge you, if it is not unpleasant to you, that another visitor arrives, whom I expect every instant. Also I can arrange a retired chamber for you, where nothing will disturb you, and you can quietly sleep till

morning-dawn. Nothing remained but to accept
the proposal. William related, while the old
woman prepared his supper, the object of his
journey, and after being refreshed he retired to
his straw bed. But he could not sleep. The
haunted appearance of the old woman, her speech
and a disgusting nasal song, which she sang to
the accompaniment of 2 cats kept him awake;
as well as curiosity to know, what sort of a visit
it would be which the old woman expected in
these deserted woods. Meantime it had become
midnight; the moon began to spread her magical
light over all things, and lent to them in the
eyes of the excited youth, all sorts of frightful
figures. The wind rose and clattered the loose
panes of the rotten, window-frame, sounding like
wisperings of approaching men. Thick drops of
rain, struck against the thin walls of the hut
toned like light steps of an inimical person secretly approaching with menace to the solitary.
Suddenly a report was heard, frightening him
from his bed: at the same time he was aware
of a rattling as if some heavy object was falling
through the chimney, and an exchange of voices,
convinced him, that his hostess was not alone.
His hair stood on end; he rose, and peeping
through a door-chink the frightened saw the
figure of a man, sitting at the glowing hearth.
On the fire something was cooking in a large
kettle, and from time to time shot out of it a

blue flame, by the shine of which William could
see the stranger more distinctly. He wore a
buff-coat, and a hat of the same colour; his face
was covered with a thick beard, and had concealed his feet in the ashes of the hearth. His
flashing, piercing eyes regarded the old woman,
who stood humbly before him, and his manner
bore the expression of anger. What they spoke
together, the listener could not understand; it
was a secret, zealous talking. He was not the
less frightened by the sudden movement of the
old woman to his bed. He threw himself hastily
on his bed, to give himself the appearance of
sleeping, and he had scarcely closed his eyes for
this purpose, when his arm was seized. „Wake
up, young man!" screamed the witch, „quick get
up, you are to make the acquaintance of a man
from the distant Orient. He can spare you your
journey there; for he is full of wisdom. Speak
and beg·him, to teach you what will be of use
to you."

William rose, to follow the old woman, he
trembled before the unknown, but the desire for
the secret art, and the thoughts of ·his beloved
overcame every other consideration. His whole
body shook as he stood before the stranger,
whose watching eye, the deadly charming glance
resembling a serpent's, stared at the young man
from the broad brim of his hat. The flame coloured mantle, which he drew about his shoulders,

while his half stretched right hand tried to
tranquilize the spluttering and bubbling in the
kettle, at last the old woman had meantime crept
to a corner of the hearth, so that only her face
was visible; all this, by the light of the turf fire
had something of a demoniacal character, and
completely perplexed the young man. In his
anxiety he entreated the protection of all the
Saints, so that no Evil one could have power
over him. For a long time the enigmatical frightful guest kept his eye fixed on William, then he
asked him in a deep hollow voice, as if it came
from a distance: „What do you wish from me?“
The young man related, scarcely master of himself, and in almost unconnected words, his accident
and the cause of his journey; he had scarcely
spoken, as the fiend broke out into a loud laugh.
„I know, what you wish to know“, he said with
changed, almost inaudible voice, in inclining to
William, „but I do nothing without payment.
For the means which I here give you and which
contains all that is useful to you, I condition only,
that you belong to me, from the day when you
will make use of your newly obtained art. Seven
years and seven months I present to you, that
you can procure the advantages I procure you,
so as to enjoy your life. If you agree to my
proposal, it is good for you, if not you will
never return from the Orient to see your Martha
again.“

William was too insensible to reflect; besides love **was** powerful in his breast; he subscribed, therefore with a pen dipped in the boiling fluid, his name on the presented parchment, and received for it a well sealed letter, which he had scarcely received before the figure disappeared.

The unfortunate passed the rest of the night in feverish excitement, and with distressing dreams. Towards morning he enjoyed refreshing sleep, and the sun was already high when he left his bed. In the hut he found neither the old witch, nor any living being, and hastily as if chased by furies, he left the haunted lodging. Half dead with exhaustion, and after long wandering, he found pitying peasants, who nursed him, and conducted him on the way to his home.

Master Ruthard was exceedingly astonished, to see his workman, whom he had already believed far away, return so soon. He thought the young man had repented of his intention, and must have reflected on something else. But how frightened was he as William related him all, handed him the lettered secret, on the seals of which was stamped a tongue of flame and a sword.

„God avert“, said the pious Master after hearing all, and after thinking profoundly for some time: „avert God that your great love for my daughter should ruin you eternally. This lucky or unlucky bringing paper shall never unfold either your hands or mine; it shall rest in the most concealed corner of my chest, till better days, till once my grand-son, over whom the devilish power can not stretch, unseals and uses it."

And so it happened. William became on the next Christmas-eve the husband of his beloved, highly delighted Martha, and Ruthard gave him workshop and customers, resigning himself to quietude which his old age required. Diligence and Perseverance accomplish even the most difficult things; after the course of a few years the wealth of the house increased, so that the old man was delighted.

After many years, when Ruthard was dead and William advanced in years also deceased, his son found the letter in which was a description how to forge blades equal in quality to the Damascene blades; and from that time the blades of Solingen are so excellent and renowned.

Gerresheim near Düsseldorf.

Gunhilde.

Gunhilde, the pious, moral and in youthful gracefulness shining Nun had awakened in her Confessor's heart an impure inclination, the existence of which she had not supposed.

The unworthy priest spared nothing to seduce the inexperienced, but all his shameful exertions failed against Gunhilde's innocence. Consumed by passion, and full of impious plans, the seducer at last tried to persuade her to fly under the promise of returning to the world, and would unite himself with her in the holy bonds of matrimony.

Gunhilde did not resist such promises and his oaths. She escaped with the priest, during a dark night from the encircling walls of the cloister, and now he believed his object attained. But it was not so; the anxious maiden resisted with unconquerable constancy every improper request and demanded the fulfillment of his promise. To grant this, the wicked priest was not at all inclined; but resigned himself, in seeing every means to satisfy his passion remained fruitless, to a vagabond, dissipated life. By this daily more demoralized, he was, at last, connected with a band of robbers, in whose society he committed numerous crimes.

But during a marauding excursion, the former priest was seized, and soon afterwards hanged, as a fitting reward for his vicious life. The news of his terrible death soon reached Gunhilde, who lamented their days in the greatest seclusion and wept their precipitation. She had it is true remained innocent; however she was a culpable fugitive, a sinner in the eyes of the world, which is ever inclined. to believe the evil than in virtue and moral greatness. Notwithstanding the unfortunate determined, to return immediately to the cloister, and to atone for her crime, by subjecting herself to the most severe punishments. She threw herself at the feet of the Abbess, and implored her to accept, an undutiful, lost but yet repentant and unhappy daughter with clemency and mercy. „Rise“, said the superior, „rise my dear child; why do you accuse yourself? have you not indeed since unceasingly prayed to God in your chamber and honoured with your charming sounding voice, and more pious you stand there, than your sisters, more pleasing to God, than I.“

And to her cell the Nuns and Abbess accompanied the astonished. On entering her cell all was clear to Gunhilde; for from her resting-place an Angel rose and disappeared, who during her absence had been her substitute, prayed for her, and praised God with pious songs.

Xanten.

Siegfried.

In the very old times Siegmund, a Netherland prince, with his wife inhabited the castle of Xanten. They had a son Siegfried, whose bodily strength developed extremely early, but not less his insolent, untamed mind, which mocked all teaching and admonition.

Scarcely 11 years of age, the vigorous boy found the monotonous quietude of his father's castle insupportable; he fled, therefore, one day in order to wander about the World to seek adventures. He wandered up the Rhine, and met at the foot of the Siebengebirges the celebrated armourer Mimer, whose occupation pleased him so well, that he resolved, to be apprenticed to him, in order to finish his own arms.

Mimer's workmen were very soon obliged to feel the combativeness of Siegfried; very often he threw them down or beat them soundly. As smith he was useless, for he cut through all iron-bars, and by powerful blows drove the anvil into the earth. The Master, in order to get rid of such a wild fellow, sent him, one day, charcoal-burning in a forest where was a fearful Dragon. This Dragon was the giant Fafner, transformed on account of his cruelties, watched an immense treasure of gold, pearls and precious-stones, which

at certain times could be seen glistening in the
clefts of a hollow cave.

Siegfried lit at the place a large charcoal-
kiln, and he had just brought it to a glowing-
fire, as the Dragon rushed towards him with
wide extended jaws, to swallow the new charcoal-
burner. „Ho, ho!“ cried Siegfried, „that will give
a very welcome adventure! now it is called,
defend yourself.“ And from the fire he drew an
oak trunk, the burning end of which he thrust
into the Dragon's jaws, just as one allows a wild
boar's onset. Stung by pain to the wildest rage,
the dragon rolled on the ground, and tried to
overpower Siegfried by the contortions of its strong
tail. But he dealt it repeated blows, and knew
how to avoid the attacks of the Dragon, and
watching his opportunity he cut off the Dragon's
head. Then he threw the carcase into the fire;
but with astonishment, he saw flow out a large
stream of fat, forming a lake at his feet. At the
same time a bird sang over his head:

You shall bathe yourself in Dragon's fat,
That no enemy's sword can on you act,
And your body for every struggle dress'd,
Be surrounded with scale armour and bless'd.

Siegfried did not fail, to obey the received
direction; he threw himself undressed into the fat,
and this anointed all his limbs, with the excep-

tion of a spot on his right shoulder, which, by
a leaf falling from a tree had been covered.
With the head of the slain Monster, the Blessed
returned to the forge. Here he slew the malicious
Mimer, and after selecting an excellent sword,
as well as splendid armour, and saddled the best
charger in the stable, the racer Grani, he left,
anxious for new adventures.

After travelling down the Rhine to the South,
he arrived at the sea and embarked. The storm
drove him on a rocky, steep coast; his active
charger however climbed up, and brought him
near a bewitched castle standing in flames.

The young hero was undecided what to do;
the bird sang, that had already given him instructions, with clear voice:

> Only fresh, with firm courage forwards,
> And leap into the fire's glow towards!
> The finest maid to win you can
> And unloosen this magician's ban.

He spurred his horse, but it struggled and
reared, and Siegfried himself was almost suffocated
by the terrible heat; however he forced the dis-
obedient animal — an extraordinary leap placed
him in the middle of the flames, and directly
the fire was extinguished. The castle was now
displayed in its complete, and undamaged beauty.
The doors sprang open, and Siegfried did not

delay to enter and inspect the interior. Admiringly he regarded the splendid apartements, in which the stillness of Death reigned; but still more was he astonished to see the inhabitants immovable, and apparently sleeping in the same positions, in which, without doubt they had in the moment of enchantment. The cook stood at the fire-place, the groom with the horses, even the animals stood immovable at their mangers.

As Siegfried entered the castle-hall, an exclamation of surprise escaped him; for there lay, on a divan as if cast, ornamented with infinite charms, surrounded with royal pomp, but bound with brass bands, as his heart seemed to tell him the promised maid.

Hastily he cut her bands, then he pressed a-glowing kiss on the rosy lips. This kiss was the sign of deliverance from 100 years enchantment. Brunhilde, so was the beauty called, opened her eyes, thanked the knight, whom to his no little astonishment she called by name, and promised to be his. All in the castle was in the same moment disenchanted, and moved as if it had never been enchanted.

Siegfried hoped for the sweet reward of Love; but Brunhilde knew how to restrain him by the magic of love, too proud, to wish to give herself entirely to a man. So she enchained him a long time, till finally, his restless spirit could not longer support this inactive yearning, and his inclina-

tion for adventures, awoke again in him too
pow erfully.

This propensity was especially stimulated by
the known bird, which did not cease to sing before his window of refuges in the Nibelungen-
lande, of great actions, still to accomplish, and
of beautiful women, whose love was still to be
won. So, one day the Hero recovered his courage, armed himself with all manfulness against
the seductions of Brunhilde, and like a thief in
the night, he left secretly the enchanted castle
with all it contained of charming and seductive.
His guide was the wonderful bird; turning to the
north it flew ever before him, from branch to
branch, house to house; and did the young Hero
listen to it in the cool shade, it sang thus:

In the North lies, still unknown,
The Nibelungen beautiful throne.
Lives cunning folk of small measure,
Who labour to hide a great treasure,
Worth for you, I give my word,
A fine cap and magical sword,
The former making you invisible, ·   ·   ·
The sword of the latter to enemies, terrible.

No wonder, that Siegfried desirer such excellent things, and continued his journey with all
possible dispatch. After a long tour he reached
the Nibelungenland, and in stretching himself

fatigued on the earth, a troop of dwarfs surrounded him, who regarded him with looks of admiration, and then wished to make him their prisoner. The young Hero however resisted energetically, bound their leader Alberich with his own long hair, and compelled him to disclose where cap and sword were concealed. The acquisition of these treasures was however not easy. Firstly Siegfried was obliged to overpower the furious giant Wolfgrambär, who watched a subterraneous treasure, the dwarf Alberich, who wished to betray him still once punish, till he showed him the place, where the invisible cap was concealed, and finally Wolfgrambär was obliged to deliver the sword Balmung to the Hero, who had bound him so well. After all this was accomplished, Siegfried set his enemy at liberty.

Having attained his object, and also slain a Dragon guarding an immense treasure, the Hero felt home-sickness, and set out on his return to his father's castle. After several months traveling, he arrived there, to the great joy of his parents, tho whom he related of his wonderful adventures.

Cleve.

The Swan knight.

The young Countess of Cleve was profoundly
sad and in great distress. A bold daring Vassal
had not only had the temerity to announce his
disobedience, but made himself master of her
castle, and her liberty, even demanded her hand
and with it the government of her lands. She
saw no means to save herself from her rebellious
subject; for no knight of her country would venture to challenge an opponent, whose dexterity
in arms, gigantic figure, and bodily strength allowed no hope of a successful result. Unceasingly the severely oppressed Lady directed her
fervent prayers to Heaven, that an assistant might
appear in her need, and the heart of a combatant might be roused, to free her from the bur-
densome importunate Vassal. On her chaplet,
according to the legend, is said to have hung a
small silver bell with the wonderful property,
that the lightest tone of it in the distance, however only in a particular direction, won in
strength and sound, and a distant king is said
to have regarded it as a cry for help, and a
demand to send assistance up the Rhine to the
oppressed innocent. This, perhaps originating in
a dream, the king regarded as an adventurous
opportunity for his only son, and it was accepted

by him with that ardour, with which the noble
knights of Antiquity seized every occasion, to
lend their protecting arms to the weak, and par
ticularly to women.

A swan appeared on the waves of the stream;
by a golden chain it drew a boat, and so placed
itself on the bank, as if demanding to be used,
from where the king's son longingly regarded
the mysterious distance. To the young man it
seemed a manifest sign and command of the
higher powers, to step into the boat, and scarcely
had he done so, when the swan ascended the
Rhine, and disappeared from the sight of the
astonished king.

Meanwhile the day had arrived for the marriage of the master become rebel with the Countess, and she could not escape this destiny, unless
she found a knight, bould enough, to challenge
the villain to mortal combat.

The anxious one, who should dress herself
for the festival, and already considered herself
as lost, saw from her window, a swan drawing
a boat up the Rhine, in which boat reposed a
sleeping knight. Immediately she recollected,
that a pious Nun had once prophesied to her, a
sleeping youth would once save her from great
danger; and joyfully surprised, the miracle amazed
her, as the youth awoke and landed, the swan
and boat immediately disappearing.

The knight turned his steps direct to the

castle, fell on one knee before the Countess, and requested to be allowed to combat for her possession. Joyfully the request was granted, and directly preparations were made in the court of the castle for this trial by arms.

Furious, like an enraged boar, the proud Vassal accepted the combat. Many participators, partial to the Countess beating hearts, anxiously awaited this, to them, unfortunate struggle, believing the young man, although expert and strong, would be obliged to succumb to the bodily size of his powerful opponent.

But the just cause triumphed; heavily struck by the sword the villain fell dead, and with exclamations of joy, the victor knelt to the saved Countess. With glances of sincere love she uttered her thanks; but not only with words did she praise the Hero, for some weeks later, he conducted the Countess to the altar, where they were united in the bonds of matrimony.

Not easily could a wife be happier than the Countess was with her husband, who returned her love with the sincerest fidelity.

Only one thing inquieted the heart of the Countess; viz no one knew whence the knight came and to what family he belonged. Before he engaged himself with her, she had been obliged to give him her solemn promise that she would never ask him concerning his home and name; for on this question, he had warningly

alluded his destiny was connected, and if she did
so, he would be necessitated, for ever, to leave
her. The Countess had vowed to obey his wishes,
and years passed without their happiness being
disturbed, but increased by the growth of 3 sons
promising to be an ornament to Chivalry.

But the more excellent and strong the boys
grew, so much the more annoying was it to the
mother's heart, that they could not enjoy their
father's name, which was certainly of a higher
origin. Once therefore as she could not more
resist the impulse of her heart, she entreated her
husband, not to leave her sons without their
father's name, which was what the lowest inherited from his father, and not to wait till they
would be regarded as bastards and mocked.
Whence he came, and his name, therefore he
could not longer keep secret.

Pale and frightened he heard her words, and
then exclaimed in a most grievous voice: „Woe,
unhappy mother, what have you done! destroyed
our happiness by your words! From this moment
I must leave you, and never return.“ Then he
had his silver-horn blown to the waters, and
distantly it echoed in the silent night. At day-
break the swan appeared swimming over the
waves; but not bringing felicity, as before. The
husband stepped into the boat, before the eyes
of the terrified, chilled Countess, and descending,
the mighty swan returned. and was never seen

afterwards. Grief soon caused the death of the Countess; but her sons became founders of noble families, who till to day are distinguished by swans in their arms.

—————

Kevlaar.

Religious legends founded this place in the 17ᵗʰ century. The principal legend speaks of a citizen Heinrich Buschmann, who on a journey, at Christmas 1661, over the Kevlaar-plain, where at that time stood a so-called trembling-cross, prayed most fervently, suddenly heard a ,voice which called to him: „Here you are to build me a shrine. As the same event happened to him on the same place some days afterwards, without any person being seen near or at a distance, so he resolved, without informing any one of this miracle, to spare some part of his slender means, and gradually amass so much, in order to construct the shrine according to the miraculous direction. The winter passed. In the spring, when Buschmann had already the necessary sum, his wife related to him of a nightly apparition, a shrine with the figure of the Holy Mother, whereupon he communicated to his wife of the experienced miracle. The married couple informed some monks who had a cloister in the neighbourbood, and they assisted in building the shrine, so that already on June 1ˢᵗ 1642 a great multitude of persons from the adjacent country made a pilgrimage to the shrine and exposed Virgin Mary, later these pilgrimages increased, so that finally a number of houses were built and formed the village Kevlaar.

In the year 1842 Kevlaar celebrated its 200 year's jubilee, on which occasion 200,000 persons made a pilgrimage to the place.

Our patriotic author Heinrich Heine honoured this pious legend by the following poem.

The Pilgrimage to Kevlaar.

At the window stood the mother,
In the bed the son lay.
„Will you not rise William,
The procession will not stay?"

„„I am so very ill, oh mother,
That I do not hear and see;
I think on the dead Gretchen
My thoughts much pain me.""

„Rise, we will go to Kevlaar,
Book and chaplet with might;
The Holy Virgin will cure you,
And your sick heart quite."

There wave the church flags,
The holy tones I mention;
That is at Cöllen on the Rhine,
There goes the procession.

The mother follows the crowd,
The son whom she leads,
They sing both in the chorus;
With praised Mary she pleads!"

*   *   *

The Holy Mother at Kevlaar
Wears to-day her best dress;
To-day she has much to do.
Many sick in great distress.

The sick people bring
Her there as offer-benefaction,
Of wax formed limbs
Both feet and hands all waxen.

And who a wax-hand offers,
Receives on hand the cure;
And who wax-foot offers,
The foot will heal that's sure.

To Kevlaar went many on crutches,
Who now dances so stealthy,
Indeed many play now the viol.
Who formerly were not healthy.

KEVLAAR.

The mother took a waxlight,
And formed out of it a heart.
„Bring that to the Mother of God,
Then heals she your smart."

The son took sighing the wax-heart,
Went to the Holy-figure sighing;
Tears welled out of his eyes,
The words from his heart trying.

„„Thou Highly-blessed,
Thou immaculate virgin,
Thou Queen of Heaven
To thee my pain merging!

I lived with my mother
At Cöllen in the town,
The town where many hundred
Chapels and churches are noted down.

And beside us lived Gretchen,
Yet she is now dead —
Mary I bring thee a waxen-heart
Heal, for her my heart bled.

Heal thou my sick heart,
Constantly my heart purging
Devoutly praying and singing:
Praised be thou Holy Virgin!"""

*   *   *

KEVLAAR.

The sick son and the mother,
In a small chamber they slept;
There came the Mother of God
Entering with very light step.

She stooped over the patient,
And Heaven-blessing her hand laid
Quite softly on his heart,
Left, as on her mouth smiles played.

The mother beheld all in dream
And seen more but hark!
She awoke from her slumber,
The dogs so loudly bark,

There lay stretched out
Her son, and he was dead;
There plays on the pale cheeks
The clear morning red.

The mother folded her hands,
It was, she knew not how;
Meditatively she sang softly:
„Blessed be thou, Mary now!"

Heinrich Heine.

Gertruidenberg.

St. Gertrude's delight.

Many years ago there lived in the Netherlands, a young maiden endowed with rare beauty, and, at that time very seldom, full of innocence and piety. A rich proud knight became unknown to the lovely Gertrude, violently enamoured of her, and only first could she convince herself by his zealous wooing, of the deep impression she had made on him, and how strong was his passion. But her serious thoughts did not think of the delights of love, also not for family happiness, and the joys of a worldly quiet life but from earliest youth had the most longing wish, that she might be allowed to pass her days in retirement, in the cloister dedicated to the Holy John. Only a pure heart free from all human weakness, could in early youth, have formed such a resolution; her breast free from every passion, entertained one only inclination, the innocent and humane of charity, and her only grief was, that with her poverty, she could not satisfy this desire. The knights wooing therefore was without result. But allowing him to see and friendly converse with her, his passion was inflamed for the rare, most lovely, blooming maiden, and as if entangled by magical bonds,

he was involuntarily devoted to the object of
all his thoughts and the torments of his love.

He was allowed to be her companion, when
she visited the huts of poverty in order to satisfy charitable intentions, or to console, where
she could not help. He was often witness of
her sorrow and her tears, when she was only
able to give consolation and hopes; therefore he
once ventured, to offer her his well provided
purse, which she joyfully and hastily accepted.
Now there was no end to these charities, also
the knight was not tired of giving. But Gertrude
really entered the convent in her 18th year,
however much the knight tried to hinder it, and
passed a pious still life, divided between prayer
and charitable actions. This inclination she was
able to satisfy as her admirer sent means to
the convent daily for her pious object. Years
passed but not the knight's violent love. Property
and estates had been sacrificed to gratify this
alms-giving, and with deep affliction, he saw the
time approach when it would not more be possible, by bringing his gifts to win a sweet grateful smile. In giving the last, he took leave of
Gertrude, for a journey as he said, but indeed
with the firm resolution, to procure money and
property, in some manner or the other. He
wandered about the country by night, by untrodden ways, through thorns and moors, full of
all sorts of gloomy intentions.

There advanced to him, at midnight, from a thicket, a man of uncomfortable, strange manner, who adressed him in a disagreeable, hoarse voice: „What do you want, knight, that you wander through the forest, at such an inopportune time? Confide it to me, who already assisted many with good advice, and still more by deed. Do you want gold? speak one word and I shall help you, as soon as we agree; as much as it may be, I am master of great treasures. As much as you may use in 7 years I will grant you and your chest shall never be empty. For this I condition a trifle, for such help is worth the trouble. Here I have a parchment, on which a contract is drawn; you can read it by that bog-light. According to this contract you resign your-self to me after 7 long years; however you must, only for form's sake, sign it with your blood; a drop is enough. If agreeable to you we will now arrange all. and to-day in 7 years, you will be here again.“

The deluded, dazzled knight consented and signed. Wildly he hurried from the place, and arrived at home, he found sufficient gold in his chest. Continually he employed his gold for the convent; yet hungered with all his riches, as if there was no other happiness and joy in the world, that to satisfy Gertrude's wishes and re-ceive her thanks.

Meanwhile the 7 years passed and the knight

saw, with anxiety tormenting the day approach which was to be his last, and for the last time see his adored Gertrude. Despairingly he would begin his terrible ride to the thicket, in taking leave of Gertrude under the pretence of a journey, and then go to Hell. Then she begged him to drink under the protection of her patroness St. Johanna, to her felicity and pious memory, as protection against every danger. He took the drink, and as he emptied the beaker, it seemed to him as if he had never enjoyed such a fortifying and exhilarating refreshment. But after taking an affectionate farewell, and in riding to the appointed place, he was filled with gloomy thoughts, and trembling he arrived at the spot. There stood already the frightful unknown waiting for him; but as soon as he saw the knight, he sprang away terrified, raised a fearful howl, and cried, in tearing the contract: „Woe to me, I have no power over you, for behind you, on your horse is riding St. Gertrude, whose felicity you last drunk." With these words the Evil-one disappeared, and a pale brimstone vapour filled the air. The knight was released, Gertrude's charity had cured him; but in his habitation he found a great treasure, which in accordance with Gertrude's will, he employed on a charitable object; and in order to be continually worthy of the favour of Heaven, he devoted the rest of his days to the service of God and retired to a cloister.

Zuydersee.

Stavoren.

Among the commercial sea-towns of Holland 6 centuries ago Stavoren took the first place. The ships of its merchants covered the seas, and imported the productions of all zones. Such an extensive commerce raised the wealth of this town to an unknown extent. It is true there was here, as elsewhere, many poor; but the number of the wealthy outnumbered them. But also high-life, luxury, and magnificence, the usual companious of great riches, did not fail, because in foolish pride and ruinous zeal, one tried to excel the other in brilliancy, in the exhibition of valuables, splendid, extravagant feasts. The legend relates, there where many houses, like palaces, built with marble, the interiors ornamented with the most artistically inlaid-work, covered with the richest stuffs, and provided with the rarest furniture, and the doors instead of iron, were bound with precious metals:

But of all the Stavoren merchants none could compare in riches with the Virgin Richberta. The good fortune, that each of her speculations was richly rewarded, and not seldom with unexpected profits, seemed to show in her, to what degree she could lavish her gifts on a mortal, and how long allow her favours to be enjoyed.

The commercial fleet of the Virgin merchant visited the remotest seas, not only returned each time with the richest profits, but with the most expensive wares, with ornaments, pearls, and precious-stones, which were employed in the palace of their mistress, and shone on its walls.

Such unexampled good fortune the Virgin Richberta could not support with indifference, with which alone she could have enjoyed it; and if it is true, what a wise man says, that great misfortunes are easier to be borne than immoderate happiness, Richberta was destined to be a glaring proof of the truth of the assertion. Her pride kept step with the increase of her riches, and she showed it both by contempt for her fellow-creatures, and satisfying it by the most luxuriant, extravagant feasts, which she gave less to amuse and gladden the town, than to give her guests opportunities to admire the ever new splendour of her apartments, be astonished at the foreign costly food and wine, and envy the giver.

At one of these extravagant senseless repasts, offering nothing to the mind, and leaving the heart void, a strange guest was announced to the Virgin Richberta. He came from foreign countries he sent her word, had seen many royal countries, and the splendour of their courts, and had come to admire Richberta's riches of which fame had reported miraculous.

The flattered mistress begged the stranger to take a seat at her side: he appeared to be still a robust old man, in the picturesque custume of the Orient, his conduct was dignified and noble, and stepped to Richberta, expecting the welcome from her hands, which according to the usage of his country was given symbolically by the offering of bread and salt. But there was no bread on the luxurious table, which groaned under the burden of rare, palate-exciting dishes, and from which the simple nourishment of poverty was banished.

Silently the stranger seated himself, and in taking refreshments he related agreeably and instructively of his travels by land and water, of foreign nations and their customs, of his changes, his pleasures and misfortunes, of the perishableness of earthly goods, and the mutability of human happiness.

Every ear listened to the sounding words of the enigmatical guest; but not the Virgin Richberta. Her vanity could not expect anything else than that the stranger should be loud in his praises of her riches, the brilliancy of her feast, and would make comparisons giving fresh nourishment to her pride; but he was silent on such subjects, till finally, demanded by herself, he confessed only by kings to have found such splendour and extravagance; the more singular, he concluded, to miss here, the best and noblest what the Earth produced. In vain one tried to obtain a fuller explanation of the strange guest; he remained dumb, and on being questioned too pressingly and importunate, he disappeared and was not seen again.

Richberta's pride and curiosity equally excited, allowed her no more quietude. She possessed in valuables all that could be mentioned, produced by Land and Sea; however the very best should be wanting? She asked scholars and soothsayers, sent for magicians and dream-interpreters: but none knew to name what she had not long possessed.

In her restless desire for the very best she had ships equipped, to cruise all seas and lands, and not to return till it had been found.

The commander of her fleet put to sea, undecided whither to direct his ships. One part he sent to the East, and another to the West, while he himself with his ships relied on the favour of the winds. It happened, that by a leak, a part of the provisions was spoiled, and although there was no want of meat, wine, and other objects of luxury, the flour and bread had become unfit for food, and the want of it was soon felt most severely. In this need the commander recognized clearly, what he was obliged to consider the most delicious and best; not the spices and perfumes of India, the pearls from the bottom of the sea, the gold from the deepest diggings but the simple everywhere thriving gift of Nature, the indispensable, inestimable nourishing, and reviving bread.

He recognized now the sense of the obscure words, spoken by the stranger, and his resolution was quickly taken. He steered to a Baltic harbour where he took a full cargo of the finest wheat, with which he sailed to Stavoren. Scarcely arrived, he appeared before the Virgin Richberta, who had not expected him so quickly, and announced to her, that he now knew, what was the most luxurious and best of all possessions; he had found it, and in abundance brought with him. He then related to his astonished mistress, how he had obtained this knowledge, how the mysterious guest could only have meant the failing bread, and as he therefore believed, had executed his order in the most satisfactory manner.

But Richberta was not of this opinion, she cast reproachful looks at the confounded servant, and painfully suppressing her rage, she asked him, on which side of the ship he had taken the cargo; she was answered it had taken place on the right side. Well then, answered the haughty Richberta, I command you to cast the whole cargo into the sea from the left side.

In vain were all representations against this order; uselessly the faithful servant appealed to her heart, in conjuring her, not to annihilate the rich gift of God, but at least to relieve the wants of the poor with it; uselessly he sent crowds of needy persons to her to soften her hard proud feelings; all was in vain, and before her eyes, she had the rich wheat cargo which could have given bread to so many, thrown into the sea, amid the howlings and cursings of the multitude.

The bottom of the sea had received the cargo, but the grains became a sowing of ruin. Germinating in the mud, and shooting up, continually covered with new earth, shot up a forest of stalks without ears, in unnatural growth always higher, like sea fungus and spiders to the surface of the water, and as the oft moveable mass of the earth therewith found a support, an immense sand-bank was formed before the harbour of Stavoren which no human power was able to break through. The numerous ships of the town, also those of the rich Richberta did not more find an entrance to the port, and were the sacrifices of the raging waves. Commerce and riches were destroyed, and continually recurring strokes of fortune precipitated the proud Virgin Richberta from the pinnacle of her splendour and happiness into want and misery.

But the sea, to which an accustomed creek had been closed, raged with ever new anger against the bank, and during the storm of a dark tempest it broke through the dikes, flooded the town, and tore it with the foundations hastily into the sea, like a long wished for booty.

Where Stavoren once stood rolls now the
troubled waves of the Zuydersee. But when the
clear water allows its bottom to be seen. the
shippers see with horror, still now, on the bottom. the proud towers and doors, the streets
and the high gables of the palaces of this sunk
once·such a magnificent town.

H a a g.

Three hundred and sixty five children.

To the Countess Henneberg came once, with
twins in her arms, an unfortunate wife begging
for charity. Irritated at the unannounced entry
into the fine apartment, which was dishonoured
by such an unclean presence the proud wife
reproached the poor beggar woman, declaring
her visit as an insolence; and as she did not
leave quickly enough, the hard-hearted countess
called after her: „Go away directly! to pity you
would be a sin; you are an unchaste wife, for
2 children can never be from one father.“

By these defaming words the heavily afflicted
rose from her humble position, and instead of
the hitherto supplicating. expression her traits
took a threatening appearance, and an uncomfortable fire sparkled from her eyes. „Curses

strike you, Unmerciful!" screamed she in furious
tones. „As punishment for your ignominious words,
may you bear as many children as there are
days in a year."

So crying she left the apartment of the Countess; but the haughty laughed loudly and sneered
at her, as she thought, impotent menace. However
it was not long before the Countess felt herself
mother, and 9 months were scarcely passed, she
bore, under unspeakable anxiety and torment
365 children successively.

But as they were successively born, so they
died: and also the mother, become insane, died
shortly after their birth and death.

In a village church, near the Haag, one still
shows the grave of the Countess and her children,
as well as the font where the 365 children were
christened.

As many children as days in a year.

You must not believe all one relates and writes,
I will allow Critics, if they are spiritual lights.

An old man from the Haag me lately related.
This wonder concerns Countes Henneberg as stated.

A beggar-woman came to demand alms,
Two screaming twins she had in her arms.

So too-richly blessed yet poor in goods and gold,
It was demanded how she could be so bold.

Away, impudent wife, called the Countes irritated,
Shamelessly you boast with your belly to be mated,

„Away, away, clean my room of her presence rather;
Two children can never be from one father."

Then spoke the insulted: „So I wish you then, hear,
That God presents you as many children as days in a year."

The wish was expressed, the Countess complained,
She felt very strangely, soon was she much paiu'd.

Three hundred and sixty five — the days of the year.
Just as many children she bore-with many a bitter tear.

Living altogether, given to the holy baptism,
Boys and girls were christen'd without schism.

Of the little daughters, Elizabeth was the name,
Collectively the boys John then became.

The christening basin is still shown there,
The mother, from terror, tore out her hair.

From terror dead, her offspring every one,
By holy baptism God's Kingdom soon won.

It has happened at Haag not a mile wide,
You may see the grave still, if disbelief tried.

                                        K. Simrock.

At the conclusion of this work, we cannot help thinking on the beautiful and true words of the genial Briton „Byron“, who thus describes the majestic stream.

Adieu to thee, fair Rhine! How long delighted
The stranger faiu would linger on his way!
Thine is a scene alike where souls united
Or lonely contemplation thus might stray;
And could the ceaseless vultures, cease to prey
On self condemning bosoms, it were here,
Where Nature, nor too sombre nor too gay,
Wild but not rude, awful yet not austere
Is to the mellow Earth as Autumn to the year.

Adieu to thee again! a vain adieu!
There can be no farewell to scene like thine,
The mind is colour'd by thy very hue;
And if reluctantly the eyes resign
Their cherished gaze upon thee, lovely Rhine!
T'is with the thankful glance of parting praise;
More mighty spots may rise — more glaring shrine,
But none unite in one attaching maze
The brilliant, fair and soft, — the glories of old days.

The negligently grand, the fruitful bloom
Of coming ripeness, the white city's sheen.
The rolling stream, the precipice's gloom,
The forest growth, and Gothic walls between,
The wild rocks shaped as they had turrets been,
In mockery of man's art; and these withal
A race of faces happy as the scene
Whose fertile, bounties here extend to all,
Still springing o'er thy banks, though Empires near them fall.

Byron.